The Unspoken Darkness

ISBN-13:9798287346959

 @avelinaharrowauthor

The Unspoken Darkness

Playlist

All Faces - Welcome Home
Emeli Sandé - Breathing Underwater
Mike Shinoda - Promises I Can't Keep
Valerie Broussard - Some Dreams You Never Wake Up
From
Barns Courtney - Glitter & Gold
Mackenzy Mackay - London
Michael Schulte - Falling Apart
Lexi Jayde - drunk text me
Damiano David - Nothing Breaks Like a Heart
Calum Scott - Roots
Sia - Helium
Cleffy - Hide Behind My Disguise
Gigi Perez - Sailor Song
Birdy, RHODES - Let It All Go
Alan Walker, Gavin James - Tired
TALK - A Little Bit Happy
Linkin Park - Up From The Bottom
Olivia Rodrigo - traitor
Sia - Alive
Royale & the Serpent, Chri$tian Gate$ - overwhelmed
SYML - Where's My Love
Mackenzy Mackay - The One That You Call
Lana Del Rey - Cinnamon Girl
Laci Kaye Booth - Daddy's Mugshot

Darhaven Citadel is an elite underground organisation of hitmen for hire. Also known only as The Citadel is 100 years old, known to be operated out of England.

The existence of The Citadel is known in select society groups, mostly ones who's bank balances are heavy and have an extensive list of enemies they want eliminated.

The selection process for which contract Darhaven Citadel will accept is thorough, the client, the target, the motive and everything in between is investigated, vetted, reviewed, accepted or declined. Most contracts are declined, only the select few are accepted and executed without a fault. There is not a single report of a failed contract that has been placed with The Citadel.

Prologue

She looks happy sitting in the sun, smiling down at her phone. Will she still smile like that after tomorrow?

"Oh I loooove this song!" Lily shouts and cranks the volume up even louder that snaps me out of my staring match with the icy duo. I get in the car and put my seatbelt on. As Maya reverses out of the parking spot and makes her way out of the parking lot, she drives past the 4x4.

I lock my eyes with the man in the passenger seat. His eyes are warm and inviting. Something feels so extremely familiar about them. Maybe he is a brother to one of the students and they look alike and that's why I feel like I've seen him before?

"We need to make a stop, I really need a wee!" I say and cross my legs. While Maya drives, me and Lily have finished few pre-mixed cocktails and we are in a great mood. Maya scoffs as she hates missing out, but thats the curse of the designated driver. We each take turns every year, so it's not just one of us driving every time.

"Can't you just hold it? We're about 30 minutes from the apartment!" Maya says as she speeds up hoping that will change our minds about our bursting bladders.

And now it's Lily's turn to convince Maya that the pit stop is needed.

"No, can't do! Unless you want me to squat in the back and pee on the floor?" I bark out a laugh which makes my already full bladder scream even more.

"OMG! The pair of you are going to be the death of meeee!" Maya tries to keep her face straight and is failing miserably, corners of hour mouth are lifting in one of her signature mischievous smiles.

"Ok, ok! I'll stop at the next services. Big or small, I'm stopping. I don't want no pissing in my car!" That does me in and I am bending over with laughter. Would it have been as funny without the alcohol swimming through my blood stream? Possibly not. But it is and I am.

It takes another 5 minutes for Maya to pull into services on the outskirts of Leeds. We all climb out of the car, me and Lily giggle, holding onto each other. Maya links her arm through mine and all three of us make our way to the restrooms.

"I've never felt this goooood!" I say as I exit my toilet stall. "What is it about taking a long wee that makes it so good?" Honestly, the drunk conversation topics are something else entirely.

"I feel reborn!" Lily announces and she glides and I do mean- glides out of her stall. Me and Maya look at each other and burst into laughter.

I never laugh as much as I laugh when I'm with my girls. I've known them since we were in diapers. We've grown up together and have always been part of each others lives. They aren't just my best friends, they are my family. My sisters. They have been with me through the darkest times of my life, never giving up on me. Always picking me up. Always taking care of me. I love these girls, I wouldn't be where I am if it weren't for these two.

"Let's pop in the shop and get some more cocktails for tonight!" Lily announces and drags us both towards the shop as we're walking out of the service station.

I pat my back pockets and realise I left my phone in the car.

Chapter 1 - Julia

It is remarkably warm weather for mid March and I am soaking up the sun rays. I love the sun, the heat and the happiness it brings to me. And yes, I also enjoy spending my 30 minute lunch break away from the kids and other teachers. Just a little bit of quietness to recharge for the afternoon.

I close my eyes and take a deep breath as my phone vibrates next to me.

Maya: How excited are we for the weekend?

Lily: I am counting down the hours!! Work has been murder this week! Bring on tomorrow afternoon!!

Me: I'm all packed and ready to go. I'll take the bags to work with me, so you guys can pick me up at 1:30pm!

"Hun, I'm home!" I shout out as I enter my apartment. Well.. our apartment. It still feels strange saying that out loud, but not as strange as it is saying 'my husband'.

"I'm in the office!" Vincent calls out. Office is a bit of a stretch, it's the second bedroom. Which is more like a shoe box, but ideal for what we need it for. After years of saving, we were finally able to buy our apartment last summer. We had to make some sacrifices, like a very modest wedding and no honeymoon, but it was all worth it. I absolutely adore our little oasis of calm, home comfort and full of love.

"Hows your day been?" I ask my husband as I enter the office.

"Busy with meetings and preparing budget reports. I'll be out tomorrow in meetings and will probably work late." He rattles on with his eyes still on the screen.

"Do you want to get a takeaway as you're away for the weekend and I won't see you till Sunday?"

"Definitely a takeaway." He finally looks at me with tired eyes.

"Rough day at school?"

I reply quickly, before I lose his attention to his reports again "Some of the kids decided to pop a load of party poppers in the middle of the class, which scared me and the rest of the kids in class. The head teacher had to come and write the whole situation up, but I had to have a serious conversation with the culprits and inform their parents." I take a deep breath "So yeah... rough day at school and I cannot wait for the weekend!"

How is it possible for the past 30 minutes to last 4 hours? I love my job, I really do, but I would be lying if I said that girls weekend doesn't top it. Girls weekend with my two besties, who I know are already outside the school waiting for me and the clock is only 1:15pm. I slowly start wrapping up the lesson by dishing out homework for the next week, which I'm sure most of my pupils won't do. I know English literature isn't everyones cup of tea so not everyone will be as enthusiastic about books and authors and the meaning behind their words. People often say that eyes are windows to peoples souls, but for authors, I think it's their written word.

Finally the clock strikes 1:30pm, the bell rings and I am free! I swiftly tidy up my desk, put all my notes away, grab my phone and send a quick message to my girls.

Me: I'll be out in 5mins.
Lily: We're here and waiting for you.

I grab my bags and dash out of the school. Every student I pass says 'Have a good weekend Mrs Green', I nod back and say 'have a good one guys'.

There. Fresh air. As I walk towards the blue Mini parked in a visitor space another car catches my attention. It's a big 4x4 with tinted windows on the sides. As a teacher, over time I've gotten to know all of my colleagues cars, visiting teachers cars and most of the parents ones too. We aren't a big school, so it's easy to remember. I've never seen this car though. Maybe a new student joining our school soon?

I can hear the music blasting from the Mini Cooper as I near it, drivers side window rolls down and Maya pops her head out.

"Boots open, Lils in the back, you're in the front. Come on, chop-chop! Time's ticking, we're burning daylight cinderella!"

All three of us have a very similar sense of humour, we just all show it differently. Maya is top tier; she is funny, sarcastic, confident and will go full steam ahead with what she has to say. Her role as a personal trainer suits her to the point. I made the mistake of asking her to help me get in shape for the wedding, she was so full on, that I ended up faking an injury to stop her sessions. Maya grew up in a large mixed race hispanic household, if you weren't loud, you weren't heard. And she was the loudest.

Lily is the middle tier; she will always join in and be open with us, but will be a lot more reserved with outsiders. She has an artists soul and her job as a graphics designer helps her fulfil her artistic needs. Lily is much quieter than Maya, but then not many people are louder than her. But it's Lily's voice itself, smooth and calming. If there ever is an argument brewing between us, it's always Lily who will be the voice of reason and gets us all to calm down.

Me? I'm the most quiet one out of the three of us. Different life experiences have made me more of an observer, than taking an active role in every conversation. But I don't have to worry about any of it with Lily and Maya, they make me feel comfortable and safe.

I round the car to the open boot and shove by bag in. I managed to pack all my stuff in a tiny carry on. I spot a bag that has bottles of wine and spirit in. Messy is written all over this weekend. I smile, shake my head and shut the boot, then make my way to the passenger side door. As I'm about to get in the car I glance back at the Range Rover and I am met with two icy gazes on me. Turns out the windshield isn't tinted, just the side windows. I keep my gaze on both men, I don't recognise either of them and from where I'm standing- they look too young to have kids to come to this school. The man sitting in the passenger seat leans over to the driver, clearly showing something on his phone. The driver looks down, gives the slightest nod and looks back at me. Then, so does the man in the passenger seat. What the hell?

"Oh I loooove this song!" Lily shouts and cranks the volume up even louder that snaps me out of my staring match with the icy duo. I get in the car and put my seatbelt on. As Maya reverses out of the parking spot and makes her way out of the parking lot, she drives past the 4x4.

I lock my eyes with the man in the passenger seat. His eyes are warm and inviting. Something feels so extremely familiar about them. Maybe he is a brother to one of the students and they look alike and that's why I feel like I've seen him before?

"We need to make a stop, I really need a wee!" I say and cross my legs. While Maya drives, me and Lily have finished few pre-mixed cocktails and we are in a great mood. Maya scoffs as she hates missing out, but thats the curse of the designated driver. We each take turns every year, so it's not just one of us driving every time.

"Can't you just hold it? We're about 30 minutes from the apartment!" Maya says as she speeds up hoping that will change our minds about our bursting bladders.

And now it's Lily's turn to convince Maya that the pit stop is needed.

"No, can't do! Unless you want me to squat in the back and pee on the floor?" I bark out a laugh which makes my already full bladder scream even more.

"OMG! The pair of you are going to be the death of meeee!" Maya tries to keep her face straight and is failing miserably, corners of hour mouth are lifting in one of her signature mischievous smiles.

"Ok, ok! I'll stop at the next services. Big or small, I'm stopping. I don't want no pissing in my car!" That does me in and I am bending over with laughter. Would it have been as funny without the alcohol swimming through my blood stream? Possibly not. But it is and I am.

It takes another 5 minutes for Maya to pull into services on the outskirts of Leeds. We all climb out of the car, me and Lily giggle, holding onto each other. Maya links her arm through mine and all three of us make our way to the restrooms.

"I've never felt this goooood!" I say as I exit my toilet stall. "What is it about taking a long wee that makes it so good?" Honestly, the drunk conversation topics are something else entirely.

"I feel reborn!" Lily announces and she glides and I do mean- glides out of her stall. Me and Maya look at each other and burst into laughter.

I never laugh as much as I laugh when I'm with my girls. I've known them since we were in diapers. We've grown up together and have always been part of each others lives. They aren't just my best friends, they are my family. My sisters. They have been with me through the darkest times of my life, never giving up on me. Always picking me up. Always taking care of me. I love these girls, I wouldn't be where I am if it weren't for these two.

"Let's pop in the shop and get some more cocktails for tonight!" Lily announces and drags us both towards the shop as we're walking out of the service station.

I pat my back pockets and realise I left my phone in the car.

"Maya, can you give me the car keys? I've left my phone in the car, just gonna give Vince a call while you grab more drinks." Maya hands me the keys and as I walk away I shout back "Can you get some Harribos as well please?" Both of them gives me the thumbs up and I make my way back to the car. I fish my phone out of the side pocket of the door and stand next to the Mini with my door open as I dial Vince.

After several rings it goes to voicemail "Hi hun, just thought I'd give you a quick call. We're about half an hour from Leeds, stopped at services to have a wee break. Just waiting for the girls at the car now. Don't work too late, I'll text you when we get to the apartment. Let me know when you get home. Love you. Bye."

It's just gone 3pm so he'll be knees deep in his budget meeting, talking figures and numbers, and projections, which just bores me to death, but Vince loves it. As I hang up I still have a smile on my face, I take a quick turn around to stretch and my smile vanishes.

The beastly Range Rover from the school parking lot, is parked 3 rows back from where we are. Same 2 men in the car. Staring at me.

What the actual fuck is going on? Swearing in my own thoughts nearly knocks me as much as seeing the creepy duo.

I lean against the side of the car and cross my arms over my chest and stare back at them. No, I won't be intimidated by them. I won't be intimidated by any men ever again. I uncross my arms, unlock my phone, click on the camera and I take a few photos of the car and the 2 creeps sitting in it. I make sure I zoom in as much as I can and also take a photo of the number plate. If anyone finds my dead body, at least I've done 50% of the investigators job by giving them the suspects.

Surprisingly, me taking a picture of them doesn't seem to have phased them at all. What is going on?

Luckily I am saved by my friends bouncing towards the car with a bag of more booze and an open bag of Haribbos in Mayas hand. I dip my hand into the bag, grab few of the sweets and climb back into the car, not giving the creepy duo a second glance. But my senses have kicked into overdrive and I can feel two pairs of eyes on me.

Chapter 2 - Julia

It's nearing 6pm, we have settled in our little AirBnB apartment and unloaded our, seemingly endless, supply of drinks. Our plan for tonight is simple- dinner at the pub down the road, a drink while we're out and then make our way back to our home away from home for the weekend with hours of chatting.

Me: We're settled in the apartment, will go out for dinner now and will be back later on. Are you home?
Vince: Hi love, yes, just got home I've picked up a pizza on the way, will have that and watch some TV. Have a lovely night.

The black Range Rover is still on my mind as I make my way to the living area. I contemplate telling my friends about it, but… what would I even tell them? That I think I've seen a common car twice today?
No, I can't do that. I know my friends well enough to know, that they will want to change or even cancel the whole weekend, as they will be too worried about me. Ever since the incident 7 years ago, they get extremely protective over me if they think there is a slightest chance of my distress.
I love them dearly and I know they would do anything for me, but sometimes that can be too much. So I plaster a smile on my face and stride into the living room.
"What are we talking about?" I ask

"Lily has a new boyfriend that she has not told us about!" Maya says while sipping from her wine glass.

"Wait what? Lils, you have a boyfriend? Why haven't we heard anything about him?" I look at Lily in a shocked surprise.

"He is not my boyfriend, we've just been out a couple of times." Me and Maya look at her with raised eyebrows.

"We need to know the details." I say.

"Every. Little. Bit." Adds Maya.

The pub is busy, as you would expect it to be on a Friday night, but we get seated quickly. Our table is by one of the windows, which is looking out to the street. Perfect spot for people watching.

"Sooo....." I say dragging out the 'ooooo' "what's his name?"

Lily blushes, she takes a sip of her cocktail to try to delay answering. "Why are you so shy to tell us about him?" I prod her further.

"Because he's different."

"What do you mean 'different'?" I continue my questioning, not letting her off the hook.

"Just different. Like, he's ruff and dark and mysterious. He is the exact opposite of the guys I usually date. He feels dangerous and off limits, you know what I mean?" She looks at us with blushed cheeks.

"No." I reply same time Maya says "Yes!"

I look at Maya in surprise "Do you?" And she gives me a mischievous smile. "You're up next Maya. I need to know what that smile means!" Both of us look back at our friend, she rolls her eyes and starts telling us more about him.

"Alright, his name is Christian and the name suits him so well. He is tall, about 6 foot, well built. Dark hair that matches his eyes. He is absolutely drop dead gorgeous." I've never seen her with this sparkle in her eye while talking about a guy. A warm, genuine smile spreads to my lips.

"How did you meet this mysterious man?" Maya asks

"Really randomly at a coffee shop in town. I don't even remember how we started talking, but we kind of clicked."

I reach my hand across the table and place it on top of hers, giving it a slight squeeze.

"I haven't seen you this excited about a guy, ever. I'm really, really happy for you Lils!"

We spent the better part of Saturday strolling around Leeds city centre, shopping, drinking coffees and cocktails. I bet my liver cannot wait for Monday to have a respite. We are heading out to some trendy club that Maya heard about while chatting to the bartender earlier in the day called Azalea. From the photos we found online- it's the place to be on any night. Only a certain number of people are allowed in each night, ou have to put your name down beforehand and only an hour before it opens at 10pm do you know if you've got in. It sounds very exclusive and part of me wants to go and the other part is absolutely terrified.

"WE GOT IN!!! OMG!! OMG!! OMG!!! I'm ordering a taxi to come pick us up at 10:30!!! I'm so excited, I cannot wait!!!" Maya screams at the top of her lungs while she runs around the apartment with a G&T in her hand!

I take one final look in the mirror before we head out. I am wearing a cream colour mini dress with a puffy sleeve on one arm and the other shoulder bare accompanied by white strappy high heels. The lighter colours compliment my olive skin tone perfectly. My dark brown naturally wavy hair comes halfway down my back, which has always been a security blanket for me. Usually I don't wear much make up, but tonight I've gone for a cheeky smokey eye with dark red lips.

The photos of Azalea we found online are not doing the club any justice. The whole room is circular, with a bar being in the centre of it on a platform. There are booths on the left hand side with dark upholstered velvet seating and a marble table in the middle. On the right hand side of the bar is the dance floor, which is slightly lower than the main level. At the back there are stairs that lead to, what I would assume, are private VIP areas. The rest of the floor is filled with either bar tables with stools around them or smaller sofas with tables. Every group gets assigned a spot, so you don't have to worry about not finding a space to sit down. We had to provide credit card details when we put our names on the list for tonight. As my two besties have already maxed their credit cards, I had to provide mine. I am seriously worried how much this night will cost me.

"Good evening ladies, my name is Harper and I'm gonna be your waitress for tonight. Let me show you to your table." An absolute goddess of a woman is walking us over to one of the booths. "There are no printed menus in the club, everything is ordered through the app. When you scan this QR code on the table it will automatically link with your booking. You order your drinks through that and I will bring them over. We don't serve any hot food, but we do have a variety of snacks you can get if you'd like. The bill will be charged to the credit card proved at the time of booking. I'll let you ladies settle in and I'll be over with your drinks once you're ready."

I take a look around, the club drips luxury, money and privilege. How the hell did we even get in here? There are crystal chandeliers that are muted to give just enough light to create the perfect atmosphere. The whole club is dressed in black, gold and dark purple. This, is how the other half lives.

I think all three of us are still shocked by what we are seeing, so I take my phone and download the app, low and behold- our booking, with our names and details.

"Girls… I'd just like to pre-warn you that, none of the drinks on here have any prices against them. Are we happy to go ahead with it?" This situation makes me feel slightly uneasy.

"Fuck yeah! When do you think we will go to another club like this? I tell you when- Never! We live this night like it's our last!" Maya stands up before either myself or Lily can say anything "We will drink. And dance, flirt and have the best night we've ever had!"

We do.

We have been here for nearly 3 hours and I am having so much fun. Maya has managed to talk herself all the way up into the VIP area and is shamelessly flirting with a very good looking man. Lily is on the dance floor with another group of girls and laughing with a drink in her hand.

As cute as my outfit looked with my strappy heels they are slowly but surely killing my feet. Sat back down in our booth sipping on another cocktail, I've not ordered the same one twice, wanting to work my way through the whole list. I'm not so sure that tomorrows' me will be that impressed with todays' me.

One minute I am in my happy buzz era, next I'm frozen in place as 2 men slide themselves into our booth. One positions himself right in front of me, the other sits on my left hand side, blocking my escape. My breathing stops the moment I recognise them. The creepy duo from yesterday. Why are my lungs not working? Where has all the oxygen gone?

"Please don't be scared, we won't hurt you." Says the man opposite me.

"Isn't that exactly what someone would say, who would intend to harm me?" Well done Jules, antagonise the men who have stalked you for two days.

The man takes a long look at me, but I don't break eye contact, even though the last particles of air are about to leave my lungs. He is intense, but…. But I am inclined to believe him. He won't hurt me. He slowly nods his head before he speaks.

"I suppose you are right on that. How are you enjoying the night?" Then gives me a wide smile. A friendly, warm smile.

I blink. And blink again.

"Why are you following me?" My heart is racing, I am surprised it hasn't jumped out of my chest and spluttered on the marble table in front of me. The time has slowed and all the background noise has been muted. It's been a while since I've felt this, but I recognise it well.

I keep looking at the man sitting across from me. Dark brown short hair, few day old stubble covers his jawline. He's got lovely olive skin complexion, slightly darker than mine. But it's his eyes I can't keep looking away from, I tilt my head slightly to the right. They are brown with specs of gold in them. What are the chances of the creepy guy having the same eye colour as me.

His smile doesn't falter as he says to me.

"I'm Brandan and this is my friend Theo." I had completely forgotten about the other man sitting next to me. His build is similar to Brandan, strong, but confident. Both of them must be over 6 feet tall. Theo is looking at me with his round green eyes, he has boredom written all over his face, whatever he has been dragged along for, he is not a fan. He's black hair is messy, like he has been running his hand through it several times. While Brandan is sporting a black suit with a white shirt, Theo is wearing a black t-shirt and trousers.

I turn my head back to Brandan in front of me.

"You didn't answer my question. Why are you two creeps following me?" That earns me a quiet snort from Theo, but I keep my gaze on the brown eyes in front of me.

"Well Julia… or would you prefer me to call you Jules?" My eyes widen at the mention of my name. How does he know that? "Actually, I'd prefer to call you my sister."

I freeze.

Everything freezes.

If the world was spinning in slow motion before, now it has stopped all together. The world is not spinning anymore. My heart is not beating. I am not breathing "And I'd like you to call me your brother." He smiles at me.

The bastard has the audacity to smile at me while I'm being pulled into the darkness.

The only sound I hear is blood rushing through my ears and a glass breaking against the marble table, before my world turns dark.

Chapter 3 - Julia

"Told you this was a bad fucking idea. She is having a full blown panic attack in the middle of the fucking club." I feel Theo grab me by my upper arms to guide me out of the booth. "Careful of the glass Julia, don't cut yourself." His voice is low and smooth with a hint of authority.

Cuts. Blood.

That stirs old, but never forgotten memories.

"Shit! I didn't know she would have a panic attack, did I?! She hasn't had one for at least a couple of years." How does he know that?

My vision is still dark, I blink my eyes to clear it, but my world it still fuzzy.

I hear a door open, I'm ushered in by Theo, who still has a strong hold on me, he leads me to a sofa and I sit down. "I'll get some water" he says and leaves the room.

I stare at the door.

"Keep breathing. Here, hold this." I look down as Brandan hands me a pebble, I take it in my hand and wrap my fingers around it. I close my eyes, focusing on my breathing and the pebble in my hand. I count to twenty and back and do that several times.

The sofa dips next to me as Brandan takes a seat. I open my eye and he holds a glass of water in front of me. Theo is nowhere to be seen.

"I didn't mean to freak you out, if I knew you'd have a panic attack, I would have never have done it this way."

I look at him as I down the whole glass of water. There is genuine remorse on his face.

"Can you start from the beginning?" My voice comes out as a whisper.

He nods, takes a mouthful of his whisky and sets the glass down on yet another marble table.

"I'm 29, so a few years older than you." And then he stops and just looks at me. He looks… confused? No, Brandan is nervous, the easy talker who dropped this major, life altering bomb on me and caused me to have a panic attack, is nervous.

"I'm afraid I'm going to need a bit more details than just your age Brandan." I coax and give him a weak, unsure smile.

That seems to relax him, he takes another gulp of his drink and continues.

"I've had this conversation with you in my head so many times, but doing it in real life is very different." He gives me the most boyish smile, I can see a little bit of my own smile in his "Long story short, my dad.. our dad… had an affair with a woman from Cambridge about 27 years ago. Not quite sure of the exact timings or how long it lasted… He didn't know you existed. He only learned about you 4 years ago when my mum passed away."

He really did make a long story short. There is too much information to unpack to even begin to understand what is going on, so I say the only thing I am sure of now.

"I'm so sorry for your loss Brandan." I can see the sadness and grief in his eyes, he lowers his gaze to the floor as he takes several deep breaths.

"It was my mum who told dad about you. She knew he was having an affair at the time and kept tabs on the other woman. She loved my dad, so she never raised it with him. She let him have his fun, go through whatever phase it was and waited for him to return to her. And he did. But she always kept an eye on the other woman. 8 months after the affair ended .. your mum gave birth to you Jules. My mum, she…she died of cancer, it wasn't easy. But before she passed away, she handed a shoebox to my dad and said 'Go find your daughter. She is beautiful. You should be so proud of her'." He takes another deep breath and his eyes are covered in sheen. "The box was full of photos of you, from when you were just born to your graduation photo. There was even a photo from your wedding. It was easy to track you from there, as mum had all your details." Brandan refills my empty glass of water, to give his hands something to do.

"But why are you contacting me now? What's changed from 4 years ago?" It's only for moment, but I catch Brandans expression change.

"I know it's a lot to take in, and trust me, it took me a while to get my head around this whole thing. Not just that I had a sister, but also that my dad cheated on my mum. I've always looked up to him, so for a long time I felt betrayed by him as well as being angry with him. How could he do that to my mum, to me, to us, you know?" He might have had 4 more years to digest this whole Hollywood movie script playing out in real life, but he still feels hurt, he is in pain. I just don't know who's the cause of his hurt- his dad.. my mum… or me..

"There are so many things I'd love to talk to you about

and answer why I'm here now, but now is not the time nor the place. We're staying at The Bells in city centre. Come for breakfast tomorrow morning and I'll answer as many questions as I can. I promise."

My head is swirling with all the information that has just been dumped on me. Brandan is talking like this is all certain, that we are siblings. That I have a father somewhere in the world. He cannot know that. This cannot be happening.

"How do you know any of this is true?" I blurt out, with more bite than I intended. He pulls his eyebrows together and tilts his head slightly, not understanding what I'm asking "This" I gesture between us "How do you know that it's true? Some photos in a box doesn't prove anything." I take a breath and look at him with pleading eyes "Why are you doing this to me?" My voice breaks on the last word and tears are threatening to escape.

Brandan takes my hands in his and instinctively I lean back. I recognise the look in the mirror eyes of mine. Hurt.

"Jules… I don't expect you to trust anything I've said to you, and I'm glad you're not. All I'm asking is for a chance for me to explain all this to you in more-" he looks around the room "relaxed environment. And to put your mind at ease, we did a DNA test, we're related."

"You did what?"

"We had a DNA test done to confirm what mum said is true."

"You couldn't have done, because you never asked me for a sample." Brandan smiles like he expected this to be my response.

"I know this is a lot to take in, but I swear, everything I've told you, is the truth. Please, come to breakfast in the morning and I'll explain and answer as many question as I can." Before I get a chance to say anything the door opens and Theo walks back in.

"Theo will drive you and your friends back to the apartment." My eyes widen and he chuckles shyly. "Don't look so freaked out. Yes, I know where you're staying and the door lock combination, trust me, it's for your own protection."

My remaining patience snaps at his words and clear invasion of my privacy.

"My own protection? Are you serious? And who will protect me from you two?" I point my finger at the pair. Brandan is about to say something, when I stop him with putting my hand up "You have just dumped a ton of life altering information in my lap, I am half drunk and I don't know what is really going on. But I do know, that I need time to process this all, before I even start considering going for a breakfast with either of you." I take a quick breath before continuing "You have stalked, watched and followed me, invaded my privacy which doesn't exactly scream 'I'm safe with these guys'!"

"Jules, we don't have time. We nee-"

I cut Brandan off "I'll make you a deal. I'll take your number and call you when I'm ready to talk. In the meantime- you will stop following me."

Both men look at each other and a quite conversation passes before Brandan takes my phone and adds his number. Theo doesn't look happy with this turn of events.

With that I take my phone back and walk out of the room, but before I close the door behind me I look back at both of them "Do not follow me. Or I swear to God, there will be a hell to pay!" My words come out stronger than I feel. My knees are wobbly, there isn't enough oxygen in this damn club and my eyes are close to betray me with tears,

10 minutes later we are on our way back to our apartment, but I cannot focus on anything Maya and Lily are talking about. I gaze out of the window and close my eyes, resting my forehead against the cool glass. Is this the last normal night of my life?

Chapter 4 - Julia

Me: Hi hun. Back from the club, heading to bed. I'll see you tomorrow.

It's nearly 4 in the morning by the time I crawl under the covers and lay my head on the pillow. Before I close my eyes and let the nightly slumber take me- I check my phone. No messages.

I'm about to fall asleep when my phone buzzes, I reach for it, squinting my eyes, looking for a text from Vince, but it's not my husband who has messaged me.

Brandan Your New Brother: Hi Jules, it's Brandan. Your brother. The one who gave you a panic attack, which I am really, really sorry about.

Brandan Your New Brother: I know we agreed that I'll give you time to think things through, but I really need to talk to you.

Brandan Your New Brother: I know you're reading my messages. Please. It's important.

Me: I need time, I told you - I'll contact you.

Me: Wait a minute! How did you get my number?

Brandan: …

Me: Brandan?

Brandan: There is no good way to answer your question without freaking you out even more.

Me: …

Brandan: Jules?

Me: …

Brandan: Julia?

The Unspoken Darkness

Me: Promise me I'm safe?
Brandan: You're safe. I promise.
Me: I'll see you in the morning.
Brandan: Goodnight Jules.

An old fear is rearing its ugly head and a knot is forming in the pit of my stomach. I want to trick myself in believing that what Brandan told me is a lie, but deep down I know it's not. And it terrifies me. Panic is rising in me and I know I'm on a one way road now.

I close my eyes and fall into a dreamless sleep.

It's 8:50 in the morning, I'd gotten few hours sleep, but that's what coffee is for. Before I head out to meet Brandan, I check on Maya and Lily. They are out cold, luckily we don't have to check out until mid-day, so they have a few more extra hours to sleep. I send them a message on our group saying I'm going out for a walk to clear my head.

I make it out to the front of the apartment building at which point I remember to check my bank account and see how much money we spent last night. I close my eyes and take a deep breath before I look down on my banking app and I see.. nothing. What? How is that possible? I refresh the page again, but still nothing. This cannot be happening, did I put someone else's bank details on the app and they will be hit with hundreds of pounds worth of bill?

Oh my God! Oh my God!! On a normal day, I could handle this with a calm head and not spin into a panic whirlwind, but last nights conversation is having a much larger impact on me than I thought.

Before I completely lose myself to a downward spiral, I log into Azalias app and check the account.

'Your account has been settled successfully. Thank you for visiting Azalea. We hope to see you again soon!'

What do you mean the account has been settled successfully? I haven't settled it. What is going on in my life right now.

"I'm glad I don't have to go upstairs and bang on the door to wake you up." I lift my head to see Theo looking at me through the open passenger side window of the same Range Rover they have been following me in. He's expression changes from playful to serious as soon as I meet his eyes. "Whats wrong?" he is out of the car and in front of me in a few long strides. "Tell me what's wrong." He demands.

"I… I don't know. The club has made a mistake, or… or I did. I don't know." I stammer as I try to get the words out while I desperately try to solve the problem in my head.

Theo's gaze bores into me. "What do you mean?"

"You know how you need to add your details when you do the booking thing with the club? I must've added someone else bank details, as there is nothing in my bank, but the app says my account has been settled." I rush the words out out as I shove my phone in Theo's face showing the message. My chest feels heavy and the air feels thick.

Theo holds me by my upper arms again and lowers his head so our eyes are at the same level "Julia, breath.

Deep breaths." I reach in my jackets pocket and grab the pebble Brandan gave me yesterday. Why did I keep it? "It's all ok. Bran settled your bill last night. He wanted to make up for causing you to have panic attack and dropping the major news on you." Seven… eight… nine… ten… "That's it, keep breathing. You're all good." Theo is still holding me by my upper arms and is following the same breathing pattern as I am. "He's new at being the big brother in real life, give him time to adjust."

"He better adjust fast, as I can't keep having panic attacks every day!"

"I'll let him know."

As we're about to reach the car I ask Theo "What do you mean 'brother in real life'?" He ignores me and proceeds to open the door for me. "Theo?" I repeat in a slightly urgent tone.

"Not my place to say." He motions for me to get in the car, I narrow my gaze on him, but I am greeted with the same unimpressed bored look he wore yesterday in the club. "Get in Julia." Why aren't my stranger danger alarm bells not ringing? The better question is - why am I getting in a car with a complete stranger?

Less than 10 minutes later I am in Brandans room where a breakfast table has been set up. He is standing anxiously by the table, unsure wether to come towards me or just wait for me to reach the table.

"You need to up your game Bran, you gave your newly acquired sister yet another panic attack this morning." Theo says casually as he strides towards the table and sits down.

I look back at Brandan and he is white as a sheet.

"I'm fine. Really. I'm all good." I give him a weak smile as I take the seat at the table and I give Theo a '*Really?*' glance.

"What… what happened? What did I do?" The poor guy can barely get his words out as he joins us at the table.

"What didn't you do is a better question?" Theo keeps going as he leathers his bread with more butter than needed. I scrunch my nose at that.

"Don't listen to him. Honestly, I'm good." I give Brandan what I hope is a reassuring smile.

"No. You weren't good, you were trembling like a fucking autumn leaf." What is wrong with this man? Why can't he keep his mouth shut? "And you nearly passed out from hyperventilating." I don't think much as I kick Theo under the table. Hard.

"Ouhhh!!" He gives me a hard look "Did you just kick me?"

"Oh, I'm sorry, must've been a leg spasm." I answer with my most innocent voice.

"You kicked me in the shins on purpose and it fucking hurt!" For a big muscular man, he sure has a low pain tolerance.

"Good." I don't even look at Theo as I reach to fill up my cup with coffee. "That'll teach you to keep your mouth shut next time." Theo grumbles in response and Brandan chuckles.

"I knew you two would get along." Colour has finally returned to Brandans face.

We spend the next several minutes serving ourselves with an assortment of food. With all the stress, my appetite has weaned, so I select a few different fruits I can nibble on, while I re-fill my coffee.

"So… why did you decide to finally contact me?" I break the silence with the question that has been plaguing me since the moment we stopped our conversation last night.

Brandan shifts in his seat as he begins.

"Dad runs a business that has been in our family for a couple of generations now. We provide high end security and protection detail to the rich and famous. It could be for a single event, it could be for a period of time or… some contracts are for life. Over the past few months we have been in discussions with other parties to expand our business, but one of our competitors who are bidding for the same business, have started playing dirty." He takes a couple of bites of his food, I don't say anything, I stay silent as I absorb his words. "About 3 weeks ago we started to notice things that were… odd. In our line of business some hostility is expected, but this time it has turned personal." Brandans easy going and cheeky demeanour has changed to something darker. There is no sign of the light he had in his eyes only 5 minutes ago. "We have started receiving threats against us as a business and as a family. Some of our operations have been disrupted as well." And with that my already non existent appetite disappears all together. He nods to Theo who produces a black folder that he hands to me. I take it with shaking hands and open in.

My eyes see black ink on white paper. I flick through the pages. I read the words. I understand them. But I don't know what they mean.

The words on the pages are starting to blur. I raise my eyes, looking from one man to the other, I finally ask in a choked voice

"What… what is this? Why do you have my photo in here with a different name?" I barely get the last word out before my throat closes up. The file contains my photo, but a different name with a different date of birth. It has 26 years of history written up, but it's not my past.

"People who issued the threats are good at finding anything to use against George Brentwood." Theo says matter of factly, but the only word I hang on to is - George. My fathers name. "They will dig until they find something or someone. In Georges case the someone is you." How is he saying all this so calmly.

"The threat against your life is too great to ignore. We will protect you, you will be safe. I promise." Some of Brandans warmth has finally returned to his eyes, but the darkness is still lingering. "We need time to give you a new identity so there is no link back to your life as Julia Green. It will be safer for you and everyone you love."

And finally the blurred words on the pages in the black folder make sense. I look back down at the folder in my lap. I scrunch up my brows as I franticly start to flick through the pages. It's not here.. I can't see it.. where is it??

The Unspoken Darkness

"Jules... Jules... Julia" Brandan raises his voice to get my attention "they're not in there."

All it takes is one look in my brothers eyes to know that there is only one file. One file for me and me alone. He is asking me to leave my life, my world behind and I can see his heart breaking for me.

"No.."I whisper and shake my head "You cannot honestly think that I will do this. I met you less than 12 hours ago and I don't know if any of this is true. I don't even know you! I can't just take your word for it." I finally stand as my emotions are overwhelming me.

Brandan gets up from the table and brings the folder to me on a page I hadn't seen before.

"Here, these are the DNA test results." I look down on a medical report which I don't understand, but the summary below is clear. I have a brother and father, who have found me. Under weird and suspicious circumstances, but they've found me.

"You two don't need a DNA test to tell you that you're siblings." Brandan and me both look at Theo "See, even that 'what are you talking about' look is the same." He finishes and returns to his plate of food.

I look at Brandan as I say "No one knows I exist or am related to you. Why would anyone be looking for me, there is no reason to. I can't do what you're asking me to. I have a husband and friends and family and job. I can't just up and leave it all for... I don't even know for what." I pick up my bag and head for the door. Thoughts racing through my head with unanswered questions of my past and not so clear future.

"Jules please." I look back at, who I know, is my brother. There is no doubt in my heart "I can't tell you everything, not now, but you have to believe me, that we will do everything to keep you safe. But we can't do that while you're Julia Green."

"Why can't you create files on mum and Vince and Maya and Lily. For all of us. I can't leave them." Tears are threatening to escape my eyes. "I won't leave them."

Brandan walks towards me, stands in front of me and for the first time I notice how tall he is. I am not short by any means, but he towers over me. He pulls me into a warm hug that I don't resist, as he says to me "I'm sorry little one. It has to be just you to keep you and them safe." I don't let my brain think too much about it as I embrace my brothers hug for the first and last time. It's warm and protective. I wish I'd known him when I was younger.

I pull out of his hug and look up at him "You are asking me to do the impossible. You are asking me to walk away from my family. If the scenario would be reversed - would you forgive me for abandoning you?" Brandans jaw is set in a tight clench. "I need to get back to the apartment before the girls realise I've been gone for too long." Without another glance back, I leave the room.

Chapter 5 - Julia

I feel like I've been living in a haze for the past three weeks. I am going through the motions, but I'm not really there. Things have been strange at home with Vince as well, he feels more distant. His work has been crazy and with me living more in my head than I have for years, it has made it a challenging few weeks. Every time he asks me 'what's wrong' or 'what's going on with you'- I open my mouth to tell him the most bazaar story, but then nothing comes out. So I just shake my head and reply that I'm tired and feel run down.

In my haste of leaving the hotel I had stuffed the black folder in my bag, which I didn't realise until couple of days later. I've gone through the folder countless times, remembering all the details of a person that doesn't exist. When I close my eyes at night, I dream about Raegan Brentwood, the woman who doesn't exist. I dream about being free.

During this time one thing that I have learnt about Brandan - he is persistent. He has called me every morning and night and at least sent one message every day. Sometimes it's just a 'hello, hope you're well', other times he sends me information, photos and videos of his life and Brentwood Global. There have even been several ones of George Brentwood. My father. And I have to agree with Theo, we don't need a DNA test to confirm that all three of us are related.

The Unspoken Darkness

George has passed on his olive skin complexion, dark brown hair and golden brown eyes to both of us.

Brentwood Global is the leader in personal and event security protection worldwide, with its head office in London. Brandan and Theo both work at the company, different divisions. George is the CEO, a position he took over from his father over a decade ago.

Despite all his calls and texts, I am yet to answer him. Even with the limited drip of information coming my way now, I am extremely overwhelmed with it all. My anxiety and panic attacks are only half a step behind me these past few weeks.

I have just pulled into my parking space at work and Brandans name is dancing across my phone and for the first time I hit the green button on the phone.

"Hi." My one word answer has startled him.

"Oh, Hi! How... how are you doing?" I can hear the nervousness in his voice. I may have ignored his calls, but that doesn't mean I've not done any google detective work. The few interviews I could find of him, he comes across as smooth talker who exudes confidence and power. But him being nervous to talk to me, his sister, that brings a little smile to my face. Which has been a rarity recently.

"I'm not sure. Nothing has changed, yet everything is different. I feel lost, but I'm here. I keep replaying our conversations in my head to try and make more sense of it, but all it does is confuse me even more." I answer honestly and choke the last words out as I take a deep breath and look out of my car window. When did it start to feel different? "I'm sorry I haven't answered any of your calls or texts. It's…."

"I know. But I'm glad you answered today."

"Me too." We both stay silent for a little while, it's a comfortable silence, like we've done this before. "Look, I've gotta go and prep for my lessons, but are you free tomorrow evening? We could have dinner."

"I'd love that."

Chapter 6 - Brandan

"So, she wants you to meet her parents?" I huff out a laugh as I throw a jab at Theo's jaw. It skims him lightly before he turns away.

"Yeah, she also wants us to go on a holiday to spend some quality time together." I duck and spin away from Theo's right hook.

"And, what's the problem with that? You've been going out with this Heather girl for what.. 6, 7 months?" we exchange a few more jabs before he answers.

"We've been on a few dinners, that's it, and she spends most of the time taking photos to post on her social medial account. The rest of time time we've spent together has been in bedrooms… or other rooms." He dances around me light on his feet. Theo and me have been best friends since we've been able to walk, but in a fighting ring? I don't trust the fucker. "I don't spend time with people. And I sure as shit don't plan on going on holiday with anyone, that sounds like fucking torture!" I burst out laughing as it's not every day someone ruffles Theo's feathers. "How is it going with Julia?" He asks, the sly fucker.

I kick his feet out "Nice change of subject." I jump back to avoid his kick. "It's going well, I'm seeing her tomorrow again. Her husband not knowing what's going on makes it trickier to catch up, but she's making it work." We've stopped the sparring as I continue to talk "She seems much calmer than when we first met her, she says she hasn't had any panic attacks, but I think she's lying about that." Theo nods.

"When is the old man meeting her?"

"I've not asked either of them the question, but I think dad is the one who will be prolonging it. Honestly, I'm just enjoying it to get to know her and doing things together." I jump off the sparring ring and head to the bench for some water "Regardless what happens, I won't leave her life, not now."

My phone is buzzing on the bench and I answer it without checking the caller ID while gulping down some water.

"Hello" the line is quite, I pull the phone away from my ear to check who's calling me. Julia

"Jules? Is that you?" Alarm bells have started going off in my head.

"Bran…" I can barely hear her. Is that traffic I hear in the distance? "I think I've broken my hand. It's swollen and it's starting bruise…" what the fuck?

"You need to go to the hospital. Get Vince to drive you and I'll meet you there." I'm already pulling my shirt over my head and shoving feet into my shoes. Theo is doing the same.

"I can't." I can hear the tears she's cried in her voice, I stop.

"What do you mean you can't?"

"I'm on the side of the road." Cold shiver runs through my body. Mental images of car crash flashes through my mind.

"Were you in an accident?" I can see Theo has already pulled up the tracking app to see where she is. I've installed trackers in her car and phone and I'm tracking her bank cards.

"No, not an accident. Bloody car ran out of petrol and I had to pull over to the side." There is so much more to this story than she's telling me right now.

"Ok, stay exactly where you are. Do not move. We're on the way." We are walking towards the car as I hear Jules say my name.

"Bran?" Her voice sounds weaker that it did a second ago.

"Yes Jules." My heart is pounding faster with each second.

"Can you stay on the phone? I don't want to be alone." Fuck. Whoever caused this will be so very, very sorry.

"I'm not leaving you, I'm right here with you. We're about 35 minutes from where you are, we're on the way."

We've been driving for about 10 minutes now. There are 2 things I can hear on the line - traffic in the background. And my sisters crying.

"Jules?" I ask gently "How did you break your hand?"

A weird laugh hiccup combination escapes her "After a day from fucking hell-" this is bad, I've never heard her swear, not even that first night in Azalea. "I got home early wanting to go curl up in my bed and forget about the world. But what I got instead was a view of my husband being balls deep in another women in the very same bed I had planned to curl in." She swallows the tears and continues on, her voice barely above a whisper "One thing led to another, he grabbed my hand to stop me from leaving and I punched him to get away. The sad things is, I probably didn't even leave a mark on his face, yet I ended up with a broken hand." There is not even a second between Jules last word and Theo putting his foot down, the speed limit is non existent.

That fucker hurt my sister and he is going to pay. As I contemplate the ways of which to torture that waste of space Vincent, I glance over to my friend, and for the first time in my life, I cannot read his expression.

The longest drive of my life comes to an end when I finally see Jules sitting in the grass on the side of the motorway, away from her car.

"I see you." With that she lifts her head and rises to her feet walking towards her car, cradling her right hand against her chest. We pull behind her car and I jump out and jog towards her. As I near her I can see her red, puffy eyes from all the crying she's been doing.

A sob escapes her and I pull her into a hug. "I didn't know who else to call."

"You call me. You always call me."

When I was a little boy every Christmas and birthday there was only one thing I asked for a baby sister. Somewhere deep down I believe I already knew about Julia, but I never stopped asking for one. When I got older, I stopped asking, but the feeling of protectiveness never faded, it only grew stronger.

"Let's get you to the hospital to have that hand looked at." I turn her and we walk back towards the car. Theo has opened the back door and is waiting there with his jacket in his hands. As we get to the car, he drapes the jacket round Jules shoulder, which seems to swallow her whole. He helps her get in the car, secures her seatbelt and closes the door. Without a word Theo walks back to the drivers side, gets in and pulls back onto the motorway towards the hospital.

Jules is looking out of the window as she asks in a broken voice "How quickly can you arrange for a divorce to be finalised?"

"I'll take care of it." Theo says with coldness in his voice. I turn to look at him, his knuckles are white from how hard he is gripping the steering wheel. I would bet all the money in the world, that he is imagining his hands wrapped tight around Vincents throat.

A&E is busy as always. We walk towards the check in window and a middle aged woman with black rimmed glasses looks at Jules and raises her eyebrows.

"I'd like to see a doctor, I think I've broken my hand." As soon as the words leave Jules mouth the snarky looking receptionist glares at Theo and me.

"Did you two have anything to do with the young ladies broken hand?" She asks with an accusatory look in her eyes.

"No, no they have nothing to do with my broken hand. That's my brother and his friend, they just brought me here." Her brother. That's the first time I've heard her call me that, and my chest tightens.

"Name and date of birth love"

"Name.. my name…"

"Yes love, I need your name to get you check in"

"My name is……"

"Her name is Ju-" I start to say when Julia finally says the words I never thought she would.

"Raegan Brentwood. My name is Raegan Brentwood."

Chapter 7 - Julia

Earlier in the day.

These past few weeks have been one of the best ones I've had in a long time. I've met Brandan for dinners and walks to get to know each other. He has continued to share information about his life, growing up and his childhood. I sense that he wants to ask if I'm ready to meet George, but I think he's worried that it will freak me out. Theo has joined him a couple of times, so I'm getting to know him as well.

I know they've been friends since they were little, they are more like brothers than friends, and that is a relationship I understand really well.

I haven't told Vince or my two closest friends about my newly found family. I know there is only a certain amount of time I have left before I need to tell them. It's not just the possibility of threats that are issued against the Brentwoods, but every time I meet up with Bran, I have to lie to Vince about working late or catching up with the girls. Everything that is happening in my life feels new. I don't fully understand it all myself, how am I to explain it to other people?

But there is one person I've been meaning to talk to to get some of the answers. And a final confirmation that what Bran has told me is not a lie.

The Unspoken Darkness

It's mid-morning on a Friday and I'm driving to my mothers house. I may have told my work a little white lie that I'm sick and have a stomach bug, so I had to go home. I have questions I need answers to and I cannot wait. Not anymore. My relationship with my mother has always been strained. It wasn't until I was older when I realised my mother and I are two very different people.

"Hello darling, what are you doing here?" She kisses my cheeks in greeting, but there is no warmth to them, not like the hugs Bran gives me. "I didn't know you were coming by today. Wheres Vince?" She looks behind me, searching for my husband.

"It's just me mum. Haven't seen you for a few weeks, so I thought I'd pop by. What have you been up to?" We spend the better part of an hour of her talking about all the gossip from her club. I finish my cup of coffee and finally ask the question I've been burning to ask.

"Mum, do you know who my father is?" Her carefully composed demeanour changes and a cold mask is slipped on my mothers face.

"That is an extremely inappropriate question to ask Julia. You know I do not like to talk about the past." She quickly gets up from the settee, we've been sitting on in the living room.

"But you do know who he is, don't you? Why don't you want to tell me?" I follow her in the kitchen in an attempt to keep the conversation going.

"What has gotten into you? Why are you asking such things." She is getting angrier with every word, but I am not letting this go. I can't. "Leave the past in the past. We have to look to the future. When are you and

Vincent having a baby?" Not this again. She asks me this every time she sees me and it is not a conversation I want to have with her now or ever. "You've been married for a year now. Clarices daughter, Catherine, the one who married the investor from London. They are expecting, and they've only been married for 8 months." We were never rich, but we lived comfortably, I never needed for anything. Grandma and grandpa were the most down to earth people you could ever meet, so I never understood why mum cared so much about image and status in society.

"Mum. I am not having this conversation with you and I am not going to live by some imaginary timelines set by your club. I am asking you about my father, because I want to know. I have the right to know." I am all but shouting at her. Not because I'm angry, but because I am lost and confused and I feel so very alone. I am floating between people, truths and half truths. All this uncertainty is awaking part of me that I've worked hard to keep locked away.

My mother doesn't just have a cold mask on her face, she is red with fury. She starts washing up our cups and looks out the window with longing in her eyes "I was a gorgeous young woman with my life ahead of me. I had plans to go to university and live a life I had always dreamed of. I planned to meet a husband who would spoil me rotten, wine and dine me, take me on holidays. I would be the perfect wife. But as you know, my life did not turn out that way." Now, she is facing me "I met a man, absolute drop dead gorgeous. He was everything I ever wanted in a husband, the looks, the money, the power. I knew he had it all. We started a whirlwind romance and I was besotted with him. He gave me everything I wanted. But then, a few months into our relationship he disappeared. Never came back, never called or wrote to me. I tried to find him, but I only had his first name. Silly really, with all the excitement, I never learnt his last name. It wasn't long after he left, that I found out I was pregnant with you. And I knew my life would never be the same." And by the look in her eyes I know she doesn't mean for the better. She means she lost the life she wanted. Because of me. "At first I was in shock. I didn't tell anyone. I hoped and prayed for the pregnancy to end, but you survived." Cold sweat covers me. Is this where it all started? "Nine months later you were born and I was damaged goods. No respectable man would ever want to date, let alone marry a woman with a child who is not his." For the first time in my life I've seen a side of my mother I knew deep down existed, but I never thought she would turn it on me. She didn't just wish for me to never be born, she absolutely loathes me. A sign and a reminder of the life she lost.

"You have resented me for 25 years, because YOU had an affair with a man that resulted in you having a child." My voice comes out steady, calm and low. She doesn't say anything, but regret does not cross her face either. In fact, she looks relieved by having this off her chest. "What is my fathers name?"

She doesn't hesitate before answering "George."

I got what I came here for and more. I've received a lifetime of hate from her with no fault of my own.

"Goodbye mother." These, I know are the last words I'll ever speak to my mother.

All I want to do now is get home, get in my bed and cuddle up to Vince. I want his hugs and I miss his smell. Ever since Leeds we've grown more distant and I know it's because I've been living in my head all this time. I want to tell him everything that has happened and why I've been so different lately. I want to go back to my safe space with him.
I need him to ground me, to hold me close.

As I unlock the door and step into my apartment, a weight seems to have been lifted off my shoulders. I head to the kitchen to splash my face with water, to wash my tears away and grab a glass of water. I close my eyes and lean against the kitchen counter and take several deep breaths. Breath in… and…. Breath out….

"Oh baby! Yeah! Harder, harder! Aaa!!" It's a female voice coming from inside my apartment. I step out of the kitchen in the lounge as I hear "You feel soo tight, I'm gonna come!" Is that…. Is that Vinces voice? In a trance I make my way to our bedroom and open the door. And my world shatters along with the water glass that has met the wooden flooring. At the same time a groan escapes from Vince's lips as he comes inside another woman. A second later two heads turn towards me and they're both pale. "You shouldn't be home yet." are the first words my husband utters to me with his dick inside another woman.

"Is that your defence for fucking another woman? That I shouldn't be home yet?" There are defining moments in every persons life. Moments that forces them to make the decision that otherwise would have been too hard, too unimaginable to make.

This is one of those moments.

There is no hesitation as I turn and head towards the door. I should feel pain, anger, betrayal, hurt, but all I feel is numbness. I know the rest will follow. They always do. There is only so much I can take, before my mind and body goes in self destructive mode. And numbness is the safe zone.

"What are you doing?" He shouts as he runs after me, trying to put his trousers back on.

"I'm leaving." I don't even look back at him.

"You can't leave me. We're married."

"Marriage didn't seem to stop you shoving your dick in another pussy, so it means fuck all to me." He grabs me just before I reach the door.

"And where are you gonna go? Mmm? You will be crawling back to me by the end of the week, so you might as well just stay." He grabs me tighter "And don't pretend that you're all innocent in this, you've been sneaking around for weeks as well, so we're square. Just calm down."

The arrogance of this man. Has it always been there and I never saw it? Have all the people I considered my closest family been hiding their true selves from me? This realisation is like a punch to my gut and my vision blurs.

"Let go of me you asshole!!" I shout and try to wriggle out of his hold, but he is holding my hands tight. So I do what every classy woman would do, I kick him in the crotch, as he lets go of my hands to cup his dinky size dick and balls, I curl my right hand into a fist and land it on his cheek. I hear a crunch, but I've got no time to waste. I open the door and run towards my car.

Only when I'm already on the road I'm hit with a wave of pain coming from my right hand. But I don't stop, I keep driving.

I don't know where I'm going, but my heart is saying head south.

Chapter 8 - Brandan

"My name is Raegan Brentwood, 9th March 98." I'm looking at her, completely dumb founded. Did I hear it right? I'm rooted in place by what she has just said.

The receptionist prints out a wrist band with personal details, Theo grabs it and puts it around her left wrist. She finally looks at me, all the light and joy I've grown to recognise in her eyes are gone. Julias eyes are empty "Do what you need to do, I'm going home with you." I clench my teeth together to stop the lump in my throat to come to the surface. She's coming home.

Theo leads her to the waiting area and sits her down, his jacket is still around her slender shoulders.

"Do you want anything?" He asks her gently, which is not a voice he uses often.

"No."

I slide down in a seat next to Julia, no - Raegan, and take a deep breath. I know I need to ask her to confirm what she just said, but I'm also afraid of her changing her mind. Or that I imagined it all.

"Are you sure about this?" She nods her head, looking straight ahead at the wall that's plastered with all sorts of medical flyers. She keeps nodding her head as she gathers her thoughts.

She begins her re-telling of todays events, Theo brings us water and he sits on her other side. With every sentence my chest feels tighter and tighter, my patience levels are running low. How much damage can I do to both, her mother and Vincent, before I upset Raegan?

"In the space of couple of hours, the life I've known, no longer exist. Two of the people who were supposed to love me unconditionally and be my safe space have been lying to me for as long as I've been alive and Vince? I don't want to know. I've been through this once, I can't do it again." She turns her head and looks me in the eyes with silent tears running down her cheeks. "I don't know what my life as Raegan Brentwood will look like, but I want to find out." The last dregs of the fight has left her and she slums back in the chair.

"Hi son, where the hell are you? You were supposed to see me earlier." Yes I was, but a single phone call changed my plans for the day.

"Jules is in hospital." I don't bother with apologising for missing our meeting, making sure my sister is safe takes priority over quarterly budget figures. I hear my fathers sharp intake of breath "She is fine. Well, she's broken her hand, but she's all right. They're putting her hand in a cast now."

"What? How did that happen?" There is no wavering in his tone of voice, it's direct, hard and promises no mercy. This is who George Brentwood is to the outside world. Only those close to him sees another, kinder side. "She walked in on her husband banging some other chick, she ended up punching him to get out. Theo is arranging divorce papers and I'll be hand delivering them tomorrow morning." There is a slight pause on the line, but George Brentwood wouldn't be at the top of the food chain if he hesitated long.

"Theo is a criminal and cooperate lawyer, what does he know about family law to get divorce papers done correctly?" Because we operate in two kinds of businesses, it is handy to have real degrees that can help in either businesses. The more ways you know to keep yourself out of the claws of the law, the better. When we were in our early teens, Theo and I had to decide which parts of the business we will be involved in, that will shape and guide us to take over one day. I always found computers fascinating so I went down the programming and business degree routes.

"He knows what he's doing dad." Even if he didn't, the way Theo was, I wouldn't even dare tell him to find another lawyer.

"I know he's more than capable, it's just that…"

"This is important, he knows it. And dad?"

"Yes."

"Raegan is coming home." The line goes quite, but I can feel the emotions rippling off my father through the phone. This is as much of a shock to him, as it was to me no more than 15 minutes ago. We have spoken about the possibility for years and in more detail recently, but how it were all progressing with Julia, it didn't seem likely to happen.

"I'll get everything ready for when you get home."

As I finish my call Raegan is walking out of one of the side rooms with right hand in a cast halfway up her arm. She looks absolutely exhausted, with empty look in her eyes. Theo is right on her heels, he hasn't left her side since we picked her up. I look at my friend and he gives me a slight nod. She's all right.

Chapter 9 - Raegan

It is dark by the time we leave the hospital. I am in the back of the same Range Rover they were following me in, but it's not fear that grips me, it's numbness. I'm looking out of the window as the traffic lights go past me. I look up at the sky and there is one lone star blinking at me and she is my sole focus for the rest of the drive.

The car slows down and stops at a massive wrought iron gate, there are three guards stationed here. They must recognise the car as they swiftly open the gate and we drive through. The driveway is long and windy, but as we come out of one of the bends a grand old English mansion rises from the darkness. There is not much light, but I can see a circular water feature in front of the house that has a circular drive way around it. Lights have been strategically placed on the building to give it a menacing look in the dark. And it works. Theo stops the car at the bottom of the stone stairs that lead up to enormous wooden double doors.

I climb out of the car and slowly turn around in a little circle to take in my surroundings. This all feels surreal. As I finish my 360 spin, the front door is open and I see a shadow standing in the doorway. It might be dark and I can't see his face, but I know exactly who that is. George Brentwood. My father.

"Come on." Brandan encourages me with his hand on my back and says quietly to me "It's going to be OK. Dad knows what kind of day you've had, he won't expect small talk from you." I nod, relieved he said that and grateful I have him by my side. I'm grateful to have both of these men by my side, they have kept me calm and stopped me from spiralling into the darkness that I know awaits me. They've done all the talking at the hospital as my mind is all over the place and no place at all. Their presence alone is giving me strength to keep going. To breath. They've become my lifeline. While being lost in my own thoughts we have reached the open door.

"Welcome home sweetheart." are the first words George says to me in a deep, crisp voice. He stands a touch taller than Bran, mid fifties, strong build which must be a result of years of working in security. He is wearing a dark grey suit with a white shirt. But it's his eyes that catch my attention, they are the same as mine and my brothers. Everything I've read and heard from Bran, George Brentwood is at the top of the game, he is cold, calculating and ruthless in business. Right now that is not who I see. I see a man, a father, standing in front of his daughter with guilt, regret and pain written all over his face. His eyes wanting, but not daring to ask or plead for her forgiveness.

I don't know if it is the culmination of everything that has happened over the past few weeks. Or if it is the mere fact that I've lost a parent today, but I'm gaining another. I take a step closer to George and wrap my arms around his back and give him a hug.

"Hi." Or maybe the hug is more for me than him. I hear his sharp intake of breath as this has caught him completely off guard. And I'll be honest, it has me as well. But he doesn't hesitate for long in wrapping his arms around my shoulders and pulling me close.

"Hello sweetheart." With me being much shorter than he is I can hear his rapid heart beats. Surprisingly my own heart is beating it's normal pace. I suppose a broken heart has no where to run. No one to beat for but it's inevitable end.

I step out of our hug and I face Brandan "I'd like to go to bed."

"Come, I'll take you to your room." Bran leads me up the grand staircase, to the right, through several hallways and some more stairs. I'll need to get a map to not get lost in this manor, as it feels like a maze. He opens a door that leads into a grand and luxurious living room. On my right there is a fireplace and a window on each side of it. An elegant coffee table sits in front of it and is surrounded by an ornate velvet sofa and a couple of arm chairs to match. In the middle of the room is a round table with a vase of fresh flowers. The left side of the room is lined with bookcases and a writing desk has been put up against a window. There is another seating area with smaller, more comfier looking sofas in the middle. In front of me, behind the round table with fresh flowers is another door. Bedroom. It's more modern than the room just outside it, with a king size bed and white linen bedding. The back wall is covered in floor to ceiling windows. There is also a built in wardrobe on the opposite wall with a vanity unit in the middle.

"And the bathroom is just through here." has Bran been talking this whole time and I haven't heard a thing?

"You know, this isn't just a room, it's an apartment, right?" I finally say as I peak inside the bathroom. Shower, bath, sink, toilet and counters.

He just laughs "You'll get used to the space. As it was such short notice of you coming home, we didn't have time to prepare much, but they managed to get you some pyjamas." he motions to the ottoman at the foot of the bed "The bathroom is stocked with all the toiletries you might need and we'll sort the rest out tomorrow."

With every passing second I can feel the energy draining out of me, I can't even muster enough of it to say 'thank you' so I just nod. Nodding seems to be my choice of communication as the day has gone on. English masters coming in handy! He gives me the biggest bear hug I could ask for while holding on the tiniest thread of self control to not let my tears fall again. "I promise, I got you. Have some rest now, I'll see you in the morning."

I strip out of the clothes I've been wearing and put them in a bin. I adjust the shower head to not get my cast wet and while holding my right hand above my head, I take a shower. I wish I could stand under the shower for hours, but I neither have the energy to stand nor hold my hand above my head for that long. I dry myself, brush my teeth, put on the clean pyjamas. After what has been the longest day of my life I climb into the bed. I turn off the bedside lamp and stare up at the ceiling. I let the silent tears roll down my cheeks, into my ears, down my jaw and into the pillow. My heart is too broken to sob or cry out loud. With every blink another wave of tears leave my eyes. With every blink my eyes become more heavy. And my heart more broken.

Chapter 10 - Raegan

I am awoken by a throbbing pain in my right hand. What the hell? I open my eyes and panic takes over me-where am I? Two heartbeats later memories of yesterday start flowing back and suddenly the broken hand is a tickle of pain compared to how my heart feels. I reach for the painkillers and a glass of water on the bedside and lay back down. The room is dark, but whispers of daylight are sneaking through the curtains. I slowly raise from the bed, making sure I don't move my right arm too swiftly, I slowly pad towards the window and open the curtains.

A picturesque countryside view greets me with the sun just above the horizon and morning dew is still covering the grass. There is no sight of a car, road or another house in my line of sight. It's peaceful. I think I'm going to like it here. I stand there for a while longer watching the world wake from it's nightly slumber.

Now that there is daylight and I'm a bit more alert to what is around me, I take a proper look around the room I'm in. My room. On the chair by the door is a small pile of clothes with a note on top

I know these are not exactly your size, but better than walking around in your PJs.
Bran

A pair of grey jogging bottoms, black t-shirt and a pair of socks have never looked more appealing than they do now. Before changing out of my PJs I decide to take another shower, but try washing my hair this time, as I can still feel the heaviness of yesterday linger on me.

As I finish getting dressed, which is much harder with one hand than one might expect. My stomach growls and demands it gets fed, I can't even remember the last time I ate. I wonder how long it will take for me to find the kitchen. I'm about to open the door to the hallway when I hear a couple of soft knocks. I open the door as the last thud of the knock echoes and George is standing in front of me. He looks more composed this morning than he did last night.

"Morning." I seem to find my voice first.

"Morning sweetheart, just wanted to check in to see how you are doing." I see the same nervousness I saw in Brandan that day back at the hotel. As to answer my question my stomach lets out another deafening growl "Would you like some breakfast?" He smiles at me softly.

"Yes please." I close the door and we walk side by side through the halls, down the stairs, weave through different rooms, I have to keep pulling my jogging bottoms up as they are several sizes too big.

"We have several dining rooms, but we're going to the sunroom. It's on the east side of the house and catches the light perfectly in the morning just in time for breakfast." Several dining rooms? How many rooms does this house have? Oh, I'll definitely need a map to navigate these halls. We finally enter a room, that I presume is our breakfast room. It's bright, not just from the sunlight beaming in from the windows covering 2 of the walls, it's also the colours chosen for this room.

Nearly in the centre of the room is a round dining table with 8 chairs around it. The table has already been stacked with fruits and pastries and I can feel myself salivating in my mouth.

"Isn't it dangerous to have whites and creams in a dining room?" I ask, trying to think of something light to say. George pulls out a chair for me and I sit down.

"Only if the conversation turns violent." Somehow, I believe his statement. He takes a seat a couple of chairs over so we can see each other more easily.

"Good morning Mr Brentwood and Miss Raegan." An older lady, dressed in a black skirt, white blouse and kitten heel shoes is making her way towards us.

"Ahh.. Right on time as always Patricia. Raegan, this is Patricia, head of the housekeeping, she pretty much runs this place."

"You are too kind sir. Nice to finally meet you Miss Raegan. If you need anything, please let me know."

"Nice to meet you Patricia and thank you. Please just call me Raegan."

She nods and gives me a smile and I take an instant liking to her, there is a cheeky spark in her eyes and I want to find out what it means. "What can I get you both to drink?"

"Could I please get coffee with milk please?" My stomach makes yet another growling sound and I shake my head.

"The usual for me Patricia. Thank you." He pours both of us a glass of water "How is your hand feeling this morning?"

"It's throbbing, but I've taken painkillers the hospital prescribed, so should start easing the pain soon."

"And how did you sleep?"

"Surprisingly well. I took a shower before going to bed and I fell asleep pretty quickly. I think the past few weeks have finally caught up with me and with yesterday on top of it, there wasn't much energy left in me to stay awake." George maintains eye contact with me while I talk. I expected to feel anxious and possibly even scared to talk to him, but I'm not feeling either. I'm feeling calm. My heart is beating it's normal pace, I am not hyperventilating. How can this all feel so normal? Before I can travel further down this rabbit hole in my head, Patricia returns with our drinks. She sets mine down in the most elegant cup and saucer I've ever seen. "Thank you."

"What would you like for breakfast Raegan?" I'm so glad she dropped the miss. There will be a hundred and one things I will need to adjust and get used to, 'Miss Raegan' won't be one.

"Could I just have some scrambled eggs, toast and mashed avocado if you have any. If not, don't worry."

She gives me a knowing smile and something tells me, she knew my go-to breakfast order before I stepped a foot in this house.

"Of course." She turns her head towards George "And you sir?"

"I'll have a full English." George spits out quickly while hiding behind his cup of coffee and taking a big gulp trying to avoid saying anything else, Patricia narrows her eyes.

"Of course sir, sometimes Christmas does come early." George chokes on his coffee and his cheeks have gone a tiny bit red, but before he can say anything, she is out of the door. I look at him and raise my eyebrows in a question.

"In my last check up the doctor said I had a high cholesterol, so Patricia has made it her mission I only eat foods that are low in cholesterol. I appreciate her care, but the only problem is, I don't like most of those foods. She is like a German shepherd, she sniffs out any snacks I get and takes them away." I press my lips together in a thin line to stop myself from laughing. The formidable George Brentwood is being schooled by his housekeeper. I can't hold all the laughter in and let a little huff of a laugh out loud

"It's nice to hear you laugh, even if it is at my expense." He tries and fails to keep the smile out of his voice.

"I'm glad I'm finally not the only one who openly laughs at you dad." I turn around to see Brandan and Theo striding into the breakfast room. Both men dressed in three piece suits and ties. It's Saturday, isn't it? Why are they dressed so official? And for breakfast.

Both men take their seats. Theo sits next to me and Brandan opposite me, next to his dad. Patricia returns with their usual drinks and a re-fill for my coffee.

"You need to sign these." Theo passes me a wad of documents. I move my cup of coffee to the side and take the pile from him. I scrunch my eyebrows together as I can't believe what I'm reading.

"What is this?" And even I can hear my voice has gone weak as I raise my eyes back up from the pages in front of me.

"Your divorce papers. And to answer your question, 15 hours." I keep looking at him and I know I must look like the idiot I feel I am right now. "Yesterday in the car to the hospital you asked 'how quickly can you finalise a divorce', the answer - 15 hours." I blink my eyes and hope that what he just said is going to start making sense soon.

I look back down at the papers and I read through some of them.

"Is this real?" I ask as I look back at him. His look has softened and what looks like sympathy has crept into his piercing green gaze.

"Yes Raegan, the documents are real." I nod at him and hold my left hand out to him. Theo reaches in his jacket breast pocket and retrieves a gold pen, that he places in my outstretched hand. Without hesitation I flick to the last page and sign. Well… sign might be a bit of a stretch as I'm right handed, but it looks close enough to what my signature is.

I will need to come up with a new signature for Raegan Brentwood. When I'm done, I hand the pen and papers back to Theo. While moving my hand back to reach for my coffee a sun ray catches my engagement ring, proudly sitting on my left ring finger along with my wedding band. I shove my hand back towards Theo "Take these off!"

He blinks at me as if giving me the chance to move my hand away. I don't. He expertly removes both of my rings.

Five years of my life, have been removed from my life in less than a minute. The laughter and joy I've experienced with Vince has been shattered. Broken pieces of my heart slowly pull me towards the dark abyss I've not visited for years. I thought I would never be in this position again.

"What do you want me to do with these?" Theo's voice brings me back to the room.

"Sell them, pawn them, throw them in the river or shove them down his throat. I don't care."

"Careful Raegan, you're giving him ideas" Bran says with a smirk and before I can ask any further questions Patricia comes back in the room with 4 other staff members, who lay our breakfast down in front of us

"You will be officially divorced by the end of the day." Bran pauses and thinks a little "Lunchtime. I think we can get it done by lunchtime." I look at all three of them as I feel like I'm the only one who wasn't included in the memo "Theo and I are going to pay Vince a visit after we have our breakfast." I look back at Theo who has a devious glint in his eyes, he trows the rings slightly in the air, catches and then puts them in his suits chest pocket. Right next to the gold pen.

Rest of the breakfast goes by in a blur. I'm siting at the table, listening to all three of them talking and I realise that I haven't got a single thing to my name.

"Bran, can you do me a favour?"

Chapter 11 - Raegan

George and I are sitting in a comfortable silence in the breakfast room. Brandan and Theo left not long ago to pay Vince a visit. Part of me is intrigued to know how it goes, the other part- doesn't want anything to do with it.

We hear a knock at the door and both of us turn to look, a middle aged man, wearing a black suit enters "Sir, Mr Hughes is here to see you."

"Thank you Simon." George looks at me "Simon is our butler, welcoming guests, arranging transport and keeping an eye on things."

"Nice to meet you Simon."

He nods in return "Nice to meet you Raegan" I smile, grateful Patricia has informed him about my name preference.

"Please take Mr Hughes to the office, I'll be there shortly." Simon nods and leaves the room, George looks back at me "Will you be OK on your own for a while?"

"I will."

After George leaves I get up and walk to the window to look out. My bedroom window must be facing another direction, because what I see here is different, a beautiful garden with well manicured flower beds, shrubs, bushes, and trees framing the garden. The sun has half-risen, casting a warm, golden light over the garden. All of a sudden I get the urge to be out there, in the garden, walking and getting lost between the paths, instead of my own thoughts.

I walk out of the breakfast room in search for the kitchen, where I am hoping I will find Patricia. As I'm rounding a corner Simon is exiting another room, presumably the office.

"Simon? Do you know where I can find Patricia?"

"She is usually in the kitchen at this time. Come, let me take you."

The kitchen is not your normal kind of kitchen. It has high, exposed beam ceilings and a floor to ceiling bay window at the end. Three deer antler chandeliers are hanging from the ceiling, sparkling in the morning light. Right in front of me is an enormous kitchen island, with charcoal coloured cabinets and marble tops. On the left of the island is an industrial size cooker that has been integrated with matching cabinets. Visually all the cabinets, appliances and decor suit the victorian era of the house, but they are all modern.

"She's right at the end." I follow Simons gaze towards the bay window where Patricia is sat down and talking to three young girls. Everyone is wearing black, which seems to be the uniform.

There is a built in seating around the bay window with a table in the middle. As I approach, two young girls draw their gaze away from Patricia to look at me, the third one keeps her gaze facing downward towards the table. Patricia follows their gaze and meets mine, she stands right away.

"Raegan, is everything all right? Was there something wrong with your breakfast?"

"Oh, no, no. Breakfast was lovely, thank you. I was wondering if you could help me?" I say sheepishly, as I don't think there is a non-awkward way to say this "I am… I don't have any clothes with me… and I wanted to go for a walk around the garden… Do you have any spare boots and a coat I could borrow?"

Understanding softness enters her sharp eyes "Girls, can you go have a look in the supply closet? Shoe size 5 and medium for the coat." She knows my sizes and that makes me like this woman even more.

All three of the young girls scoot out of the seating and scurry down another hallway at this end of the kitchen, I follow them with my eyes.

"All three of them started only a couple of weeks ago, they're still in training. They'll do most of their daily tasks together to not feel too overwhelmed by the jobs or the sheer size of this place." Patricia explains.

"Do you often have new employees?"

"No, Mr Brentwood informed me that you will be joining the household soon and we needed to accommodate for that. They're all in their early 20's, all escaping one thing or another, but eager to learn, work and prove themselves. Don't worry, all staff have their full background checks performed and are fully vetted. Mr Brentwood doesn't take any risks." Just as I'm about to ask 'do I really require 3 housemaids', they bound back into the kitchen bringing bright yellow wellies and a green parka.

"Perfect. If I ever get lost, just look for the yellow wellies." I say as I shove my feet into the boots. Patricia gives me a smile, but the girls look extremely timid.

"All right girls, why don't you go and make Raegans room while she is out?"

"Yes miss." All three say and go back out the same corridor they just came through.

"Did I say anything wrong?" I ask Patricia as she helps me put the parka on.

"No, they're new, like you. They want to do everything right. They're not used to interacting with the masters of the house yet."

This is by far, the most beautiful garden I have ever walked around in. I have no idea what any of the plants are called, but they are beautiful, even in spring. It must look glorious in summers full bloom.

The walk has helped me calm my racing thoughts and the beauty of the garden is making me feel at peace. The air is fresh and apart from the odd conversation between the staff, there is no noise. Even with the sun in the clear sky, there is a pinch of chill in the air, which somehow, makes this whole experience just a bit more magical. I find a wooden bench, nestled between a couple of shrubs facing the sun.

For years my life has been a constant 'go-go-go' mode without much of a break. This is the first time in my life when I don't have to be anywhere, do anything and there is no one relying on me. It feels liberating, but at the same time I'm overcome with guilt.

I've lost my husband, who I thought was my best friend. I've said goodbye to my mother who has never loved me, which I think is something I can make peace with.

The Unspoken Darkness

But the deepest cut is yet to be made. My two friends. I have to say goodbye to Lily and Maya and I can't even imagine how I will do that. I've made the decision to be Raegan and I know I can't bring them into my new life, but I also don't know how to let them go.

Panic rises within me.

Darkness crawls towards me and I see my old friend standing at the edge of the abyss. Smiling at me.

Fear.

Fear of knowing what this means and where this road leads.

Pure fear overtakes me and I'm frozen in place. Flashbacks of my past rush through my mind.

The blackness. My lungs are contracting.. begging for oxygen, but none is coming.

Fear has wrapped its hands around the shards of my heart and squeezing… and I am reminded again, that even a broken heart still hurt.

Every part of my soul hurts. And *It* knows it. *It* knows it's got me. Again.

And *It* knows I will pay the dues it asks.

"There you are sweetheart. Mind if sit?" Darkness around me retreats to its corners and breath returns to me. I blink. The garden and George comes back into focus. I nod, unable to form any words for second day running.

George and I sit on the bench for a while before I gather enough courage to ask the question I've been meaning to ask since breakfast.

"Is it weird for you that I'm here?" I turn to look at him

"What? No! Of course not. What makes you say that?"

"Well.. this wasn't exactly planned. And I don't just mean about me turning up yesterday. I know you've known about me for several years now, but that's different from actually being here and … and existing. Does that make sense?" I finish my rambling, unable to find the right words to voice what I truly want to ask.

He looks at me, really looks at me, deep into my eyes "I don't regret a single thing that has led us here. Do I wish I knew about you from your first heart beat? God yes." The knot of emotions is rising up and I have to keep swallowing and blinking to keep the tears at bay. "I can't change the past nor can I be a part of it, but I will do whatever I need to, to earn your trust and love to be part of your future. You are my daughter and that will never change. This house is as much your home as it's Brandans' and Theodores. I don't expect you to call me dad by the the end of the day, I know it will all take time." He takes a breath before adding "So that's all I'm asking for- your time." His voice cracks a little, but he covers it up with a cough "Time for us to get to know each other."

I can hear the sincerity in his voice "I'd like that." I smile at him "I'd like that very much."

This isn't just new for me, it's new for George as well and I want to give this a real, full hearted try. After a long moment I say "This garden is serene and beautiful."

"My wife was passionate about flowers and plants, and everything to do with gardening. She would spend every spare minute out here pottering about. She would drag me to the most random plant places, because she'd heard some rumour of one plant or another." Georges face has lit up in happiness of these memories

"Did Bran inherit her joy of gardening?" I ask

"He did. The gardeners don't allow him to work in this garden, they've banished him to the greenhouse. But that doesn't stop him from planting a plant here and there, just to irk them." His last statement makes me chuckle, as all I can imagine now is Bran sneaking around the garden with a spade and a plant under his arm.

"Come on, I've got a few more things I'd like to show you."

"Am I meeting Alvin today as well?" George gives me a confused look, I raise my eyebrows in question. He shakes his head, still looking non-the wiser "Alvin and the chipmunks. You've got 2 out of the three, Theodore and Simon, and now I'm hoping there is an Alvin somewhere in the ranks, to make the full set." George lets out a laugh, It's deep and hearty. There is no fakeness about it.

"Oh my God!! I have never noticed that!" He continues to laugh "There is no Alvin, but I'll make sure we complete the set!"

Georges office is all masculine, a couple of leather sofas as you enter the office with a coffee table in the middle. By the back wall a sturdy looking mahogany desk with a leather chair behind it and a couple in front of it. Walls are lined with bookcases, art work and antique weapons. Even though the furniture is of dark wood and all decor is as well, the room looks remarkably bright. The large windows framing the room might have something to do with it.

"Please, sit down." he gestures to the sofa, two steaming cups of coffee are already sitting on the coffee table, awaiting our arrival. George sits down next to me with his laptop and couple of envelopes and a small box in hand. "I know this must be all extremely overwhelming for you and this is not how I expected all this to come about. But certain people in your life made choices that pushed your hand, and in turn - mine." I sit, holding the steaming cup of coffee in my hand.

"First things first, this is your new phone. It's all set up with all your contacts. I know Bran has explained the security business we're in." I look down at a white Apple box in my lap "Over the next coming days, we will need to discuss and finalise the plan of how we tie up Julia Greens' life." I swallow hard. My life as Julia Green has an expiry date. Is it really that easy to erase a life? A lifetime of memories?

"In this envelope is your new passport, birth certificate, driving licence and national insurance number." Deep breaths… deep breaths "And here is your new bank card. It's current balance is £150,000 thousand pounds, I think that should cover all the essentials you'll need. And th.."

I raise my broken hand in the air to stop him. I hear the words and the meaning behind them, but they're not linking up.

"Raegan, take a deep breath. It's all right, just keep breathing." I am hyperventilating with a panic attack on it's heels, so I follow Georges instructions.

"That's it. Keep breathing." With every breath my mind clears. "Deep breaths." A moment later he asks the question Brandan hasn't asked yet. "When did you start experiencing panic attacks?" He asks cautiously.

Knowing how protective Brandan is, I can only guess what George would do if he would even find out what happened 7 years ago.

"Several years ago. I've had therapy to help and I was doing really well, until…until all this."

"Would going back to therapy help?" There is zero judgement in his voice, just warmth.

Do I want to go back to therapy and open old wounds? It's one thing remembering and having flashbacks in my mind, it's another to have to give those memories voice.

"I'll be all right, I just need some time to adjust." I give him a reassuring smile, but I don't think he is buying it. George lets the silence be, which I am grateful for.

"Ok." He gives me a long look before continuing "Right, where were we. Your finances and trust fund is managed by Mr Hughes. A monthly allowance will be put in your account that should cover most things. I'll arrange a meeting between you two for him to explain all your investments. And in this envelope" he holds out the second yellow envelope to me and I take it "are several properties that are in our family. When we turn 21 we can chose one of those as our residence or holiday home, or whatever else you might want to use it for. Bran and Theo got apartments in London, but there are some gems in there." George takes my broken hand in his and I realise how much smaller it is, even with the cast on "I know you are overwhelmed and this all feels alien to you, but I am here for you."

Why does this feel so normal? So safe?

A soft knock sounds at the door.

Chapter 12 - Raegan

"Come in!" George raises his voice slightly for the person on the other side of the door to hear. I take a long sip of my coffee "These are your bodyguards."

I slightly splutter my coffee. "I'm sorry, my what?" Surely not, I must've miss heard him. Why would I need a bodyguard, let alone two.

Two tall, extremely handsome men have stepped into the room.

"This is Christian" George motions to the man standing on the left. He looks in his late twenties, dark hair that match his dark eyes. If there ever was a template to what bodyguard should look like - he fits it. "And this is Leo." Leo is much younger than Christian or me, he looks the exact opposite of Christian, light, dusty brown hair, bright blue eyes and a happy smile on his face.

I place my coffee cup down, get to my feet and reach for the two men with my broken hand extended.

"Nice to meet you both, but" I turn to look at George "I don't think I need bodyguards." Before George replies, both, Christian and Leo shake my hand with "Nice to meet you too Miss Brentwood"

"No, no miss Brentwood, just Raegan please." Both of them nod in acceptance, not uttering another word, while waiting for George to answer.

"Sweetheart, this is not negotiable. When you leave the manor, Christian and Leo will escort you and be your shadows." The sweet and caring look on Georges face has morphed into something else. Something darker. A worry.

Not wanting to add to his list of things to worry about, I agree "Ok, they'll be my shadows."

It's not until I return to my room, a short while later, and see myself in a mirror I remember I am still wearing Brans clothes. I turn around in the room and head to the wardrobe, but it's empty. Of course it is, I haven't got anything with me. As I am staring into the empty wardrobe the outer door to my rooms open and I hear female voices. The new housemaids. I step into the living area and they all freeze in place, not expecting me to be here.

"Sorry miss, we didn't know you had returned to your room." One in the middle with auburn hair speaks "We're not quite done yet, erm-"

"Could you please get Patricia, Christian and Leo please?"

"Of course miss." all three of them near enough run out of the room in search for the requested people. While I wait I make my way over to the bookcases in my room and take stock of the books on the shelves. Mostly classics, but plenty enough romance novels. A warm feeling kindles in my chest.

"Raegan, you called us?" I spin around and see Patricia, both of my bodyguards and the three housemaids.

"Yes. I.. I haven't got any clothes or make up, or… or anything really. Would one or two of your girls be able to go and get them for me?" Patricia looks slightly shocked by what I've asked, but she schools her features quickly.

"Of course Raegan." She turns to the girl and says "Indy and Sarah, your assignment has changed for the day."

Indy, the auburn haired girl and Sarah, black, pixie cut girl, can't seem to hide their smiles. Patricia looks back at me "Anything in particular you are after Raegan?"

I look at both of the girls "Something of everything. Go wild!" They finally let out a squeal, as they cannot hold their excitement anymore "Christian and Leo, can you please escort Indy and Sarah?" I reach into the envelope that is still in my hand and pass my bank card to Christian "Pin number's on the other side."

From the look on Christians face, I can tell that this isn't sitting well with him. "Miss Brentwood, sorry, Raegan. We're your bodyguards."

"I know." I answer him.

"Our job is to protect you." He protests.

"Christian, the only choice of clothes I have are either my brothers humongous jogging bottoms and t-shirts or bright yellow wellies and a green parka. I am way too tired to leave the house and go shopping. When you take Indy and Sarah, I will take one of those books" I point behind me to the bookshelves "and go crawl under a blanket on a sofa somewhere. I won't be leaving the house, so I will be safe. And you will keep Indy and Sarah safe while you're out." I can see him clenching his jaw wanting to argue with me. Before he can, I whisper "Please. Just this once."

Christian doesn't break eye contact as he replies. "Just this once."

After they all leave I decide to look at my phone. My old phone.

Seven missed calls from Vince and two, semi, threatening messages.

The Unspoken Darkness

Three missed calls from Maya and Lily and 7 messages in our group chat.

I read them all. I type my reply several times before I finally settle on the one with most honesty, without giving anything away.

Me: Hey girls. I'm good, nothing to worry about. Just need some time away to think about a few things. Love you.

I leave my phone on the dressing table and stride towards the bookshelf. Without much consideration I pick a book and head out of my room to find a sofa with a blanket.

I hear rustling and voices, but the slumber is so sweet, I don't want to open my eyes. I feel my legs being lifted, the sofa dipping and then my feet are resting in someones lap. A warm and soft blanket is laid on top of me and someone tucks me in. I don't think I've ever been tucked in.

A loud noise of clanking bottles finally forces me to open one of my eyes.

"Brandan for Gods sake! Can you keep it down, your sister is sleeping!" Georges whisper shouts forces me to open my other eye.

"Not anymore she isn't!" Bran exclaims with a grin and points at me while dragging a trolley into the lounge room with bottles and, what I assume, food under the covered plates. I look down where my feet are and Theo is sitting at the end of the sofa with my feet in his lap.

"You are a bloody nuisance at times!" I can hear the frustration in Georges voice and then the sofa dips just a bit further away from my head and he sits down with a huff "Pass me a beer before I write you out of my will!" Bran just laughs at him.

I crane my neck to turn my head to face George "How long have I been asleep for?"

"Few hours." Bran hands him and Theo a bottle, places plates of food on the coffee table and lays down on the remaining empty spot on the massive L shape sofa. "You're all right if we watch football?" George asks.

"Yeah." And I turn my eyes towards the wall mounted TV. Every time I enter a new room in this manor I am left speechless of how big it all is. And this room is no exception. The TV is mounted above a stone fireplace. It looks immaculate, as if it's never had a real fire in it. A low coffee table is opposite the fireplace with a massive cream coloured L shape sofa surrounding it. Artwork and bookcases cover the walls and rich green curtains shoulder each window, making it feel warm and cosy inside. There are lots of plants dotted around the room, which I'm sure are Brandans personal touches in the room. There is an extra armchair by the fire place and a couple behind the sofa, creating an extra seating area.

I see my book has fallen to the floor, I don't remember much from it, I must've read myself to sleep very quickly. I reach for it and place it back on the coffee table.

"Was it any good?" Theo asks as he takes a sip of his beer.

"Honestly? No idea, think I fell asleep as soon as I opened it." He nods in response.

Not long after the game starts I start to dose off again, but suddenly I feel the gentlest touches on my feet. I pry my eyes open and look at Theo. He continues to look straight ahead, focusing on the game. No, he is definitely massaging my feet and it feels so good, so relaxing. I'm struggling to keep my eyes open when he turns and says to me "Sleep."

"Did you say something son?" George asks to which Theo replies.

"Raegan's asleep again." It doesn't take more than few more moments, before I am fully asleep.

When I wake up the room is dark, only illuminated by the glow of the TV, which has been turned down. I turn my head where Bran and George were sitting - they're not there. I turn to look where Theo was and he's still here. Asleep, his arms crossed over his chest. I slowly lift the blanket off me and then move my legs off Theos lap and sit upright on the sofa.

"How did you sleep?" Theos low voice startles me.

"Did I wake you?"

"No." I know I'm not much of a talker when I'm just woken up, but I can muster a few more than just one word answers "How did you sleep?" He repeats the question.

"Yeah, slept good." I'm about to get up from the sofa when I ask him "How did it go with Vincent earlier?"

"It's taken care of." Before I can ask him anything else, he is up, extending his hand towards me "Come on, let me walk you back to your room."

We don't talk on our way back to my room and I'm grateful for that. 'It's taken care of.' Four words to signal the end of my marriage. I always thought we were happy together. Of course we had our arguments and disagreements, but every couple has those. Right? We fit together so well. He helped me overcome my trauma, he didn't know everything, but enough to be considerate and thoughtful. As cliche as it sounds, I thought that one day we will have our own family and we'll grow old together.

"Who did all this shopping?" Theos voice brings me back to the present and not the future I will never have.

"I asked a couple of Patricias girls to go and get me a few things." I look around the room. Shopping bags and boxes cover every inch of the sofa and table. I can barely see the carpet beneath all the treasures "Maybe more than just a few things." I wince at the expense sitting in front of me.

"Do you need help putting this all away?"

"No, but thank you."

"I wasn't offering my services, I would've gotten one of the maids to help you."

I look back at him and he's got an unreadable expression on his face "Good night Theo." He grunts a 'night', turns on his heel and leaves.

Knock - knock - knock.

"Come in!" I shout and hear a door open and close, footsteps coming towards my bedroom.

"Oh wow! Leo was not kidding when he said they bought all the shops!" Brandan waltzes in and plops himself down on the bed, while I'm sitting crosslegged on the floor taking tags off my new wardrobe and folding clothes away.

"Well, I didn't want to borrow another pair of your humongous sweatpants, so I sent Indy and Sarah to get me my own humongous sweatpants"

He laughs at me. "Good for you!"

We sit in silence for a while until I'm confident enough that my voice won't betray my true feelings before I speak. "Theo said it's all taken care of."

"Yes. It will be filed first thing Monday morning to make it official and by the end of the day it'll be done." My breathing quickens as my eyes start to burn with todays lot of unshed tears. I do wonder how deep is the well of my tears. The clothes in front of me turn blurry and I'm folding a t-shirt by touch only. Bran slides on the floor next to me and pulls me into a side hug. With my head on his shoulder and his arm wrapped around my shaking frame, I let the tears fall. Brandan doesn't say anything, he is just here and that is all I need.

Chapter 13 - Raegan

Even though I have nowhere to be and nothing to do, my days quickly fill up and they pass rather quickly. I like the little routines I have managed to establish.

In the mornings I go for a nice long walk around our estate. It wasn't until later that I found a woodland trail, leading me over a mile to the other side of the property on a slight uphill. From there I can see the whole estate. The trail looked slightly overgrown, people have probably forgotten about it. Some days I would turn around and go back straight away, some days I take some time to just to sit and enjoy the quietness.

Before breakfast this morning George asked me to see him in his office, a room I haven't been in since my first day here.

"Come in sweetheart, take a seat. Coffees on the table." I take a seat on the sofa which is exactly the same spot I sat in no more than a week ago. George comes and sits on the sofa opposite me. "There are a few things I need to talk to you about. Your old phone, Bran has changed its GPS settings to ensure the location is showing as being up north. He has done the same with VPN to match your IP location. If anyone ever suspects anything, there won't be a digital trail. Camera function and microphone have also been disabled, when you speak to your friends, Bran will enable them."

I sit with this information for a moment before speaking "Doesn't that seem a bit excessive?"

A tired smile forms on Georges face like he expected me to say that, clouded by a saddened look in his eyes. "I thought you would say that. I know you may think it's cruel of me for asking you to cut yourself off from everyone you've ever known. And it is. But there is no other way I can protect you. This situation we're in, how things are developing...we need to be extremely careful."

"Do you worry about Bran and Theo as much as you do about me?" I ask genuinely.

"I worry about all my children, but you more so. Brandan and Theo have been raised differently, suited for a life in all facets of Brentwood Global."

"I understand. You're trying to protect me from not just physical, but also emotional harm. If something were to happen to people I, Julia, loves because of me, I would never forgive myself for it." He nods in a confirmation "There is more to Brentwood Global than just security, isn't there?" George looks at me in surprise and I'm not entirely sure he is breathing. "Don't look that surprised, I might be quiet, but I pick up on things." I take a mouthful of my coffee to let my brain form the right question. "Is the threat from this *other* side of Brentwood Global?"

"Yes." He doesn't hesitate to answer. "Raegan, what Bran said to you back in Leeds about a competitor playing dirty due to us bidding for the same contract was a lie. It wasn't a lie in a sense that it has happened in the past, but right now, that is not what is happening. I don't want to overwhelm you with every part of our businesses, but I also-"

I cut him off "I'm not sure if I want to know yet." He closes his mouth "But… if there comes a time when I have more questions, will you answer them honestly?"

"Always, but not if that would put you in harms way." There is a war being waged in his eyes, I can see him being torn between telling me more and keeping his secrets safe. One gives him trust and the other puts a wedge in the gap we've been trying to breach. He continues "That is also why you have two bodyguards. Christian is well versed in the *other* side, understand the risks and the threat we're under fully. Leo is young and eager to learn. He doesn't know about the *other* side. Anytime you leave the house, they will be with you whether it's on our premises or outside the gate, that is non negotiable."

"I understand." I answer honestly and a weight of worry seems to lift off Georges shoulders. My stomach makes a growling sound, begging to be fed. "Can we go to breakfast now?"

He smiles "I think we should."

Despite George being busy with Brentwood Global, endless meetings, social events and interviews- he insisted we have breakfast every morning in the sunroom.

Bran and Theo joins us when they're staying at the manor, but half the time they are in London, either because of working late or having actual lives and going out, meeting people.

"Tell me about uncle Carl?" George gives me a look that is so very similar to Brandans. One they have both been giving me, when I'm calling someone else in a familial name, but not calling them brother or father. But he doesn't dwell on it too long before he answers.

"We grew up in this house, same as Brentwood Global, this house has been in the family for generations now. Even though we were already well off, my dad wouldn't let us get spoilt with presents or buying everything we thought we wanted. When we were about 10 or 11 we wanted a go-kart to go around the estate and play whatever imaginary things we thought of at the time. But our dad wouldn't buy us one, so.. we did what every other boy would have done- we built one. The first one was not very good and neither was the second or third one. But by the time we got to our fourth cart, we knew what we were doing. I've lost track how many we actually built over the years. When we got older, that turned into a passion for cars. We would buy old, beat up cars and restore them. Make them work. We never sold a single one of those. We have a garage, on Carls farm, full of all the cars we've restored over the years."

"That is amazing. Do you drive them or just have them in the garage?"

"We drive them. Every year we will take couple of them and go on a road trip. The business we're in, it can wear you down, so having a week or two away, with just my brother, recharges my batteries."

"Which has been your favourite road trip?" I ask.

"Mmmm...I suppose, any road trip that lets us explore something different, whether it's a new culture or trying a new experience or discovering something new about yourself, those are my favourite ones. And what about you?" I look at him in confusion "You and your friends go on yearly road trips as well."

"We do. Nowhere near as exotic as your trips, but the location never really mattered. It was about us being together, listening to each others ranting about work or having one too many drinks and singing a very bad karaoke while having the time of our lives. Being in each others company brought the calm that was always out of reach in our day-to-day lives." A blanket of sadness rolls over me. I will never experience that again, that comfortable feeling of just being with someone. Two souls that understand me, who know me.

I need to say the words that have been building on my tongue from our safety briefing earlier when I saw how torn he was about them lying to me and still not fully telling the truth. I want to put his worry at ease.

"What we spoke about earlier, it doesn't change anything between us or the relationship we've built." Relief fills his eyes. "We all have our secrets."

"You have secrets little bear?" I whip my head around towards the door to see Bran walking towards the breakfast table. The nickname seems to have stuck after I told him his hugs feel like a big bear is hugging me. So… I'm the little bear now. He seats himself next to me and starts piling food on his plate, which makes me scrunch up my nose.

"Maybe you should start using the serving dishes instead of the plates?" I tell him, as the amount of food he consumes concerns me at times. He looks at me with a raised eyebrow then narrows his eyes on my plate and unease fills my stomach. I should've kept quite.

"I'll make you a deal, you finish your plate and I'll start using serving dishes!" He suggests with a smirk. I know why he's saying that. With everything that has happened I've lost my appetite. I am trying to eat every day with every meal, but.. I can't seem to swallow the food. And I am well aware that my plate is always monitored like the most prized possession. I even suspect that Christian and Leo report back to both of them about how much food I've consumed while I'm with my shadows.

So, to prove a point that I am trying to eat more "Deal." I extend my cast covered right hand and we shake on the deal. I look at my plate of scrambled eggs, mashed avocado and half eaten toast. And I tuck in.

As I'm about halfway through the food of my plate, Bran adds a couple of strawberries and a pot of yogurt.

"Hey, what are you doing?" I nearly shout at him, which only earn a deep chuckle from George and a grin from Bran.

"You love fruit." He answers.

"You're cheating."

"Nope. I never said anything about not adding food to your plate."

I narrow my gaze on him. "You sneaky bastard." I feel my eye twitching as this competitiveness in me is new and unexpected. He just grins, damn well knowing that he's got me. I huff out a big breath and continue eating.

With a corner of my eye I can see him moving again and I don't waste a moment to turn to him with my fork held in my left hand and glare at him. "I swear to God Brandan, if you add one more piece of food on my plate, I will stab you with this fork."

He drops a piece of pastry back on it's plate and put's his hands up in surrender. "I'm done. I'm done. Not touching your food."

George chuckles at our exchange before saying "You definitely got the Brentwood genes."

Chapter 14 - Brandan

Growing up with Theo, we always played pranks and teased each other, just like any blood related sibling would. I thought I had grown out of it, but as it turns out - I haven't.

I knew I was pushing Raegans buttons to the limit during breakfast, but that made her actually eat a full plate of food for the first time she's been home.

"What are you doing today?" I mutter out while stabbing a piece of meat on my fork and a bit of it slides off the side of my plate. Maybe Raegan has a point of me eating off serving dishes.

"I was planning on going to the shops and get myself a laptop." Both dad and I look at her in curiosity, as technology can be a dangerous thing. In understanding Raegan sighs "I used to write a lot, before uni mostly. But I think writing will help me sort out a few things."

"OK, I'll take you and I'll set it up for you." She nods knowing that there is no debating this.

A couple of hours later we stroll out of a shop in the city with Raegans new laptop.

"Thank you for coming with me." Raegan says as we walk down the busy street in London. Both her bodyguards a few paces behind us keeping her safe. "Why don't you have guards?"

The question startles me a bit, as I try to come up with as close of an answer to the truth as I can.

"I do when there is a need, but most of the time I can ensure my own safety." I can see her nodding. I wonder how long we have before we need to share more of what Brentwood Global is. Will her knowing change her decision? Change our relationship? We walk for a while longer, enjoying the warm spring air.

"You know I try." I look at her with questioning look, but her gaze is faced forwards "To eat."

Guilt burrows low in my gut "Rae, I didn't mean to point it out in such-"

"I'm glad you did. And I also know you have all been watching my food intakes like hawks." She turns to look at me, I squint my eyes closed. "All five of you!" Shit. Thought we were more stealthier. "But as I said, I'm glad you did. I know... I know I have a lot to process. That" she points at the bag holding her new gadget "will help. Writing is like a therapy for me. To get the thoughts curdling in my brain out, arrange and understand them. It'll get better." She gives me a tight lipped smile that, I know is hiding a lot of hurt "I promise." She turns and we continue walking "Anyway, are you going back to work or are you gonna treat your sister to a drink?"

"Shh, be quite and stop tripping up!" I shush Raegan as we stagger up the manor stairs. I cannot remember the last time I was this drunk.

"You shush and if you think you're whispering - you're not! And your lip is split by the way!" She gives me a crocked look.

"What?" I reach my right hand to my lip and fuck.. it's split. And the motherfucker hurts. I keep hold of her with my left arm, I'm not sure if it's for her or my benefit.

We finally manage to get up all the ten thousand steps and nearly fall into the hallway as the front door opens.

I might be drunk, but I would know that thundering look of anger on dads face anywhere. But both of us try to do our best to straighten ourselves up. Dad closes the door and stands in front of us not saying a word.

"Did we wake you?" Rae whisper shouts and then hiccups.

"You're not whispering either!" I say back at Rae. "I don't think anyone in this family knows how to whisper."

Dad just glares at us. So she turns to me "I think he's angry." Which make me laugh, but one look from dad has me choking down the rest of the laughter.

"Did you wake me? No. Why? Because I never went to sleep. You know why?" We shake our heads and my head spins. "Because my adult children, insisted to their bodyguards to go home as they are in capable hands. Your hands" he looks at me "The pair of you went pub crawling around the city and got in a fight. And by the looks of your split lip you didn't even win it. You are totally drunk and can't even walk up the damn stairs."

Rae sounds way too enthusiastic when she announces "I learnt how to throw a punch though!" Her speech slurring on 'throw'.

"That was a good punch Rae, next time aim a bit higher, to get their cheek, instead of their shoulder!" I try to mimic the movement with my hand.

"You punched someone?" Dad nearly shouts.

Rae looks back at dad proud "Yeah, and didn't even break my hand this time!" She waves her left hand in front of her in proof. "Look! Still in one piece!" Dads golden brown eyes land back on me and I know I am in a shit creek without a fucking paddle. "But we're all good!" She looks at me and winces "Maybe not you. You need to put some ice on your lip, looks like you've got your lips done, but they're wonky!" I blink and so does Raegan, and then both of us burst into laughter.

I can hear dad muttering something under his breath sounding like "you two will be the death of me", but our laughter drowns him out.

"Come on you two, you need to go to bed and sleep it off." The anger has left his voice and he gets between us, wrapping his arms around each of our middles and walking us to our rooms. Even though I am not much smaller than he is, this makes me feel like a teenager again. And I'm not entirely mad about it.

Chapter 15 - Raegan

It took me nearly two days to recover from the hangover of the century. I've been like a hermit in my bed, barely moving and mostly communicating in grunts. At some point during the recovery Bran made his way to my room, followed by a couple of people carrying a TV in my bedroom.

"I think I'm dead." He says as he sits on my bed looking pale. "Just set it up on the dresser and pass me the remote. I think I'll hurl up all my intestines if I move again." Staff quickly set up the TV, pass the remote to a very grumpy and rough looking Brandan and rush out of the room.

I look over at him laying down and pulling the duvet to his chin. "What are you doing?" Even my own voice seems to ring in my ears and makes my head pound.

"I'm making you watch me die, as this is all your fault. 'Treat your sister to a drink'" he says in a mocking voice and huffs out a breath, while flicking through the TV.

"I never said 'let's go drink London dry', *that* was your idea!" I reply.

"Shut up!" And I do, with a slight smirk on my face.

"I had fun though."

After a moment he says. "Me to. But next time we go out, I'll arrange an IV bag for when I get home. As this is not fun."

"Part of the experience." He glares at me "Sort of."

"Shut up." But he is smiling.

Not long after the movie starts, Indy comes in the room and freezes by the door.

"You all right Indy?"

She shakes her head before replying "Yes, sorry. Excuse me Mr Brentwood, I wasn't aware you were here, I didn't bring any food for you, just for Raegan."

"No Mr Brentwood, just Brandan please. What did you bring Raegan?" He asks as Indy arranges a tray on the bed by my side, after I pull my legs up to my chest.

"All the good stuff that helps with a hangover." Indy replies, he leans over and picks a slice of bacon off my plate and shoves it in his mouth. Bran seems to have perked up a bit.

"Can you bring me the same. And coffee. And coke. Lots of those!"

"Yes Mr Brent… Brandan." Her cheeks turn a little pink.

"Thank you Indy" we both say at the same time.

"Aaaa… so you two are awake!" George comes in my room next. "And alive!" Have they changed my bedroom door to a revolving one? There are way too many people coming in my rooms for my liking. "How are you feeling?" And there is a hidden smile on his face, thoroughly enjoying our misery. "You both look-"

"Dead! We know!" We reply and that seems to add to Georges amusement as his smile widens.

"I was going to try and come up with a punishment for you both for being so reckless, but seeing as you're both sick like dogs, I think thats punishment enough." He laughs. "I thought my days of looking after drunken teenagers were behind me, but I'm not going to lie - this is highly entertaining." I am sure both Brans and my glares at him are exactly the same, which only makes him laugh harder. "On a serious note, I think it would be good for you Raegan to spend some time in the training ring, just to learn some self defence moves."

I didn't see this coming, but can't say I'm surprised. With a splitting headache and nausea rolling through my stomach I reply.

"If I agree, will you please shut the curtains and lower your voice?" I don't fully remember getting to my room last night, or was it early this morning? When the light came streaking through the windows as the sun rose, I wanted to close them, but even the slightest movement was making me feel sick. So I pulled my covers over my head and hid.

"Deal."

George has walked on my side of the bed and drawing the curtains close as I twist to look at him. "Can it be with Christian and Leo?" He gives me a questioning look "The self defence lessons." He thinks about it for a while, weighing the pluses and minuses.

"Yes, we can make it work."

A couple of days later I'm in a sparring gym in the basement, which seems to have all the latest state of the art gym equipment anyone could ever ask for.

"Is this where you all train?" I ask my two guards while I'm having some water.

"We? No, this is Brentwood private training hall. You only get inside here if you're invited!" Leo replies.

If truth be told, I've grown to like my two bodyguards. They're the perfect duo for me, a real grumpy x sunshine romance. Leo is always upbeat and smiling, talking to anyone and everyone, whereas Christian is quite, observing and calm.

After being thrown in this life, the situation I'm in, they've been the constant since the first day I arrived. At the beginning they just walked by my side as I roamed and got my bearing inside the house and outside. Once I got more used to having them with me wherever I go, I started talking to them. To get to know them and for them to know me as well.

"Oh? Where do you guys train?"

"We have a facility further away on the compound." I nod, not wanting to pry any more. I am well aware there are secrets held within Brentwood Global. Now is not the time to learn them.

"Right you two chatter boxes, let's do a few more moves and then we can call it a day." Christian has taken on the roll of my instructor with Leo being the dummy. As according to Christian "if all you're gonna do here is crack wiseass jokes, then being a dummy is an upgrade for ya!" That shut Leo up and made me laugh.

I am not a fit person, I don't exercise, I don't run or lift weights. I never have. The only form of exercise I've ever done is walking and my muscles, or lack there of, shows. My arms, even my right one, feels heavy, my legs are jelly and I am sure I will feel much worse tomorrow. And that is only after the first training session. I'm not entirely sure I'll survive the second.

I have showered, changed and making my way to the kitchen where I know I will find my two guards. As I make my way there, Theo is on the stairs, with an unreadable expression on his face.

"Is everything all right?" I ask hesitantly. Apart from that first day, where he was extremely tentative, he has been distanced. To be fair, he isn't spending much time here, so I've not had a chance to get to know him much.

Instead of answering, he just looks at me, still with the same, unreadable expression on his face.

"Okaaayy… looks like you're having some internal discussion, so I'm going to leave you to that. See you later Theo."

I continue my way down to the kitchen, just as expected, Christian and Leo are sitting in the booth at the end of the kitchen and munching down their lunch. I slide next to Christian and before I can blink, Indy puts a plate of food and coffee in front of me.

"How are you feeling after the session?"

"Are you worried you've gone too hard on me on our first session coach Christian?" I ask teasingly.

"Yes." His answer shocks me and I can see the worry on his face.

"Christian, I'm fine. My arms feel heavy and my whole body feels like jelly, but I'm fine. Honestly, I'm good."

He scans me from head to toe, or as much as he can see us sitting at the table. "You'll tell me if the training is too much."

It's not a question "I will."

It doesn't take us long to finish all of our lunch. It takes a bit longer for me, but I manage to eat most of it.

We are walking through the house, past the main stairs when I hear Theos voice from behind us. He is still standing on the stairs, by the looks of it, he hasn't moved at all.

"Where are you going?"

All three of us twirl around to look back at the staircase, Christian is the first to reply "We're going to get her gear."

Theo makes his way down the stairs and walks towards us "I'll take her."

I'm glad I'm not the only one stunned, Christian and Leo have gone still beside me.

"You don't need to take me, I'm more than happy to go with the guys."

Somehow I think that was the exact wrong thing to say, as Theos face twists, but I still can't read what his face is hiding.

"I'm taking you, let's go." He marches towards the front door without waiting for me.

I mutter a quite "I'm sorry." To my guards and follow after Theo.

When I reach the bottom of the stairs outside, Theo is standing by his car, with passenger door open for me.

"How very gentlemanly of you." I say as I slide into his car, he closes the door and in few long strides he is already on the other side and getting behind the wheel.

He doesn't say anything for several long minutes while we make our way down the drive and through the security gate.

"Is everything all right?" I ask for the second time.

"Everything's fine."

"Did Bran ask you to do this?"

"No."

"Then why are you taking me to the shop? Surely you have more important things to do."

"Don't assume you know what's important to me."

I turn to look at him. He's calm behind the wheel, completely oblivious to the fact that I'm getting more frustrated with him with every single answer he gives me.

"I'll ask again - then why are you doing this?"

"Can't it be that I simply want to spend time with you?" He finally glances over to me, that makes me narrow my eyes on him.

"I doubt that." I can see the corners of his mouth twitch slightly upwards.

We continue the rest of the way in silence, which I don't mind. For the first time in a while, I feel calmer, almost content. My thoughts don't race as they have been for weeks now. I can breathe deeper. So I close my eyes and my memory jumps to yesterdays conversation.

"Sweatheart, come, sit down. We have come up with a plan to close the Julia chapter." I sit on the same sofa in Georges office as I did my first time here. He is sitting opposite me, Bran next to him and Theo on my sofa "In your next call with your friends, you will need to arrange a catch up in Cambridge in 10 days time."

"10 days? That's.." I look from one man to the other to the next with wide eyes "That's... so soon."

"I know, but we can't leave it longer, the risks are too high." I swallow and nod "Bran and Theo have already started putting everything in place for it to work. We need it to run seamlessly, so there are no suspicions about Julias death." George stops and looks to Bran to continue with the plan

"It's a simple switcheroo, you don't need to worry about anything, only to get out of the car at the right time."

Chapter 16 - Raegan

"Raegan… Raegan we're here…" I jolt awake, my breathing quickening. I look around and I'm greeting with emerald green eyes intent on me. Theo. He was taking me to the bike shop. I relax.

"Sorry, I didn't mean to fall asleep."

Sleeping has been another struggle I've been facing. There has rarely been a night where I've had more than 3 consecutive hours of sleep. I can't seem to fall asleep, and when I do, I don't seem to be able to stay asleep for long.

"How long was I asleep for?"

"Couple of hours."

"Couple of hours? How far have we driven?" I look out of the windows to see if I recognise anything. I don't.

"We're about 40 minutes from home." My eyes widen at that "You were sound asleep, there was no point in waking you earlier." He must see the question in my eyes "The shop will close in about an hour."

"Afternoon, how can I help ya?" A bearded tattooed man greets us as we walk in the bike shop. There are few bikes on display and tons of accessories, helmets and clothes.

"We need a AGV K6 black helmet with fully tinted visor, black Dainese leather trousers and a matching jacket. Torino gloves and nice black boots to finish the assemble. Clothes in small and boots in size 5."

The shop assistant looks Theo up and down and then me, and I get why. Theo is dressed in a suit with a flashy watch, while I'm in jeans, an oversized jumper and a broken hand.

"Right away. Please have a seat by the changing rooms, I'll bring it over."

Fifteen minutes later I am in the changing room with all the gear. I undress as quickly as I can, given my limitation with only having one working hand at the moment. I'm struggling to put the pants on, but I do the best wriggle dancing I can to get them on.

"How much time do we have before closing?"

"They'll stay open for as long as we need them to."

I finish lacing up my boots and step out of the changing room.

"Can you help me with the helmet please?"

Before he takes the helmet from my hands, he reaches behind my head, pulls all of my hair into a ponytail and secures it at the nape of my neck and then takes the helmet out of my hands.

"Look at me."

I do.

He puts the helmet on.

"Tip your head back."

I do.

He fastens the straps at my chin.

"All done."

I step to stand in front of a mirror and that is no longer Julia looking back at me. This is Raegan Brentwood. A lump of sorrow is building in my chest, threatening to spill. So I lower the visor and hide in the dark.

"Everything fits all right?" The shop assistant ask.

"I think so." I say quietly

"We'll take it all." Theo says with enough confidence for both of us, I walk back into the changing room while Theo settles the bill.

"Theo?"
"Yeah."
"Erm… is there a female shop assistant?"
"Why? What's wrong?" His tone is urgent and I can hear him move to be just outside my changing room.
"Well.. I'm stuck in the trousers and I can't get out with-" he barges in my changing room "with one hand."
He is trying to look the usual bored Theo, but his smile is betraying him.
"Can you at least pretend not to look so amused by this?"
"Never Alora." Alora. The code name they've given me during our operation. "How did you get them on?"
I huff out a long breath before answering.
"I shimmed and wriggled my way into them. I didn't think about how I would get out." The most beautiful sight unravels before my eyes. Theo is chuckling, doing his very best to not laugh out loud. His green eyes are sparking with.. what is that? Joy? No. Something else. Something… more. "Can you please find a female shop assistant to help me?"
"They don't have any and that bearded fucker ain't coming in here."
I blink at him. "Right.. fine.. I'll get Indy to help me when we get home." I turn to sit and put my shoes back on when Theo grabs my arm.
"Let me help you."

I am caught off guard by how genuine he looks. "No, it's fine. I'll-"

"Stop being so fucking stubborn and let me help you. I'm not going to hurt you." A zing of fear from years ago ripples through my body. A voice I've not heard in so long seems to be whispering in my ear. Trudging up memories. Hurt. Humiliation.

I didn't realise I've been stood, frozen in place until Theo has my face in his hands, leaning down with his nose to mine. "Raegan. What happened? Tell me." A mix of worry and plea covers his face.

"Nothing happened, just zoned out thinking about all this." I am surprised by how calm my voice comes out. But from the look on Theos face, I know he is not believing what I'm telling him. I swallow to keep the sting in my eyes at bay and the tremble out of my voice. "Will you help me out of the trousers?" I ask quietly.

And he does.

We're about halfway home and neither of us has spoken a word. Usually I don't mind the quite, but something inside of me is niggling to start a conversation.

"How do you know so much about bike gear?"

"Because I ride bikes."

"Do you? I've never seen you on one."

"Best time to ride is at night when you're safely tucked in bed."

"Mhm."

"Have you been on a bike yet?"

"No. Christian will show me tomorrow."

"Of course. Christian." His hands tighten on the steering wheel.

"Why don't you like him?"

"I don't like most people."

"That's true, but you are always extra arsey with Christian."

"I just think you can do better."

"I'm sorry- What?"

"He's not much of an upgrade from your husband. Sorry, ex husband." His tone has turned nasty. So very different from the guy at the shop. "You really know how to pick them." I am so shocked that my brain has stopped working, no words are forming. Just a darkness threatening to pull me under. Where is this coming from. Where is the smiling green eyed man from minutes ago telling me I'm safe? An unknown feeling twists inside of me.

Intercom flashes with a caller ID Heather, he answers.

"Hey babe, where are you?" Female voice dripping with fake sweetness and seduction rings through all the speakers.

"At the manor, had to run an unexpected errand. Took longer than planned." Really? I didn't even ask him to go with me, he didn't leave much of a choice, but to go with him.

"Oh.. you always do such important things."

"No, this one wasn't important, waste of time really." My ears are ringing. My tears are threatening to fall. He will not see me cry. The bastard.

"Are you coming into the city tonight? There's an exclusive party happening that I thought you might get us in." Her voice is like nails on a chalk board.

"Sure, I'd like to go out and have a good time, instead of being tucked up in bed." He is using his own words he said to me against me. Why? Why is this drive way so damn long. The air is thick and I need to get out of this car.

"Yeeey!! I'm so excited. Love you."

"See you later." Theo ends the call.

The car stops at the bottom of the stairs, exactly at the same spot it was when we left. Both of us sit in silence. Blood is rushing in my ears, heart is beating double its normal pace. I clear my throat and steel my nerves. "I don't expect you to like me, but there is no need to be this cruel. I didn't ask you to take me to the shop. I didn't ask for any of this."

"Raegan, I didn't-" I don't hear the rest what he has to say, I am already halfway up the stairs. "Fuck!" Is the last I hear as I head into the house. Rushing footsteps follow me. He is gaining on me. Damn him and his long legs. I quicken my pace. "Raegan wait!"

I don't turn to look, my focus is on my door at the end of this hallway. Few more steps. "Will you fucking wait?!" I reach for the handle, open the door and step inside and I turn to look at him. He is right here. Face covered in so many emotions I can't decipher any of them, his chest heaving.

A wave of tiredness rolls over me. I know this feeling.

There is only one thing that can help me, to keep me from fully being pulled into the abyss.

"Get fucked Theo." I say on an exhausted breath and slam the door in his face.

"FUUUCK!!" He screams in frustration. I click the lock. He slams both of his hands on the door making it rattle. A quite darkness has settled over me.

Chapter 17 - Raegan

"You're sure you want me here for it?" Bran asks for the tenth time.

"Yes, just stay out of the camera, I don't want them asking more questions than necessary."

I've set up a call with Maya and Lily to arrange our catch up. We've been messaging a little ever since I left, but this will be my first time seeing them.

I'm scared of what they will see.

I'm scared they will see through my lies.

"Ok, if it gets too much, just give me the sign, I'll cut the connection and end the call." He fiddles with whatever set up he has going on to monitor it and cut the call if needed. From the happy gleam on his face I can tell he absolutely loves this kind of stuff.

"I never properly thanked you for coming to get me when I called you from the side of the road. Even though I didn't know you well at the time, deep down I knew I could trust you. Through all of this you've been the steady constant, keeping me tethered. Safe. You are the best big brother I could ever ask for. And your big bear hugs are my favourite!"

I've only ever seen my brother in a jovial mood, his easy going personality charming everyone. Him showing me his vulnerable side now, sheen covered eyes and unable to speak, this is precious. With two large steps he has enveloped me in a hug and a single broken part of me settles in it's rightful place.

"I love you little bear." He squeezes me tighter.

"I love you too." Last truth I voice before my call.

"Heyyy.. how are you guys doing?" Maya and Lily come on the screen and the severity of how much I miss them hits me like a wrecking ball.

"How are we? How are you? Where have you been hiding?" Maya doesn't hesitate to start the soft interrogation.

"Yeah, you've not told us anything in the texts, we need to know." Lily manages to add before Maya can continue her line of questioning.

"I know you won't believe me, but I'm good. You know.. my hand is still broken, but healing well. The couple who have graciously let me stay here have been wonderful. And I've had time to think about everything that happened in peace."

"What did exactly happen?" Lily asks softly, being careful to not reopen the freshly closed wounds.

"I got home from work and found Vince in a bed with another woman. I tried to leave, he wouldn't let me, so I punched him in the face. Drove until I was nearly out of petrol only then I realised my hand was throbbing in pain." I am glad that most of what I'm telling my two closest friends isn't a complete lie.

"And you got the divorce done in like a day? I didn't even know that was possible!" Maya the true crime detective never misses anything.

"I know, was surreal to have it done and dusted so quickly, but the couple here have a son who is a lawyer and he took care of it."

There is an awkward silence on the line and I've got a sneaky suspicion I know what question will come next.

"Why didn't you call us?" Yep, that's the one. Lily might be the one asking, but I know both of them are hurt beyond measure. But telling them the truth would undo everything I'm doing now to keep them safe. To protect them. So I settle on the half truth. Again.

"In a space of few seconds the person who was supposed to protect, support and love me, pulled the rug from under my feet. My whole world shattering alongside it. I didn't want to talk. I didn't want to deal with it. All I knew was that I didn't want to be there and be myself. So I ran." I take a few moments to collect myself "On a more positive note, I'm coming down next week and I wanted to-"

"YES!! YES!!" Both of them shout at the same time "Whatever day or time - yes. We can make it." Maya adds.

I smile, but it's bitter sweet. I will get to see my two best friends, but I will also have to say goodbye to them.

The girls catch me up on some more news in their lives, work and dating and fifteen minutes later we hang up. Promising to see each other next week.

For the final time.

"How do you feel?" Bran ask from the other side of the coffee table while putting all his tech equipment away "Are you still up for going to dinner with uncle Carl?"

"Yeah, I'll be all right, I just need a moment." My moment is spent in the bathroom, that has become my dark therapy. I open the top draw, that houses make up, brushes and hair items, but the only thing I am interested in is the gold keychain knife. I never went looking for it, I found it by accident while exploring the draws in my living room. Despite it's small size, the blade is incredibly sharp.

I close my eyes inhaling deeply.

Chapter 18 - Brandan

"Hey, Patricia. Do you know where I can find Indy?" I give the head of housekeeping my best boyish smile, which she knows means nothing, but mischief. I poke my finger into one of the mixing bowls in front of her on the kitchen island "Mmmm.. tastes good. What is this?" She slaps my hand away as fast as a lightning strike when I go in for seconds.

"Stop dipping your grubby little fingers in my cake batter." She has never stopped scolding me like a little boy. "Indy is in the library, we've been tasked with re-arranging some sections as per Mr Brentwoods instructions. May I ask why?" She doesn't lift her eyes from mixing the ingredients.

"Just a chat, that's all." I dip my finger in the batter and nearly run out of the kitchen, before I'm slapped around the ears with a wooden spoon.

"You are banned from my kitchen Brandan!"

"Love you too!" I shout back at her.

I've never known anyone to devour books like Rae has since she's been here. She's said several times she will re-organise the library as 'one cannot find any damn book in there'. I bet dad has instructed Patricia to do it, before Raegan makes true on her threat and starts moving books with her broken hand.

I stop just outside the library doors, as the conversation happening inside is far too intriguing.

"Don't you think?" A female voice I don't recognise asks

"Think what?" A quite soft voice I recognise as Indys asks.

"That he's hot!" Another voice.

"Who?" Indy asks again, sounding exasperated. I wonder if this is how the conversation often goes.

"Brandan!" Both the voices I can't place names against nearly shout at the same time.

"Oh! Erm.. I suppose he's an all right looking guy!" An all right looking guy? I've been called a lot of things in life, but 'all right looking' is not one of them.

"You're joking! He is so hot! What can you tell us about him?" The first woman asks.

"What do you want me to tell you Sarah. I don't know him, the few interactions I've had with Mr Brentwood, he has been nice to me. Just like everyone else."

"But you're friends with his sister, you must know something!" Ah… yes, Sarah. One of the girls that did Raes shopping when she arrived.

"I'm friends with Raegan, but we don't talk about boys, let alone her brother." Is that a slight disgust in her voice? Towards me? Mmm… I do love a challenge.

"Do you know what?" One who's name I don't yet know "I prefer his friend! His broodiness is really sexy!"

"Theo?" Indy asks in surprise.

"Yeah! He looks like he knows his way around a woman!" I bite my fist to prevent me from laughing out loud and give my position away.

"He's scary. He even upset Raegan the other day." Theo did what? I step out of my hiding place and into the library.

It's a large, bright room. Floor to ceiling windows, with double doors leading to a garden patio. Sides of the room are lined with bookshelves and some of the books are currently on the desk, chairs and the floor. Any free wall space has a hanging art piece, either a painting or a wall sculpture. The windows make it feel bright and airy, when the sun is out, it streams through the windows, casting the room in a golden light. I can see why Raegan loves this room.

"Afternoon ladies!" My voice startles the three maids in the room, one of them, Sarah I think, even drops the book and has turned bright red. I try not to let my mouth curve into a knowing smile. "Indy, could I please have a word?"

She places a handful of books back on the shelf "Yes Mr Brentwood." I open the door to the patio and let her through.

"I've told you before Indy, just call me Brandan." I shut the door behind us with a satisfied smirk. Sarah and the other girl heard that and will grill Indy about it. 'An all right looking guy' needs to get his kicks where he can. "Please take a seat."

The patio outside the library is already set up for the warmer weather, with a couple of outdoor sofas and chairs around a coffee table and an electrical fire in the middle.

"I wanted to talk to you about Raegan."

"OK." She sounds hesitant and I know I am on dangerous ground here.

"Have you noticed any changes with her? Anything different? I know you two are close and-"

"And you thought I would break Raegan's confidence? Just because you asked me?" I look at Indy's brown eyes and I can see a fire burning in them. I have messed this up. Badly. "Raegan's trust has been broken by people she thought would never hurt her. She has to rebuild her faith in people and decide who is worth giving a piece of her heart to. If she would find out you are asking me or anyone about her, instead of talking to her, it would devastate her. Both of us would lose her."

I am taken aback by what Indy is saying deep down I know it's true. Raegan would never come to me for anything if she found out I've been trying to wrangle her secrets from people around her. Indy's fierce loyalty to my sister is admirable. I can't ruin their friendship, Rae needs Indy in her life.

The way Indy speaks about pain and betrayal makes me uneasy. There is a story behind this fierce red haired girl that is calling me, wanting me to uncover it.

"I'm worried about her." I finally say "She's been... different the past few days." Indy nods at what I'm saying, which I'm taking as a silent agreement.

She rises from the sofa we're sitting on and turning back to the library door. When her eyes lift from looking at the ground to my eyes she says "You have grown up in this world-" she gestures with her arms around us "Raegan hasn't." She goes back into the library, leaving me alone on the sofa to think.

Chapter 19 - Brandan

I'm driving all four of us to Carls farm, that is less than an hour away from where we live. We only have one security car following us. Despite the pressure we're under, we always try to move about our lives as normal as possible.

As long as I can remember Carl has always lived on this farm. Over the years him and his wife Audrey have restored and modernised the house and other buildings on the land.

"That building on the far right, that is where we keep all the cars we've restored." Dad says and Raegan leans slightly across to the right to see out of the window.

"Do you have a garage there as well where you do the repairs?" they must've talked about his and Carls car restoration hobby.

"Yeah, it's got everything a petrol head could ever want."

"Can you lean back so I can see out of the window?" Raegan is asking Theo, who is looking down on his phone, sitting in the back with Rae.

"It's just a building, you're not missing much." Is his muttered, bored response.

"Would it kill you to be nice?" She bites back.

"It might." Raegan releases an exasperated breath.

"You're an utter ass." I nearly choke on air.

"You all right you two?" Dad asks, as shocked as I am by the short exchange. There is something going on between both of them, and that something - is affecting Raegan far too much for my liking.

"We're good." Theo replies while finally looking at Raegan, who has elected to ignore his existence.

"Sweetheart, are you all right?"

"I'm good." She continues to look out the window.

A short while later we're standing in the foyer of Carls farm house that leads to the open space living and dining room. Dad introduces Raegan to Carl and Audrey, and then to our twin cousins - Evelyn and Olivia. Lyn and Liv just turned twenty and are enjoying their two year gap year.

If Raegan is nervous about meeting the family, she doesn't show it. She looks relieved.

"Have you two been looking after your sister?" Carl asks after giving me a warm hug.

"She's not my sister." The cold way Theo says it makes all of us stop short with a 'what the fuck' look on our faces.

"If we were related, he would have better manners." Rae answers and Aubrey leads her away into the living room.

"I don't envy you Raegan, having to put up with three strong headed boys! Come on, let me show you the house."

That's two strained exchanges in a space of five minutes. Dad gives me a look that I know means I need to get Theo's head out of his own ass and soon. Dad turns his focus on his two nieces and how their horse trails are going.

I motion to Theo to follow me in one of the side rooms.

"What's going on between you and Raegan?" I don't even wait for him to close the door behind us before I snap at him.

"There's nothing going on." But his strained face suggest otherwise.

"Nothing. Do you wanna try that again?"

"There is nothing going on between us. Just because she's your sister, doesn't mean we're going to be best friends."

"But I do expect you to not make *my* sister cry." That changes his expression and I swear gilt flashes through his green eyes. He turns towards the window and runs his hands through his hair. After a long moment he released a breath and finally speaks.

"I never meant to upset her, it just... it just kind of happened." He admits.

"Let me guess, you were being a dick like you were just now and in the car?"

He does't hesitate to answer "Yeah."

From the slump of his shoulders I know he is not proud by how he's acted today or whatever happened the other day between them. Theo is not one to often make mistakes and even more rarely - own up to them. Or apologise. The lawyer in him always feels the need to talk himself out of any wrong doing or pulling the fifth - no comment.

"You need to tone down your dickishness as it's having an affect on her." He spins around quickly and is right in my face.

"What do you mean 'having an affect on her'?" a lesser man would cower under his intense gaze. A knock sounds on the door and Carl pokes his head through it

"Come on, foods ready boys!"

"Coming." I reply and head towards the door to follow uncle to the dining room.

"Brandan." Theo's voice is low. I look back at my best friend. "I'll make it right."

I nod at him. "You better."

"Dinner is lovely as always Audrey!" Dad says, knowing that it is Carl who cooks Sunday roasts, but auntie always plays along.

"Thank you darling, it's nice to be appreciated for all the hard work I've put into this dinner!" Everyone is holding back laughter at the table apart from Carl.

"I don't know why you two always insist on playing this game! It's extremely frustrating." He stabs at his chicken and vegetables.

"Because you're an easy wound up job!" Dad replies with a grin.

The rest of the dinner continues with an easy conversations. Audrey and Carl are asking Raegan questions about her life, getting to know their niece.

To my surprise Theo sat himself down next to Rae at dinner table, his way of trying to make up from earlier and to uncover what damage he has done. Sly fucker.

After dinner the girls have taken Rae to the stables to show their competition horses. While we have migrated to uncle Carls study.

"She's adapted pretty well, considering the situation." Carl starts while pouring us drinks.

"She has. Next week will be hard for her." Dad replies.

"Is that when you're ending Julias life?" Carl asks.

"Yes. We can't wait any longer, the danger is too great."

"Have you got any news on the situation?"

Considering the brainpower in this room, 'situation' is the best we have come up to call it. Over the past year it's become more evident that our covert missions are being affected by external sources. About six months ago, we received our first threat. We're still unsure if they know how much Brentwood Global is involved in Darkheaven Citadel, but we need to tread carefully.

"No, I have programs running constantly monitoring different feeds, but nothing has come up. We've done checks on every Brentwood employee, nothing has been flagged." I answer.

"Darkheaven Citadel is not something you find in a quick Google search. It has been in our family for generations, there are less than 20 operatives working on the assignments and going on missions. How the fuck can we not find the leak? Putting everyone in this family at risk!" Carl finishes with a frustration. And he is right.

Brentwood Global is the heavyweight in security and everyone knows that. But the real business, the one that has made us money and put us on the map- is Darkheaven Citadel. Nearly 100 years ago my great-grandad started it with nothing more than a rage filled heart and extreme amounts of determination. After he had exacted his revenge upon the people who had wronged him, he discovered that he was rather talented at killing people. Not in any shoot-shoot-bang-bang kind of way, but in a meticulous planning, understanding the stakes and striking at just the right way. That's how

Darkheaven Citadel was born. The first underground, black market hitmen for hire. Very quickly he learnt that he didn't want to take on any job that came his way, the risks were too high for low rewards. Over the decades it has grown into a smooth operation where we have a handful of active agents to complete the missions. The principle is the same as it was at the beginning - we only accept the highest grade jobs for maximum reward. Each job is severely vetted before we accept or decline. Anything to do with politics or religion are the most sensitive ones, but most cash rewarding.

We know we aren't the only fish in the pond, but we are the biggest shark.

"We're working on every lead we have, you know that." Dad is trying to placate Carl, but I know he is as much frustrated with this as anyone. Things are escalating far quicker than we anticipated.

Chapter 20 - Raegan

It's been three weeks since I broke my hand and the boys are taking me to the hospital for my weekly check up. I don't think this is the normal practice, but George insisted I get a weekly check to ensure it heals correctly.

"So..?" Leo asks as soon as I exit the doctors office. I have grown to really like my two bodyguards. Christian is right by my other side in seconds.

"My hand is healing well, doctor has given me some exercises for me to do, to start strengthening my hand and arm."

Christian scowls and looks down at me "You're arm is ten times stronger than it was when you broke it since we've been training. What is he trying to say?"

"He doesn't know you two have been training me, this must be the standard procedure."

"Mhm." Christian murmurs and we continue walking out of the hospital to our car.

"Are you ready for the bookstore?" Leo is as excited by this visit to the most magical bookstore as I am. I've re-discovered the reading bug while I've been at the manor, we even re-categorised the library at home. But I am itching to buy new books, so I found the most magical bookstore I could.

"I am." My smile is wide "Thank you guys for coming with me, I know it's not exactly your scene." Leo throws his arm around my shoulders and pulls me closer to him.

The Unspoken Darkness

"Nonsense, I've heard book girls like bikers."

"You are not a biker." Christian corrects him while opening the back door of our car for me to get in.

"Not yet." I love their bickering, they're like an old married couple.

A while later we park up on a side street in the most picturesque little town. It is not a place you would expect to find in the outskirts of London. The main high street is still the original cobble street. There are no big chain shops here, the town has preserved it's uniqueness and originality. Each shop has an old school sign hung above it, the windows are dressed with flower boxes. The lettering in each shop window is hand written, giving every shop the same, yet completely different feel.

The bookshop takes up the corner of the street. Large, green stained glass sash windows decorate the front of the store. Hanging plants that haven't come in full bloom adorn the entrance. Above the wood and glass door hangs the sign in gold lettering - The Cosy Prophecy.

And just like that, I feel at home.

The inside is even more incredible than the outside, deceptively spacious with seemingly endless shelves filled with every book a girl can dream of. It is a two story building with a windy, black metal staircase leading to the upper floor. It takes me a moment to take it all in, but I follow my nose, that has sniffed out the coffee that I will be bribing my two bodyguards with. A calming sound of a piano being played fills the air. If this isn't heaven, I don't know what is. I am well aware that the two men with me do not share the same sentiment. We make our way upstairs and both the main shop as well as the coffee shop, are fairly busy for a Wednesday mid-morning.

"Why don't you both find us a seat and I'll go order." I gesture to a table by the railings overlooking the ground floor near the piano.

"Leo go with Raegan, I'll secure the table." Christian replies while scanning our surroundings.

There are a couple of people in front of us as we wait in line.

"Oh, did you get your theory test booked?" I ask Leo. From the first day I met him, he has not stopped talking about getting his bikers license. From what I've heard there are quite a few of the guys who are working at the house that ride bikes, they even have their own club, which Leo is desperate to get in.

"Yep, it's in a couple of weeks time. Once I pass that, I'll get the practical test booked in straight away. I've got my gear, my bike, just need the license." I can feel the excitement rippling off him and I am genuinely happy for him. Terrified for him being on a bike, but happy that it'll make him happy.

"Will Christian get you 'in' the club once you pass?" Christian is a biker as well and will be my getaway ride tomorrow.

"I keep asking him, but he won't say. There are a few other guys I know who are, but I'm not that close to them. I did think about asking Theo, but.. I don't think that will go down well."

A young woman with shoulder length blonde hair and hazel eyes greet us. She is wearing silver, round glasses and her name tag reads *Elyse*. Such a beautiful name.

"Hi, what can I get you guys?" Her cheeks pink a little when she looks at Leo.

"Hi, can we get two large cappuccino's, one large latte, two cinnamon swirls, three pain au chocolate and two croissants." She looks slightly confused at me "I promised my friends an endless supply of coffee and pastries if they come with me and carry the books I buy" I lift my right hand showing my arm in a cast.

"Yes of course, not a problem." Elyse shyly looks away as she puts our order through the register. "What do you guys read?" She asks while looking at Leo, who seems to have forgotten how to speak. I look at him and raise my eyebrows, he finally clears his throat and says

"I… I don't read." Oh dear God, this is painful to watch. A disappointed "Oh" leaves Elyses mouth.

"What would you recommend to Leo to get him into reading?" At that her eyes light up.

"Well, depends in what kind of stuff you're into. Do you like fantasy, rom-coms, drama, crime or real life events?"

"Erm… I like the Harry Potter movies?" Oh dear.

"That's a perfect choice. An easy get into fantasy is Fourth Wing, it might sound a bit out there if you're not a big reader, but definitely a must try." She then looks at me "Have you read it?"

"It is on my list of books to purchase today." I look at Leo "Why don't we buddy read it?"

"That is amazing, I love to tandem read with my friends and then discuss it. You guys take a seat and I'll bring the order across to you."

"Thank you Elyse." I smile at her and we walk to the table Christian has secured. And I do mean *secured*. He has changed the position of seat, so it's not in a direct view of the entrance, the view from both of their chairs cover the full 360 of the place. And to top it off- he has moved the other tables further away.

"That was painful to watch." Christians dry sense of humour always makes me laugh. Well… laugh more on the inside, I haven't laughed out loud for a while now. But I smile.

"It was even worse standing right next to them!" I add, keeping my face as serious as I can.

"I did consider going in to rescue you, as it was reaching danger zone." Christian looks dead serious when he says that and a genuine laugh escapes me. Christian looks at me with warmth in his eyes "It's good to hear you laugh."

"Yeah, yeah, I'm glad that you're laughing too, but not at my expense." Leo sits down with a huff "I hate you both." And he crosses his arms over his chest.

"Broodiness doesn't suit you and you won't win Elyses heart with that!" Leo glares at me, while Christian smirks. Over the past few weeks we've grown closer together, I enjoy their company. My laugh just now is proof of that. To them I am just an assignment, I know that. But to me? They are becoming an integral part of the new me, whoever she might be.

A few minutes later Elyse brings over the drinks and pastries, lays them all down and I catch her having a sneaky look at Leo with bright pink cheeks.

I pull out my phone, click on camera, turn on the selfie mode and snap a photo of the three of us.

Chapter 21 - Raegan

We've been here for a while, I would guess close to 3 hours. I know my two companions are bored and have been ready to leave for about 2 hours 45 minutes, but they have not said a word. They are taking turns to follow me around, carrying my basket of books while I browse. I've gone through every section that holds my interest- fantasy, crime, romance, thriller, dark romance, and young adult. For the first time in years, and I do mean years, I actually have time to just read. Get lost in the pages and escape reality. Maybe between these pages I'll find pieces of new me.

I've made my way to the stationary, picking out sticky notes, pens, notebooks and anything that catches my eye. I have always loved annotating and writing notes when I read books. The thought of doing it again makes me smile, not just on the inside.

"This really is your happy place." Christians voice drags me back to the bookstore and away from my reading daydream.

"Yeah, I think it is. I've always loved books, ever since I was little, even before I was able to read. I loved flicking through the pages, looking at pictures. Just arranging them in my little bookshelf. But once I could read, gosh, no one could wrangle a book out of my hands. I always had a book on me at all times. As the time went on I fell in love with literature more and more and ended up doing English at uni. But I haven't read like I used to when I was a kid since then. There was less and less spare time to truly enjoy reading, so for years I've just read for studies or work." I finally take a breath and look around the gorgeous book shop "I've fallen back in love with reading over the past few weeks. Reading just for me, for fun. And who knows, maybe these books-" I gesture to the basket that has turned into a basket-trolly, which is heaped with books "will help me discover Raegan." I give Christian a smile and he nods back at me.

"How are you feeling about tomorrow?" I bet he has been meaning to ask me that the whole day. I also bet he has been tasked to ask me that. Tomorrow is the final day of Julia Green.

There have been so many discussions, recaps, rehearsals, me repeating the plan to George and Bran to make sure I know what will happen. Not just so I know 'what will physically happen', but so my mind can get used to what will happen as well, to prevent me going into shock.

"The thing I am most anxious about is seeing my friends." I answer honestly. Despite having spoken to them several times on the phone and even video call, seeing them face to face scares me. "I have been practising different scenarios in my head, even speaking them out loud. Answering their questions about the last few weeks and me going mostly off the grid and the fastest divorce in history. But I… I can't…" my eyes are burning with tears, there is a lump in my throat and my heart is off to the races. The shelves around me are closing in and the books have absorbed all the oxygen in the shop.

The Unspoken Darkness

I've deliberately bypassed this part of tomorrow in my prep, because I know it will wreck me. Now trying to say it out loud makes it real. I blink and blink and blink, but the burning sensation in my eyes is not going away, so I give up the fight.

I close my eyes.

I feel Christian putting his hands on my shoulders and lowering his head to my eye level, but I keep my eyes closed.

"Breathe Raegan. Don't let the panic attack drag you down. Breathe through it. You can do it. Focus on your breathing." I do. I follow Christians instruction. The darkness recedes. Oxygen returns to my lungs.

Swallowing the lump in my throat I open my eyes.

My tears fall.

With a broken voice I whisper "I can't find the right words to say goodbye." The last word is barely audible to my own ears, but I know Christian heard it. He is right here with me.

Both of us allow the silence to stretch, it's not uncomfortable. It's needed. We don't break eye contact, it's a lifeline at the moment.

"This industry we're in, always demands sacrifices. The higher you are on the food chain, the bigger the price. You, Raegan, are a Brentwood. Brentwood is not just at the top of that chain - it is the food chain. The list of people who are willing and actively doing whatever it takes to change that, is ten times longer. All of us who work for you and your family have given something or someone up, not just to work under the Brentwood name, but to work in *this* world. But the people who sacrifice the most are the people who's name is

Brentwood." Christian is a man of few words, but when he speaks, he tells a lot. In the sentences he just spoke is so much information my frazzled brain cannot compute. I try to ask one of the twenty questions swirling in my head, but the words fail me. Again.

Instead my attention is grabbed by what I see in the corner of my eye. Both, Christian and I turn to look at where Leo is talking to Elyse. Her bright pink cheeks are seen from where we're standing across the shop, she is very animated while talking to Leo, but she does not break eye contact with him. After they chat for a bit longer, she gives him a book, giggles a little bit and walks back to the cafe shop upstairs.

When Leo reaches us he looks extremely confused, yet satisfied with himself.

"She gave me that book she mentioned when we ordered our coffees" he keeps looking at the open page in the book, then looks up at us "and she said 'if you want to re-create any of the scenes, my number is on the first page'." my mouth falls open while Christian chokes on his own breath. "Is.. is this a normal thing that happens in bookstores?" He asks looking at me with his wide blue eyes.

"Apparently so. What can I say, girls like bikers." Is all I say as we make our way to the checkout desk.

Chapter 22 - Raegan

How does one prepare for their own death?

When Brandan first talked to me about this over a months ago I thought he was joking. Never in my wildest dreams did I think I will actually do it. Ever.
Yet here I am, sitting in the back of the taxi, driven by Leo, on my last ever dinner with my friends. Cambridge city centre is always busy and I'm taking it all in. I won't be coming back here for a long time, committing the streets and the warm feeling of the city to my memory.
"We're here Rae." Leo looks at me through the rear view mirror "Good luck. I'll pick you up as planned."

The girls and my favourite catch up place is a small, family run Italian restaurant opposite Kings college. We usually come here on payday, straight after work, eat all the carbs we can and then continue to a pub down the road.
I open the door to the restaurants two pairs of the most familiar eyes land on me and a new set of tears are streaking down my face. Before I can even blink, they are barreling down the restaurant towards me, their faces streaked with tears to mirror mine. I will my legs to move towards them and we meet in the middle of the room in the biggest, sob full hug. All my emotions are bubbling over and I keep thinking to myself - how the hell am I supposed to get through this lunch with my girls?

It takes us several minutes to settle down at the table and get our drinks ordered.

Most people think their most valuable items are cars, houses, jewellery, rare works of art, but to me? There is no number high enough to value these two beautiful women sitting in front of me. Since Bran first told me about the threats, they have intensified. Everyone is keeping the details away from me, but luckily one of my bodyguards is more forthcoming with information. With what Leo has told me I know that a couple of our people have been attacked and a suspicious package has been sent to uncle Carl.

With the threat to our family increasing I will do whatever it takes to keep the two most important people in my life safe. Even if it means I'll break their hearts doing so.

"Have you been eating and looking after yourself up north?" Lily finally breaks the silence, a gentle start to ease us into our conversation. No, I haven't been eating much and sort of- is what I want to reply, but I know that will only make them worry more. So I open my mouth to retell my well rehearsed story of events. One I have already half shared with them.

"Before we start, I wanted to apologise to both of you. I never meant to just run away and… You two mean the absolute world to me and I love you so much. I just.. froze, panicked and ran. Ran until my hand was throbbing in pain and my car ran out of petrol." I tell them a made up story how I came across a B&B near the Lake District and the older couple running it was sweet enough to take me in and take me to hospital to get my arm looked at. I tell them everything that happened with Vince. Again.

Telling them the half truths and lies cuts deep. In normal circumstances I would never know when my last conversation with them would be. Now that I know- it's filled with lies. I am about to break their hearts and there is not a damn thing I can do about it.

"And their son is this shark of a lawyer at some fancy London firm, who took care of my divorce just like that. It was incredibly sweet of them to ask their son and he agreed, which was surreal." My friends are looking at me with wide eyes and I'm not entirely sure if that means they believe me or if they smell the lie I'm trying to sell them.

"Is he hot? And are you going to be the cliche and sleep with your divorce lawyer?" I laugh as that is the most Maya thing to ask. Images of Theo flash through my mind. Him in a suit. Him in his signature dark denim jeans and black t shirt. Him smiling at me in the bike shop. I shake my head to get rid of them as they have no place to be there.

"No and no. The only thing he was good for was to finalise my divorce."

We eat our lunch and sip our drinks as the girls catch me up on their lives, work and gossip I've missed while being away. I don't think I've ever listened this intently to anyone. I want to remember their voices, their expressions and laughs. I will miss them dearly.

"What are you doing now?" Lily asks after a short moment of silence.

"I'm still signed off work for another week so I will spend that up north. It's peaceful there, it gives me plenty of time to organise my thoughts and process what has happened. It's all still so raw that at times it doesn't seem real. Like, my head knows what has happened, but my heart and soul doesn't, does that make sense?" Apart from my geographical location, everything else I tell them is the truth "I feel lost. My head is a jumble of thoughts, and pain, and grief. Anger. How could he do that to me? Were we not happy? Was it all just me wanting it to be good so he went along with it? I feel so fucking humiliated!" I didn't even realise that I am shouting with anger. The restaurant is half empty so my voice carries. I rarely swear, but when I do, it's when I feel like this.

"Oh baby, come here." Lily is on her feet and around the table and pulls me into a hug.

"I'm in so much pain it physically hurts." I sob in Lily's shoulder "It hurts Lils. It hurts so damn much."

We spend the next half an hour reminiscing about the old times, re-living some of our funniest stories. My laugh is tinged with sadness and remorse. Maya, as always, is already planning our next girls weekend and I play along knowing I will never be part of it.

"My train is in half an hour, I need to get going." With that we settle the bill and walk out of the restaurant.

"Do you want me to give you a lift?" Maya asks.

"No, I've ordered a taxi." And right on cue Leo rounds the corner in the taxi. I hug my friends a little tighter and hold them a little longer "I love you both so, so much." To stop myself from saying anything else I released them and slide in the back of the taxi. Leo drives off and I wave my final goodbye at my friends.

The Unspoken Darkness

I hope they only remember the good times we shared.

The drive to train station will be no longer than 10 minutes, I have 6 to change out of my clothes I'm wearing and into full on biker gear. As we are about halfway to the station, we hit traffic, which is being created by a conveniently organised women's rights demonstration.

Leo is counting down to my exit "Ten more yards. Christian is already there, he will be on the right." I put on the helmet and tighten the straps the best I can with one and a half hands. "6 yards." My hands are shaking as I reach for the door handle. "3 yards"

"The crowd is rowdy, just like planned. I'm in position and waiting for Alora." Christians voice comes through the comms in my helmet.

"One yard" I swipe my visor down, and open the door at the same time the other passenger door opens. Two guys are moving a body, that looks remarkably like me in the back of the car in my vacated seat.

I am out of the car and there are people everywhere. They are masking my perfect escape. Bran, Theo and George have been going over these plans for weeks. Every possible angle has been covered, from traffic to door to phone cameras. To wondering eyes of curious people. They found a blind spot of phone coverage and the least amount of 'eyes' of all sorts on us. It is now or never. Within 10 seconds of me being out of the car, I am on the back of Christians bike and we are slowly moving through the traffic. "Alora is secure."

With that last sentence we commence our two hour ride back to the house in Surrey. With each passing mile that takes me further away from Cambridge, I am moving closer to the dark abyss.

The reality of what has just happened dawns on me with an overwhelming wave of grief and pain. The finality of Julias life. My life. Loss of my friends. My husband. My mother. Everything I've ever known is gone. I made it 'gone'. My mind is going through all my memories prior to that fateful Friday when it all went to hell. It's like flicking through a memory book of all the memories, happy and sad ones. With every turning page the grief grows bigger and the darkness grows bolder.

I don't even attempt to fight the tears, the sobs and the darkness. I let them come and swallow me whole.

"Route is clear, Alora is safe. Turning off the comms now." click "You deserve to mourn in private."

And that is exactly what I do for the rest of our journey. I hold on tight to Christian, he pats my hands every so often to check on me. We don't speak, we travel in companionable silence, that is riddled with my sniffles, sobs and hiccups. My helmet is steamed up and I can't see much out of it. Christian has switched from motorway to country roads.

He is giving me as much time as he can, before delivering me home, safe and sound, to let all my emotions out without no one but him around. From the first moment I met Christian we've clicked. There is a familiarity between us. Christian is my friend and I know I am his. I am convinced that Brandan and George will be at his throat as soon as we arrive at the house about disconnecting the comms and taking the long route. But he is doing it anyway. For me.

A familiar iron gate greets me, the guards nod and let us pass. We ride up the drive and veer to the right as we come up to the house into the garage. A sloping down road leads to it, the industrial sliding doors are already open and three, now very familiar figures, are standing in the centre waiting for us. I get off the bike first and Christian follows. We stand facing each other, my back to the three men. I tip my head up and Christian undoes my helmet straps

"How much trouble are you in?" my voice is hoarse from the lack of use other than sobbing

"Don't worry about me." He lifts his visor to look at me, but I keep mine down.

"But I do worry."

"I know you do, but I've got this. Do you need a hand to get your helmet off?"

I shake my head. Having it on is a barrier between me and the world. And I can't do 'the world' right now.

"Ok. If you need anything- call me."

"Thank you Christian."

With my full biker gear on, visor down, I turn to face the three most menacing men I've ever met and I walk straight past them. I am transported back to the night at Azalea as everything turns to slow motion.

One foot in front of the other.

One foot in front of the other.

One foot in front of the other.

Lift your feet to climb the stairs.

Lift.

The Unspoken Darkness

Lift.

Lift.

One foot in front of the other.

One foot in front of the other.

My door.

My little apartment.

Safety.

I enter my living area, shut the door behind me and I lock it.

Tonight it's only me and my dark old friend.

And for the first time I am not running from *it*, I am seeking out *its* company.

Chapter 23 - Raegan

Through the window I can see the darkness has fallen and I'm still standing under the shower. I have not moved since I stepped in. I can't recall what I have been thinking about or if I have been thinking at all. There is not a single bright feeling in my body. I'm consumed by darkness.

I want to scream yet no sounds leave me when I open my mouth.

So I turn to what will help.

My little gold hilted knife.

I press it into my left upper thigh until a droplet of blood appears. Water washes it away.

My hand is steady and heart is calm.

I press the blade deeper, I wait for the blood to pool… and then I cut.

Blood.

Relief.

I repeat it again. And again. Until I have three, semi identical 5 centimetre lines cutting across my upper thigh. In between the five already there.

With every drop of blood that leaves my body, I feel the darkness receding. The pressure that was building inside of me has been lessened.

I watch as my blood mixes with water, it swivels down the drain. And some of the pain gets washed away with it.

I've been lying in my bed for over an hour, but sleep evades me. I couldn't be bothered to close the curtains and the moonlight is dancing through the windows, performing its nightly show.

A knock sounds at my door. My bedroom door. Didn't I lock the main door?

I turn on the bedside light and sit up in the bed just as George pokes his head through the door "Did I wake you?" For the first time I notice how tired he looks. Everything that is weighing me down, is only a fraction of what is sitting on Georges shoulders.

"No."

"May I come in?" I nod in response, he comes in and sits on the side of the bed beside me. "I know this is a silly question, but how are you feeling?"

I'm sure he can see my red rimmed, puffy eyes, that only hold pain and grief. I have been pulled in two directions when it came to George and Bran and this new life - trust them and go with it or hold back. Today was the split in the road and I took the the road to trust them.

I am a pendulum of emotions. One minute I feel nothing and in the next, I feel everything. My head is full of questions that are demanding answers, but the words aren't forming. The snippets floating through my mind aren't making any sense.

Ever since I met Brandan my life has turned into a whirlwind of emotions, revelations and life changing events. I've given up everything I've ever known, everything I am. The overwhelming dread of no past and a very unclear future is threatening to pull me under. *Its* beaconing me.

"Who's body was it that you used as mine in the 'accident'?" Shock crosses Georges face, as I'm sure this is not what he expected me to ask "Did you kill an innocent girl to stage my death?" That has been playing on my mind from the moment I saw her body being put in the back of the taxi, but voicing it is making me feel queasy. A tidal wave of guilt washes over me. Am I responsible for the death of a person? Oh my God! Oh My God! OH MY GOD!!! What have I done!

"Sweetheart, take a deep breath." When did I start hyper ventilating? Why have I no control over my body?

I look into my fathers eyes and I see pain. Not because of what he has had to do to make today happen, but because of the anguish running through me. We both follow a calm breathing techniques, in for four, hold for four, out for four.

After a long moment, George finally speaks "No, she wasn't an innocent girl, she was sent to infiltrate our company and get close to Bran. This would have then granted her access to this house, Bran, Theo, you and I. When the right time came, she was to kill us." Cold sweat covers my body and I know the last remaining tint of colour has drained from my face. He takes my hand in his big, callused one "Brentwood Global is a front to another business. It's called Darkhaven Citadel. Most of the people who know about it assume that we are just the front and not involved in the Citadel. But they also know - that we have enough knowledge to get to those who run The Citadel. I don't think this is the time for me to tell you all of it, but-"

"We're the food chain." George quirks his brows at me in question "Christian told me that Brentwood's aren't just at the top of the food chain, we are the food chain in *this* world. He meant Darkhaven Citadel, didn't he?"

He releases a breath. "He did. Even in our organisation, there are only a handful of people who know. The smaller the circle, the safer it is. Both Brandan and Theo have grown up switching between the two worlds, playing both sides, learning the businesses. I won't be able to keep you away from it forever as word of you will soon spread and when the time comes I'll introduce you to the Brentwood Global arena, but we will keep you away from the Citadel."

As it turns out there is such a thing as too much information. But wouldn't it make their life easier if I wasn't here? Why did they seek me out?

"Do you wish I never existed?" A horror look paints Georges face. He sits closer and pulls me in a hug and holds me close. Mum was never affectionate with me and I've always loved hugs. I'm a hugger, I swear a hug always makes things better.

"I only wish I knew you existed much, much sooner. You'll think I'm silly or sentimental, but I often imagine how it would have been like seeing you and Bran run through the house when you were little. I'm not going to lie, he was a little shit" I snort a laugh, my head is resting under his chin and I can hear the smile in his voice "and would have gotten both of you in a ton of trouble, like your night out, but I miss it." We're both quite for a while before he asks "Can you miss something that has never happened?"

"Saudade." I can feel him turning his head to look down at me "It's from Portuguese, it doesn't have a literal translation, but it describes a feeling of melancholy for something or someone that is no more or never existed. So, yeah. I think you can miss something that never happened." George is resting his chin on top of my head, I yawn and whisper, my eye lids heavy "Tell me something."

To the sound of my father's calming voice and his warm embrace, I drift off to sleep to his story about him and uncle Carls childhood.

Chapter 24 - Raegan

It's early morning when I make my way to the family room and snuggle my way into the sofa. I flick on the TV and search for the news channel. It doesn't take long for yesterdays news to come on.

'It was here, yesterday afternoon around 4:30pm when a taxi carrying one passenger, lost control and crashed into electrical works. Causing the cars electrical wiring to short circuit, leading to sparks reaching the petrol tank and the car exploding. Authorities have confirmed that the passenger was a 26 year old Julia Green, a schoolteacher in the local community. Police have confirmed that they are investigating the driver of the taxi, who has not yet been named, as there have been reports of the taxi swerving on the road prior to the crash. Julia Greens family have asked for privacy during this extremely difficult time."

I stare at the tv as the reporter is on the scene and reporting live. As I watch my old life go up in flames, literally, a weight has been lifted off my shoulders. I only have one life to live and I am going to make it a good one.

The following week, leading up to my hand being taken out of the cast goes by in a blur. I've spent my days journaling, which has helped my racing mind to slow down. Christian and Leo have continued my training and with my cast coming off, I can only imagine what Christian has in store for me.

Leo and I are tandem reading Fourth Wing. Leo is adamant he doesn't want to message Elyse until he has read it, so we're moving through the book at speed.

The weather has been really warm, so we are lounging outside by the pool and soaking up the sun.

"Christian?" He turns from where he has been sitting on his chair to look at me "Can we go for a bike ride?"

"Now?" He asks, not sounding enthusiastic by the prospect.

"Yes. I think the open road will help me figure some stuff out." He takes a deep breath, realising this is not an argument he will win.

"Ok. Get changed in your riding leathers and I'll get it all cleared with your dad."

"Are you two really going?" Leo slides his sunglasses lower on his nose while looking at us with his puppy dog eyes "What am I gonna do?"

I turn back to Christian "Have you got a side cart?" But he doesn't exactly appreciate my joke.

"You" he points at me "Go get changed. And you" pointing at Leo "be useful and go to the range, practice on your aim." A wide smile is plastered on my face as I make my way to get changed.

Thirty minutes later we're on the road. The first two times I've been on a bike I've been a ball of anxious nerves coated in grief. But today, for the first time I am enjoying the ride. Despite being on the back of the bike, with no metal protection around me I feel safe.

Weaving through the traffic and blazing down the country roads is making me forget my life. I am here. In this moment. Breathing. No trauma or grief barrelling down on me.

How wonderful would it be to feel like this all the time?

After a while of riding Christian pulls over at a rest stop, that is surrounded by a woodland and park benches scattered around. There are several cars parked up, families with kids and dogs having a break from their road trips. We get a couple of drinks from a food van who has claimed this spot and walk to the furthest bench from the road and other people, closest to the tree line and sit down.

"How have you been doing?" Christian asks.

"You're with me every day, you know how I am." I reply quickly.

"I see what you're doing and I can guess how you feel, but I don't really know."

"Do you want to know?" He gives me a look that is between questioning and offended "I didn't mean to... I know babysitting me is below your skill set, so... I don't want you to feel like you're stuck with me if you want to move onto other things."

Christian gives me a look that makes me want the earth to open and swallow me "When I heard that your dad was looking for a bodyguard, I asked to be reassigned to you. You are Leos and mine responsibility to keep safe. In every way. So..I do want to know how you are doing."

"Why did you ask to be my bodyguard?" I didn't know that he asked to be transferred to my personal protection detail.

"I wasn't born in the Brentwood world, I just got tossed into it. I know how hard it is to acclimate and get your head on straight. I wanted to be able to help you through this, to make it easier. And less lonely." I lean my head against Christian's shoulder while holding the coffee cup in my hands "I don't think of you just as an assignment or my job, you're my friend Raegan." I weave my arm through his and squeeze his hand.

"You're my friend too Christian." We sit like that while we finish our drinks and watch the people around us before I speak "I've not been well. It's been hard. Most nights I wake up from a nightmare, feeling confused and not knowing where I am or who I am. As much as I think I've managed to come to terms with the changes in my life, something new unravels. I am scared of all the threats, but do you know what terrifies me even more?" I can feel him look at me, and I look back at him "Not knowing who I will become."

Christian unhooks his arm from mine, slings it around my shoulder and pulls me in for a side hug.

"Has this ride helped you at all?" He asks me quietly.

"It has. I've got a plan for tomorrow. Will you be able to take me in the city in the morning before my hospital appointment?"

"Where to?"

"Brentwood Global."

One thing in life I've always detested is bullying. Someone who thinks they are above everyone else. So tomorrow, I will confront one of them.

A day after Julias death.

I am on my walk back to the house, the boys didn't come with me today, as I needed some time on my own. I am heading to our lounge room where I'm catching up with Leo and Christian. There is nothing planned for today and even smaller chance of me leaving the grounds, but they like to stay with me anyway.

As I'm nearing the door I can hear shouting coming from inside, I can't make out what is being said, so I creep closer to the door and peek through.

"Both of you are in so much shit I can't even begin to explain!" Theo bellows at Leo and Christian. He has his back to me. "How can you let her just roam around the grounds on her own?!"

Leo looks scared and ashamed. Christian is keeping his emotions under better control than Leo, but anger is seeping through.

"She needed some time alone, so we let her go for her morning walk without us." Christian replies through gritted teeth.

Theo moves to stand right in front of Christian "How the fuck can you be so irresponsible. I expected that from him" pointing at Leo "but you should know better."

That last comment has snapped something in Leo "Ok, yes, we fucked up by letting Rae go for a walk on her own on a *completely* secured compound. Raes been through a fuckton, so if she needs an hour without us or *you* breathing down her neck, then that's what she needs."

"Rae? You call her Rae?" Theo turns back to Leo and is closing the gap between them. "She is Raegan to you.

You are not her friend. Or her pal. This isn't a fucking daycare centre. You are her bodyguard and you stick with her like fucking glue. Your job is to protect her, not to be her friend." I did not know it was possible for his voice to rise even higher, but he manages it. But Leo doesn't balk under Theos wrath again.

My anger at how he is speaking to my two shadows is boiling over, but my feet are staying unmoving. The next wave hits when I realise how he spoke about me, like I'm an object. And not a human being. I hate that I am reduced to this state, unable to defend them, while being rooted in a place of shock. It won't be long before the wave of guilt washes over me.

"Between the three of us, you are the least versed on how Raegan is doing or what she needs. So back the fuck up Theo." Christian takes a step towards him and positions himself between the two men. "You've upset Raegan more than once, there won't be a next time. Probably best if you stay far away from her, because when you're close to her, you're a complete and utter dick. And that just won't do."

I never knew silence could be so loud. After the longest thirty seconds of my life Theo is the one who speaks first "Your one and only job is to protect her, so don't let her out of your sight." With that he walks out of the patio doors and storms down the garden.

I am still standing by the door as a wave of guilt washes over me. Why didn't I go in there and stand up for my friends? Why did I let him talk to them like that? Talk about me like that? In one breath he says I'm precious and need to be protected, but in the next, I'm nothing more than an expensive piece of art, that needs to be kept behind a bullet proof glass.

Present day.

"Hey Rae, I wanted to talk to you about fathers day. I thought we co-" Bran has marched halfway into my living room before he stops abruptly. Looking at me like he's seen a ghost. Well.. maybe that isn't far off. First time since our meeting in Azalea I have actually dressed up today. I am wearing a dusty blue pant suit with a corset top in the same colour and a blazer to match it. My hair and make up is done, thanks to Indy. Who is bringing a pair of nude colour high heels. I sit down on the little side sofa and start putting them on. I cannot wait for the cast to be off and be able to use my hand as normal.

"Morning brother, how are you today?" I ask cheerfully.

"What are you up to?" He narrows his eyes on me.

"Why would you think I'm up to anything?" I look at him innocently.

"Because you have exactly the same look on your face I do when I'm about to do something I'm not supposed to."

"On that note... how attached are you to Theo being your best friend?" I tilt my head looking at my brother. Yes, brother. It feels to call him out out loud and not just in my head.

He opens and closes his mouth without a word.

"Do I need to turn you off and on again, you look awfully confused." I ask teasingly. Leo and Christian walk in my room and stop either side of Brandan.

"WOW! You look so different." Leo says and both, Christian and Bran turn to look at him like 'did you really say that out loud?' "What?! She does! But like good different. And you look really hot in that pants suit!"

It takes less than a split second for Brandan and Christian to crowd him and my heart stops. Leo shouts and puts his hands up in surrender "Raes too old for me!" He tried to dig himself out of a hole.

"Hey! I'm not that much older than you! But thank you Leo, I appreciate your compliment!" But my overly protective brother and my bodyguard, don't move an inch "Guys, leave him alone!" After a few more tense seconds they step back and I can see the pink tinge on Leos face. I have to bite my lip to stop from smiling.

"Ready to leave?" Christian asks finally looking back at me

"Where are you going?" Bran asks him

"The office." Is his court reply

Brandan looks at me while I collect my handbag and stand up.

"Why are you going to the office? I thought you were meeting dad for lunch later before your hospital appointment." It takes him a beat, but the puzzle pieces slot together "You're gonna rip Theo a new one, aren't you? Why?"

"He's rude and I don't like it, so I want to have a talk with him." I walk closer to him. "But I'm glad you brought up fathers day, I've got an idea I want to talk to you about." I lean slightly on my toes and kiss his cheek and my two shadows and I walk out of the room. We're a few paces down the hallway when I hear Brandan shout.

"Wait… Did you call me 'brother'?" Bran has stepped out of my room into the hallway

"Don't worry brother, I'll help you find a new best friend, as your taste in friends is questionable!" I wave back at him "And maybe have a nap, your response times are really slow this morning." I can see him grinning and shaking his head at me.

"Chris, Leo - try to keep her out of trouble!"

"She's the boss, what she says goes!" Leo shouts back.

"Fuck my life!" Is the last I hear of Bran as we head towards the garage.

Chapter 25 - Raegan

Brentwood Global headquarters are in a flashy new skyscraper in London city centre. Christian stops the car in front of the building and Leo opens the door for me. As we're walking towards the main entrance a man in a black suit is walking towards us.

"Miss Brentwood, welcome to Brentwood Global. I'm Clive." He extends his arm and I shake it as much as my nearly healed right hand will allow "Your brother called ahead and said you will be visiting. Please, follow me inside and we'll get your security clearance sorted."

Clive leads us in the building towards the front desk, cutting off people queuing for meetings, appointments, interviews. We reach a dark haired women in glasses who hands a security pass with my photo and name on it "Just show it to the security and they'll let you through"

"Thank you. Which floor can I find Mr Oakes on please?"

"Thirty sixth."

We make our way to the thirty sixth floor. Out of all the things in life that terrify me, heights is not one of them. When we step out of the elevator I see the London city skyline through the floor to ceiling windows. Beautiful.

"His office is this way." Christian guides me to the door that says

The Unspoken Darkness

Theodore Oakes
MD
Brentwood Law

I knock and open the door and I am not greeted with Theo behind a desk. Instead I am greeted with a young man sitting behind a desk looking at us with a very unimpressed look on his face.

The rest of the space is set up like a waiting room, with couple of sofas and a coffee table.

"Is Theodore in?" I motion to another door, which I'm 100% sure leads to his office.

"Do you have an appointment?" The young man counters with a very clipped tone, he must've picked that up from his boss.

"I don't need an appointment." I step towards Theo's office door.

"You can't go in there!" His assistant shouts as he scrambles out of his chair to stop me.

Too late, the door is open and I walk in. And what I see will forever be etched in my memory.

First I see is the back of a woman's head, she has bright red hair, definitely not a natural colour like Indy's and her whole body is bouncing up and down. She is facing, who I assume is Theo under her, and holding onto his shoulders while they fuck.

Momentarily I am transported back to a month ago with a vivid memory of Vincent plunging his cock in another woman.

There is a gasp behind me that snaps me back to reality. The gasp is from his assistant and low chuckling coming from my two companions.

"What the fuck?" Theo shout "Get out!"

The woman on top of him freezes in place and does not turn to look back.

"No." Is my only reply.

If looks could kill, I would be dead now.

"I tried to stop her, but-" his assistant is doing his best to dig himself out of a hole I made, but I am not giving him an easy time, as I continue striding in Theos office and taking a seat in one of the plush chairs across from his desk. Never breaking an eye contact with the blazing green eyes boring into me.

"There are a few things I'd like to discuss with you, so I suggest you tuck little Theo back in your pants." I slightly turn my head to the right to talk over my shoulder back at my chuckling bodyguards, but keeping my eyes trained on Theo "You can wait for me in the waiting room, I'm sure Theos assistant…"

"Jacob." Theo bites out.

"Jacob won't mind getting you couple of coffees while you wait."

A very unsure and trembling "Sir?" Is whispered behind me by Jacob.

"Leave." With one word answers from Theo, my conversation might be much easier to conduct than I thought. "Off." he tells the red haired woman, who is still perched on top of him. Reluctantly she climbs off him, while tugging down her already short skirt. And I am pleasantly surprised that Theo does tuck himself back in the trousers.

The red haired woman's face is nearly the same colour as her hair, either from the activities or the embarrassment. Or a combination of both.

"Theo, aren't you going to introduce me to your lovely friend?" I ask, keeping my voice casual.

But before he can answer she sits herself back on Theos lap, that he doesn't look to be too excited about. She slips on a mask of sassiness and speaks for the first time.

"I'm Heather, Theos girlfriend." Oh, this is Heather. The one who wanted Theo to go out to a party, just so she could get the invite. There is something about her I dislike. I've only ever heard her speak on the phone once and now I'm meeting her for the first time, but the darkness inside tells me we won't be friends. "And who the fuck are you?" Rude and arrogant, perfect match for Theo.

"Heather." Theo warns

"What? She's the one who barged in here. Who is she?" Heather is very demanding.

"That's not important. What I am interested in is- you, tell me about yourself Heather." This has caught her off guard and Theos gaze keeps drilling into me, making my breathing harder. I keep reminding myself that this is all his own doing.

"Erm… I'm an influencer." Of course you are "I have over three hundred thousand followers and Theo is super supportive of my career." The last bit of her sentence is meant as a claim of him and my stomach churns at that.

"What do you influence?"

Heather looks at me in confusion, then looks at Theo who is continuing to stare me to death.

"What.. what do you mean? I'm an influencer."

"No, I heard you the first time, no need to repeat yourself. What I'm interested in is, are you influencing people with your financial advice, how to build a business or exercise plans or just funny content people can lose themselves in?"

The look on her face morphs from confused, to angry and back to arrogance "I do brand collabs, showcasing all the latest fashion and travel. We were actually just discussing our next holiday to Monte Carlo and what brand deals I could get." From the twitch in Theos face I get the confirmation that what she told me is a big fat lie "The only problem is Theo cannot get any time off, his asshole of a boss won't let him have any holiday." She ends her sentence on a whine, that irritates my ears. Theos jaw is clenched so tight I can hear his teeth grinding together from across the desk. My smile hasn't faltered the whole time of this interaction and it's just changed from fake to genuine.

"Well.. good luck with that. To both of you." I even flash them a toothy smile, before returning back to Theo and the reason why I'm here "I have fully made peace with the fact that you don't like me and I no longer care to know why. But what I do care is how you speak to people under my employment. If you have a problem with my bodyguards or anyone else I work with- you come and talk to me. You do not corner them in a room and bellow at them knowing nothing of the matter at hand. Have I made myself clear?"

There is a long, tense pause between us. I can see the cogs turning behind his eyes, outweighing the pros and cons of agreeing with me. Theo is a man who always wins, so admitting defeat, especially to me, will hurt his ego greatly.

"Understood." My eyebrows shoot up a little at his acknowledgment.

"Marvellous. To make up for your wrong doings, you will personally invite Leo to join your bike club and be nothing but nice and welcoming to him."

"Absolutely not."

I cross my legs and sit back in the chair.

Theo throws his head back, resting it on the back of his chair, lets out a big sigh followed by a "Fine."

He returns his head to the normal position and I notice that, his hands are not on Heather, they haven't been this whole time. He kept them on the arms of his chair.

With a satisfied smile on my face I rise them the chair "I'll let you return to your previous activities." And I walk back towards the door

"You're being a real bitch!" Heather says to my back, which I think is something she does a lot. I turn on my heel to face them again.

"Heather." Theo's voice is a low threatening rumble and she stiffens at his tone.

"You're right. You know what? Why don't you both join me for dinner tonight?"

"Why would *we* join *you* for dinner?!" She spits while half mocking me.

"Don't." Theo grounds out, but I'm not sure who it's aimed at - me or Heather.

"I'm Raegan. Raegan Brentwood." As the colour leaches from Heathers still flushed face and the understanding dawns over her "Yes, that's correct, same Brentwood as on the side of this building. And I wouldn't throw the term 'asshole of a boss' around too much during dinner."

When I exit Theos office I see both of my bodyguards sitting on the sofa with dainty coffee cups in their hands while Jacob is sitting at his desk, back straight and not moving.
"Gentlemen, let's go find George."

We travel down a couple of floors to where Georges office is. Every time I look out of the windows there is a magnificent view of the city. The sunny weather adds an extra layer of charm over London skyline. Elevator door dings open and we step out onto the executive floor. The layout seems very similar to the floor Theo's office is on, in the middle of the floor is the main reception desk, with offices and meeting rooms filling the sides of the floor. There are seating areas between some of the offices that offer views of the city.
"Mr Brentwood's office is on the other side" Christian says and the guys lead me there. Leo opens a door which leads us into another little waiting room with a middle aged woman behind the desk. From the information George has told me about the business I know that is Nora, who has been his assistant since he started in Brentwood Global nearly 40 years ago.
"Hi Nora, I'm-"
"I know who you are love, let me see if your dad is finished with his meeting" she gets up from behind her desk and walk into his office, and I'm stood there in shock. I didn't expect anyone to know about me, even less so to recognise me. Less than 30 seconds later 5

men dressed in suits and papers in hands walk out of Georges office followed by Nora. "Go on in love, he's free."

"Hello sweetheart, I didn't expect you until lunch." George walks towards me and gives me a quick hug.

"Hi, yes, sorry. I came to see Theo." He raises both of his eyebrows in a surprise "Nothing like that, just needed to have a chat with him." I walk towards the large window and look out to the city "Did you know he has a girlfriend?"

"A what?"

"Not a 'what', but a who." He chuckles "Her name is Heather, an influencer. I've asked them to join us for dinner tonight, hope thats OK?" George comes and stands next to me, while we look out to the city.

"Of course. You don't sound too keen on this Heather girl."

"She's rude and arrogant, two things I really dislike."

"So why invite her for dinner?"

"The prospect of spending more time with her seemed to infuriate Theo more than my dislike for her."

George laughs "You are exactly like your brother."

'Mmm.. he said something similar this morning."

Me: Good news! My cast is off!!

Brandan: That's great! Are we celebrating tonight?

Me: Sort of! I've invited Theo and Heather for dinner tonight.

Brandan: You ripped him a new one, didn't you?

Me: Just a little bit.

The Unspoken Darkness

Brandan: Tomorrow you're helping me find a new friend.

Me: Ok.

Brandan: I'm being serious.

Me: Ok, I seriously will help you find a new friend!

Me: How was that? Any better?

Brandan: No.

Me: I'll see you tonight.

Chapter 26 - Raegan

George insisted on coming with me to the hospital to remove my cast, which was incredibly sweet of him. I could never imagine my mother doing that, she would have probably blamed the whole thing on me. Assigning zero blame to Vince. Anything to not cause any ripples from me that might taint her or her reputation.

We are sat in one of Georges favourite restaurants in the city waiting for our food to arrive.

"How is your hand feeling?" He asks while we wait for our food

"I'm glad it's healed and they were able to take the cast off today. But it feels strange having it out in the open."

The waitress places our drinks on our table "Your food will be out shortly."

"Thank you" George replies with a polite, practiced smile.

"I wanted to talk to you." I need to get it out before I lose my nerve.

"Is everything all right sweetheart?" Concern covers his brows

"Nothing to worry about, I'm just... I'm bored. I've always done something, school, university, work and whatever else, but I haven't got anything to do now. As much as I've enjoyed the free time and not having to rush from one thing to the next, I want that. So I was wondering, if there is anything in Brentwood Global I could do?" The words tumble off my tongue quickly, not giving myself a chance to doubt myself.

"Sweetheart-" George starts, reaching for my hand on the table, but I cut him off.

"I don't want to be a director or a supervisor or anything like that. I need a purpose. A reason to get out of the bed in the morning and not just for a walk, to read or write." I swallow the sudden lump that has formed in my throat. "Any entry level role will do. And the building is secure, so there won't be any increased risk to my life."

Same brown eyes I'm greeted with every day in the mirror are looking at me with so much warmth. George is taking his time, choosing his words carefully.

"I think it's wonderful that you feel well enough to want to go back to work. I really do and I will support you in this, but... I have conditions." A smile has spread to my lips and I nod. "One - Leo and Christian will be in the building with you. Two - if I get the slightest inkling that something is off or you're working too hard, I'm calling it. Three - you'll have to wait until I find the right position for you."

I keep looking at him "Is that it? No four and five?" I'm trying to tamper down my excitement, but I know George can see it on my face and my body.

"Four - I reserve the right to amend and add to these rules as I see fit." I clamp my lips together to stop from saying anything else, that might add the fifth rule straight away. When I am convinced that that's it, I jump out of my seat and round the table to give him the biggest hug I can.

"Thank you! It means a lot!"

He kisses the top of my head "I know it does sweetheart."

The Unspoken Darkness

We spend the rest of our lunch talking about all the different jobs we have done and the weirdest ones we've heard of. After our extended lunch break, George returned to the office, while Christian and Leo drive me home.

I have changed out of my blue pant suit into a pair of jeans and a white top and sitting at my writing desk journaling. Today has been one of the best days I've had in ages, I can't remember the last time I felt so... free? Inspired? Dare I say happy-ish? I can't find the right words to describe how I feel, but I am buzzing with this new found energy and I want to put it to good use before it fizzles out. I open my laptop and let my fingers skim over the keyboard, I take a deep breath and let my soul speak it's truth.

I'm writing non stop as years of thoughts and suppressed feelings come to the surface to be finally heard. I let them affect me in whatever way they need to. I need to feel this for the final time, to process, digest, accept and move on.

I nearly jump out of my skin as I feel a gentle tap on my shoulder "Oh my God Indy! You scared me!" I'm panting and holding my chest like my heart will jump out.

"I'm sorry Raegan, I didn't mean to. I kept saying your name, but you were so focused on your laptop, that you didn't hear me. I'm so sorry."

"That's all right, I got really absorbed in my writing that I completely lost any sense of my surrounding or track of time."

"I thought that might be the case, I came to tell you that dinner will be ready in 30 minutes and both Mr Brentwoods are in the dining room."

"Indy, could you please get the pale yellow summer dress out of the wardrobe for me? I'll quickly re-fresh."

I'm sat with George and Bran at the dining table. George at the head of it, Bran on his right, I'm next to him. And the two seats in front of us are for Theo and Heather, who have not yet arrived.

We are in the middle of conversation about the best qualities in friends, as I am now on a lookout for a new one for Brandan, when the two missing guests finally waltz in the dining room.

Theo walks towards the table and empty seats, George rises and give him a hug "Hello son." I'm not sure what Theo has told Heather, but I don't think he has said that George is like a father to him.

"Sorry we're late, had to move a couple of meetings around last minute due to the late notice." He gives me a pointed look "George, this is Heather, Heather this is George Brentwood. And that smirking bastard is Brandan and you've already met Raegan."

I have never been a very showy person, but sitting here, watching Heather squirm under three Brentwood judging glazes, gives me a weird satisfaction.

"No problem at all, please sit down. We were just talking about what are the best qualities in friends." George says as everyone settles in their seats and housemaids fill our glasses.

"I'm always up to meeting new people!" Heather says with a flirtations smile while looking at Bran. With a corner of my eye I catch Indy stiffening at her comment. It takes her a second to compose herself and continue with serving us our starters.

Brandan looks Heather over and I am so very curious to know what my brother is thinking of her. George is the one to break the awkward silence.

"Tell us about yourself Heather. What do you do for living?" Oh dear. Here we go again.

"I'm a fashion influencer." She must've done some research since our meeting earlier this morning.

"How very interesting. Do you-" George is cut off midway through his sentence by Heather trying to take a swing at me.

"What do *you* do Raegan?" Her voice has turned slightly mocking and I'm not the only one at the table that notices it. Brandan sits back in his chair lazily observing the new comer.

"I'm glad you asked Heather, as I haven't got the chance to tell Bran yet. As of next week I'm joining the Brentwood Global family in the media division."

Bran turns his attention to me in a surprise. "You are?"

"Yep. Had the interview earlier today and got it." Slight white lie, but speaking to George was kind of an interview. He called me just before I got sucked into my journalling frenzy and said there is a position in the media team. As I have an English degree and was teaching it at my school in Cambridge, I'll be writing, proof reading all media releases, statements, website updates and even some speeches. Which is really exciting. I am not entirely convinced there was an opening or if George created it. But nevertheless - I am happy.

"Congrats lil' bear!" He pulls me into a crushing hug. "Proud of you."

"Congratulations Raegan." Theo says from across the table, I nod at him with a smile on my face.

The rest of the dinner goes by smoothly with easy conversation between all of us, only when Heather adds to the conversation with her snarky remarks, the air gets thicker.

We have finished the desert and plates are being cleared away when Heather asks me a question I wasn't ready for.

"What about you Raegan, have you got a partner? Or do you just like barging in offices of other peoples boyfriends?" An evil smirk is on her lips. My brain is trying to come up with an answer when Theo answers for me. Or rather - stabs me through the shattered pieces of my heart.

"Raegan couldn't keep a man even if she tried to."

Shock. The world stops spinning. My lungs have stopped contracting. Cold sweat coats my body in less than a second. Few parts of my broken heart I had managed to piece back together are ripped apart and I'm plunged back into the darkness.

My happiness lasted less than a day.

"THEODORE!" "YOU FUCKING ASSHOLE!" George and Brandan shout simultaneously.

My heart is beating to only service my body with blood flow, not to live. It's the sobering truth of his statement that has undone me.

I look squarely in Theos green eyes and I see guilt there. A second too late.

I don't bother with answering Heather. My legs carry me away. I slide to the floor in my darkened room and blink up to the dark ceiling. With each blink a stream of hot tears slide down my temples.

Chapter 27 - Raegan

2:49am and I am still awake, I've made it to my bed from my previous position on the floor. I've been tossing and turning for the past 4 hours and I cannot fall asleep. Dark thoughts are hunting me. I release a big huff and get out of the bed, put on a pair of leggings, shove my feet into a pair of boots and I grab the first jacket I can reach and head out of my room. I haven't walked around the manor grounds in the dark before, but I've been on this route so many times during the day, that I know it by heart. The full moon is guiding my way tonight.

I reach my favourite spot which is on a slight uphill that looks back to the manor from the tree line. In the distance I can see guards patrolling the perimeter, security never sleeps where Brentwood's are concerned. I step over a fallen tree trunk and sit down, which has has become my perching station on my recent walks. Sometimes I only sit here for few minutes, sometimes it's close to an hour.

My mind races back to earlier in the evening, Theos words echo in my head.. in my soul.. in my newly shattered heart *'Raegan couldn't keep a man even if she tried to'*. My breathing shallows, my eyes are burning and my throat is closing up. I close my eyes to calm my racing thoughts.

They're racing for a reason. He spoke true. Despite how I feel about what he said or about the man himself, his words were true. He might have meant them viciously, without any thought behind it. But they're true. In both of my relationships I couldn't keep them. Regardless how hard I tried. Is that where I went wrong? I tried too hard?

Every time I feel like I've made progress, I am shoved further down. Getting up each time gets harder and harder. Making the light I reach for feel more unattainable each time I try. How many more knocks can I take before I stop the climb?

There is only one relief I crave now. Pain. Physical pain. I reach a hand towards my left thigh and I press hard. No pain. The cuts have healed.

Crack

I turn my head towards the noise and a whole 6 feet of an angry Theo is standing in front of me. I turn back to look back at the house. I hear him move closer and sit on the tree trunk next to me. He places his forearms on his knees and leans forwards. Clasping his fingers together like he is preparing himself for whatever he wants to say. Maybe under different circumstances I would care, but not tonight. And not him.

"Raegan." I can feel him looking at me, but I keep staring straight at the house. "Raegan, look at me." Nope. "Rae, please." Now that does get my attention and I turn to look at him with fire in my heart. Or where my heart used to be.

"No. You don't get to call me that." I look back straight ahead of me. Most of the time I am overwhelmed with sadness and grief, but now anger rises to the surface.

The Unspoken Darkness

"Look, I came here to apologise for what I said earlier. It wasn't fair and I'm sorry." He barks out and gets up to leave. "But I shouldn't be the only one apologising, considering all the shit you pulled today." With every word, more and more anger is seeping into his voice. I remain calm and rise from the seat I've been perched on, walk towards him and stand in front of him. Surprise crosses his eyes, but soon enough return to the status quo of indifference. I remove the jacket I've been wearing and hand it back to him and start to follow the moon lit path back to the manor.

"Why're you returning it now?"

"It's served it's purpose."

"What was it?"

I turn to look back at him "Safety."

I can't read his expression no more than I can read my own heart, but something has changed with that last word between us.

My hike back to the house is filled with my heart thumping in my chest and anger ringing in my ears. The only victory I take is I didn't cry in front of him. No tears have fallen. Numbness has it's arms around me.

When I reach my room a wave of exhaustion hits me, all I want is it to curl up in my bed. Before that is possible, I need to lessen this drowning feeling.

My bathroom has become my therapy room. Not that anyone would approve off it, but not everyone is burdened by what I am. I'm standing by the sink in my underwear and long shirt, the reflection looking back at me is one I know well. I grip a blade in my right hand and while watching myself in the mirror. I go over the cuts I've made before. With every cut *its* tolerance grows, demanding more in return for *its* quietness. Blood drips down my thigh like an offering to stay alive.

The light I can see from the bottom of the well shines a tiny bit brighter. I close my eyes and stay in this calm state where nothing else matters. Where I feel nothing.

It doesn't take me long to tidy up the sink, the blade and wash off the blood from my leg. The cuts are still open and fresh, allowing me to breath. To live.

I exit the bathroom and walk towards my bed, but I stop in my tracks when I hear him say my name.

"Raegan."

I turn to my left. Theo is standing in the doorway of my room, his jacket clutched in his hands.

"What are you doing here?" I manage, barely a whisper.

Theo takes a step closer "I don't like the way our conversation went, we need to talk it out."

My only thought is to get him out of this room. Away from me. Away from my darkness. The shirt I'm wearing is barely covering my bum... barely covering the scars when they healed. Now they are red raw with blood still seeping out. He cannot see it.

He cannot see *me*.

"You need to leave." He doesn't move "We'll talk in the morning, it's late and I'm tired." I swallow. Hoping the fear doesn't show in my eyes. "Please leave." I am holding on to final dregs of my strength and composure. His eyes drop to my exposed legs, even though the room is only illuminated by my bedside lamp, it's light enough to see the cuts. The small pebbles of blood that have started to collect in the deeper parts of the cut are easily visible.

"Leave Theo. *Please.*"

He throws the jacket I returned on the chair and steps towards me. It's not just his size that fills the room, it's his presence. Power. Authority. He cups my head with both of his hands and looks down at me. I am rooted in place unable to move or swat his hands away. Or demand again that he leaves my room. He leans his head towards me.

"Tell me."

It might be my own traitorous eyes covered in sheen and exhaustion, but there is panic in his eyes. The frown between his brow is deep. I can't look him in the eye and face his judgement. So I close them and dip my head towards the floor. I know that what I'm doing is unhealthy and dangerous, I don't need another person to tell me.

"Leave. Please just leave." I know I'm begging and I don't care. I'll beg on my knees if it'll make him leave.

"No. Was I the reason you cut yourself tonight?" His voice is full of pain and regret. My own breathing becomes heavy and a sob escapes my clamped down teeth and lips. Traitors.

With one arm around my shoulder and head and the other around my waist, Theo pulls me close to his chest. On instinct I wrap my arms around his middle and he holds me tight.

"Look at me Alora. Please look at me." I shake my head as the shame is eating me alive. I've never spoken to anyone of how deep my trauma runs, not even to my therapist. I managed to control it, kept it hidden, not letting it show, conceal it with love and hugs, and happy smiles. But now it hits me like a freight train and it floors me. I never wanted to burden anyone else with my darkness. I never wanted to taint anyone with my past.

But Theo doesn't let me fall. He catches me and holds me even tighter to his chest. There is no end to my tears or my crying, my body is fighting to keep them contained, but it's losing. Badly.

"You're shaking baby." In one swift movement Theo has moved us to the foot of the bed, he is sitting on the floor, his back against the bed frame. My bum is on the floor between his legs and both of my legs are over his right thigh. He is still holding me close and I realise I have grabbed his shirt on his back with both of my hands, nearly choking him.

"You're safe. You're always safe with me." He reaches on my bed and drags down a throw and wraps it around me and kisses my temple. "I'm so fucking sorry for what I said today and the other day in the car. I'm so sorry baby." He kisses my temple again. "I'm so sorry." Theo's voice is low, full of sorrow and guilt.

I hear his words, but they aren't making any sense, so I focus on his strong heart beat. His steady *thump - thump - thump* is centering me.

"Raegan, I need you to answer my question." I can't. I don't want to lie to him, but I can't tell him the truth. "Baby, I need your answer." He's not going to give up on that.

I nod.

I hear a sharp intake of breath followed by a loud "FUCK!" I didn't know it was possible to be held even tighter, but Theo manages. "Tell me how to make this right." I don't answer, not only because I can't, but because I don't have an answer for him. So I shake my head and stay quite.

He kisses the top of my head and whispers against it. "Next time you feel the need to hurt yourself, you come to me. Call me, text me, barge into my office, which you seem to like or drag me out of my fucking bed - I don't care. You come to me, you got it?" I nod. "Promise me Alora. I need to hear you say it Raegan."

I swallow to clear my throat "I promise."

He kisses the top of my head again and whispers "That's my girl."

When my tears have slowed and my eyes start to feel heavy, I ask him quietly. "Will you stay until I fall asleep?" I've still not dared to look up and risk seeing his green eyes.

"I'll stay." He is soothing me by playing with my hair. With every stroke my eyes feel heavier. "I'll stay as long as you need me to."

"Tell me something."

And he does. He's telling me about a cold winter day when him and Bran decided to explore an old well. I don't hear much of the story as my mind has started to drift away. *Thump - thump - thump* and the smooth narrater voice who's telling me an adventure story of two boys, is my new favourite thing. And maybe, just maybe, I won't wish for it to end tonight.

Chapter 28 - Raegan

It's been nearly a week since my breakdown in Theos arms and he has made it his mission to check in on me every single day. Sometimes it's a text, sometimes he calls me.

This week I've started my new job at Brentwood Global. It's been nice to meet new people and be useful. And be good at what I'm doing. Each lunchtime I spend with one or all three of the Brentwood men in my life.

One thing I miss about working full time is I get to spend less time with Leo and Christian, but they still drive me to and from work. And with my hand being fully healed, Christian has upped our training intensity.

Leo and I are continuing our buddy reading with our next book. Leos big motivator for continuing with reading is Elyse.

They've been out on several dates now and Leo is absolutely smitten by her. For once, I completely understand why, Elyse is an amazing young woman, she is intelligent and has a cheeky side to her as well. She's good for him, keeps him more grounded and look at life from a different perspective.

I'm sitting on my bed journalling when I'm pulled out of the writing trance with my phone buzzing beside me on the bed.

Theo Oakes

"Hello?"
"Put your riding leathers on and get to the garage."

"What?"

"Don't forget your helmet." Click. The call gets cut off. I look at the phone and see it's nearly midnight.

I climb out of my bed and head towards the end of my wardrobe that stores my riding leathers and pull my hair into a braid. Put my phone in the jacket pocket and make my way down to the garage.

Theo is standing by his bike in the middle of the garage, looking down at his phone. He is dressed in black leathers, same as me. He looks up at me and puts his phone away, I stop next to him.

"Is it such a smart idea to be dressed in black on a black bike riding at night?" That question carries genuine worry. How are drivers supposed to see us being so blended into the night?

"Was that one of the questions you asked Christian when you went on his bike yesterday?"

"Is that what this is about? I didn't ask you to take me on a ride, during the day, so you're going to take me out in the middle of the night and hope no car hits us?" I tease.

"Yes it is. And no, I'm not taking you out in the middle of the night so we get hit by a car." He steps in front of me, takes my helmet and puts it on me "I'm taking you out in the middle of the night, to show you what real freedom feels like." He secures the chin strap and tips my head back and looks deeply into my eyes "Next time you think of going on the back of a bike, it's mine you get on. Understood?" I gasp at the audacity of him. How can he be so sweet and considerate one moment and then a completely overbearing ass the next?

"You have a girlfriend to give rides to. I have a Christian." Why am I pushing his buttons? It rarely end well for me.

He swiftly puts on his own helmet and straddles the bike, without looking back at me "Get on." I do. Did I leave my spine in my room? Why am I doing what he tells me to do? I will need to have some serious talking to myself later. "Our helmets are connected like yours is to your lover boy."

Is he jealous of Christian? I roll my eyes and smile to myself.

We are zooming through the night and I am holding onto Theo tightly like a little monkey does to its mama. He navigates the country roads with ease and confidence, it doesn't take us long until we're on the motorway. There isn't much traffic on the roads and I must admit, it does feel good riding at night. Not that I will admit that to him, Theos ego is plenty big enough, it doesn't need inflating more, so I settle on "Where are we going?"

"The city." The words have barely left his mouth before he speeds up and I let out a 'wooooo' as the speed tickles my stomach and to my surprise I hear a little chuckle over the helmet comms.

"Did that amuse you?" I try to sound stern and affronted, but fail miserably. Even I can hear the wide grin on my face. His only response is to squeeze my left knee and a warm tingly feeling spreads to the dark hole in my chest.

The Unspoken Darkness

Theo is weaving us through traffic to get to the core of the city "I didn't think there would be this much traffic at this time of night."

"Nightlife, events, tourists, London never really sleeps." He responds.

We've stopped at a red traffic light, my arms are still tightly around his waist, he covers mine with his and turns his head back to look at me. Even with his black tinted visor down I can feel his pearcing gaze boring into me "How are you holding up back there?"

"Good."

"Good." He echos my answer just as the light turns green and we continue on our way.

We ride past some of the most recognisable London landmarks and they look so very different at night. Big Ben is guarding over the city from his prime location. The Thames is silently flowing through the heart of London, keeping it alive. The hustle and bustle of the night life adds a mysterious feel. But my favourite part is just right ahead us. The Tower Bridge.

There are tourists taking their nightly walk across it, snapping photos and exchanging kisses. I reach into my right pocket and pull out my phone to take a few photos on my own. In one of the photos I lean slightly back on the bike so I can see Theo, the bike and the Tower Bridge ahead of us. I make sure I click the button several times just in case. I snap some of the river on both sides of the bridge, but my last one is me looking up at the bridge.

Gantry connecting the two towers is lit up against the night sky and *snap*. It's only after I've put my phone back in my pocket that I notice that Theos hand is holding mine in a death grip. Surely to ensure I don't fall of the bike, nothing else. Tickles in my stomach return and not due to speed this time.

To break myself out of my hazy stupor, I find my voice to ask "Is there somewhere higher up we can see the city from?"

London at night has captured me and I want to see more. Theo turns left and right and right and left, even if I did know my way around the city, I would be lost anyway. So I stop trying to follow the streets and let go, taking in the sights.

I see people exiting pubs and bars. Women holding onto each other while staggering to find a black cab. Men still in their suits from their corporate day jobs. Some smoking and holding a drink, some laughing. I don't pay much attention where we're going so I'm a little shocked when we stop and I look up to see 'Brentwood Global'.

"Come on." Theo urges me, takes me a little time to get off the bike. My legs are stiff as we've been riding for a while. He puts the kickstand down and gets off it himself.

He takes off his helmet and I walk over to him, tilt my head up "Can you help me Teddybug?" I try to hold the laughter in, but it escapes as a snort. Heather used that nickname of his at the dinner last week and it's stuck with us, much to Theos dislike of it.

"Does that still amuse *you*?" He asks gruffly, trying to sound affronted.

"It most certainly does!"

He grumbles to himself, which I can't make out, but he gets to work with undoing the strap and pulling my helmet off. "Call me Teddybug one more time and see what happens." His green eyes sparkle with half fury and half promise of something I shouldn't be intrigued to find out. The prospect of which makes my throat dry up quicker than an impending panic attack. I need to have that word with myself. Soon. My lips have lost the memo as well, as they are pulled in a wide smile.

He takes takes my right hand and leads us towards the building, both our helmets in his other hand. A man I've not seen before, appears from the building.

"Good evening Mr Oakes, Miss Brentwood. I wasn't expecting you."

"Evening Michael. I'm taking Miss Brentwood to the top." My insides melt when 'Miss Brentwood' rolls off his tongue with ease and I want to hear him say it again. And again.

Get yourself together woman. You are not a desperate teenager when the first boy has given a tiny bit of attention, you are a grown woman - act like it.

Theo passes our helmets to Michael, walks past him into the building, straight for the elevators. He is still holding my hand and I'm not keen on the time when he will let me go. As I've already given up on having any control of myself tonight, I squeeze his hand tighter, revelling how good it feels.

"Wow!" Is my first word that leaves my gaping mouth as Theo opens the door to the rooftop of Brentwood Global building. It took us a couple of elevator rides and three flights of stairs to get here, but it's one of a kind view of the city "It's gorgeous!"

I spin around to have a look in each direction, I tip my head back and look at the night sky. No stars blinking down at me thanks to the city's light pollution, but it's still gorgeous.

"How high are we?" I ask, still looking up at the sky and my head bumps into something hard.

"62 floors." Theo is looking down at me with the top of my head resting against his chest. I'm not sure if it's the night sky tricking my eyes or if Theo is actually smiling down at me. I continue looking at him, waiting for the smile to disappear, but it doesn't.

"You should do that more often."

He scrunches his brows together in confusion, but the smile stays "Do what more often?"

"Smile." The night sky above him adds an extra layer to his mystery "Smiling suits you." His eyes widen slightly at my words, so before I say anything else and embarrass myself further, I tip my head back to it's normal position and walk towards the edge of the building where I can see The Gherkin building.

"Do you come up here often?" I ask while leaning against the railing and looking out to the city

"No."

"Have you taken Heather up here?" I'm still looking straight ahead, but somehow this question is making my heart race and there is a heaviness attached to it. There is a fifty-fifty chance of a 'yes', but to me, there is only one right answer. Suddenly I feel him behind me.

"This is the first time I've been up here." I'm too much of a coward in this moment to face him, so I continue looking straight ahead "With you." He adds in a low voice.

Theo moves to stand beside me, forearms on the railing, looking down 101 floors. I follow his gaze, the bike is still at the front of the building, there are a couple of security cars that we saw earlier, but not much else happening on the ground level.

We stay like this in silence, completely mesmerised by the view in front of me, until he breaks it "Why do you cut yourself?"

My breathing stops as my mind had wondered far and wide while being up here, *that* was a topic I had not wondered to. I haven't been close to my darkness for days. Theo has caught me off guard and I'm not sure how to respond. If I say nothing he will ask again. If I answer vaguely- he will drill for details. If I answer honestly - he will kill him. So I go for half truths. Again.

"Mental illness derived from trauma is a strange mistress to have. At times, like now, I feel content and some might say happy, sometimes I'm not feeling much at all and everything feels numb. But the worst is when I feel too much. Too much hurt, pain, guilt, shame. Self doubt. It's invisible, yet it wrecks the most chaos. It's hard, impossible to explain as it will be different for everyone, but for me it's like this pressure is building up and up and up and it needs to escape. The more it builds up, the less I can breath. The walls around me start to cave in, suffocating me." Finally, I turn to look at him "That's when I do it. To stop my mind from suffocating me." He gives me space to speak without the expectation to, so I add "I've never spoken about this before."

"What held you back from telling anyone?"

"Fear of being judged by someone else's rules and standards. Burdening my loved ones with the worry of what I might do or making them blame themselves for not being able to help me. They worried enough about me, without me adding an extra layer on top of it. And honestly? I didn't, and still don't know where to begin or how to explain it without crumbling to the ground."

"What made you feel like this?" His question is genuine, no hint of judgement.

"I don't want to talk about it." I cast my eyes back towards the city and add on a whisper. "Not now."

"What are you scared off? That I'm going to kill someone?" He says half jokingly.

"Yes." His face drops and in this moment I know one thing for certain - Theodore Oaks will keep me safe, even from myself. It's also clear he will not stop until he has learnt the truth. He might let it go tonight, but not for long. And that scares me the most. This strange friendship we have means more to me than I care to admit, losing it fills me with dread. And the truth will unravel it all. When did he become my safety buoy in the unchartered waters of my darkness?

After several more minutes he takes my hand again heading back towards the door "Come on, we need to head back."

The Unspoken Darkness

The ride goes by in a blur, both of us processing what has been said. I've lost track of time, which isn't unusual, but my thoughts feel lighter. Feels like *its* shed some of *its* burden and feel more at peace. Periodically Theo would cover my hands with his to check I'm still there and holding on tight. Every time he does that, I squeeze him tighter, which seems to put him at ease.

It's not long before we are back home in the garage. Motion sensor lights come on with every foot we drive deeper in the garage. He parks up and I get off the bike.

Without another thought I am in front of him with my chin tipped up and he doesn't hesitate to undo the strapping. When I feel it's loose, I take the helmet off just as he's taken his off.

"Thank you for tonight, it was different." Before he can scowl I add. "Good different."

We walk in the house in silence, the air feels too heavy with words, both spoken and unsaid. We have made it up the stairs and as we're about to walk our separate ways to our rooms, I have finally find my voice.

"Theo?"

"Yes Alora."

"You are the only one who knows, in either of my lives. It's still too hard to talk about, so I don't. But if one day I find enough courage to speak those words, I'll find you."

"I know you will." He kisses my forehead, turns on his heel and walks to his end of the house.

Chapter 29 - Brandan

After a long day at the office and several meetings with board members, I am glad to finally be home and sink into the sofa. I'm still wearing my suit when dad passes me a beer and takes a seat on the sofa alongside me.

"Long day son?"

"Yeah. And still no tangible leads for whoever is fucking with us." It's been months and I have very little to go on. Actually, I have nothing. Fortunately there have been no more threats against anyone else in our family, but I know better than to relax. "Hows Rae getting on at work?" Raegan has been working at Brentwood Global for nearly a month now. With the long hours and extra assignments I'm doing, I've mostly stayed at my apartment in the city, which has limited our interactions.

"She is doing really well. Everyone is happy with the work she's doing, it's not easy to settle in a fast paced role that requires communication with most of the people in the building, but she's doing great." Dad takes a sip of his own beer, wanting to say more "I fear she's turning into us Bran."

I furrow my brow and look at him "What do you mean?"

"She's working a lot. Long hours. Most nights Christian and Leo have to tell her to come home. When I agreed for her to work at the office, I thought it would help her. Now-"

"Dad, Raes life has been ripped open and apart. She feels like nothing she has is hers. So she's pouring herself into work. Making a mark of her own, without us."

He lets out a long and deep breath "I worry about her. She's just found her way home, I'm not ready to let her go."

"I know."

My eyes are glued to the TV, not that I'm interested in what's on, but more to try and switch my brain off from work.

"Evening gentlemen!" Rae is bouncing in the room. She looks happy and she's wearing my sweatpants I gave her the first day with an oversized t-shirt. She sits herself on the coffee table in front of me and has the biggest grin on her face. This cannot be good.

"Why are you wearing my sweatpants?" I narrow my eyes at her while asking.

"They're perfect for getting ready in." At this, both dad and I sit up straighter on the sofa, we've nearly been laying down and asleep. This has got our attention.

"Getting ready for what exactly?" I continue my interrogation.

"Going out. That's why I'm here. I want to know what's the best club to go to." Her legs are bouncing in place from the excitement.

"You are not going out." I reply, which stops her feet and she tilts her head to the right and I realise - this is not a battle I will win, but I will go down swinging.

"And why not?"

Such a simple question, yet I cannot come up with anything better than "It's a school night!" Dad chokes out a laugh and I hear him mumble "never stopped you before!" And takes a sip of his beer. Shouldn't he be more concerned about Rae wanting to go out?

"Ahaa… I have tomorrow off, so no problem there." She planned this all out, I know she has.

"Bran, go with your sister." Raes and my heads turn towards dad. "And if you plan on getting drunk like last time, don't dismiss your bodyguards, so they can carry your asses to your rooms." He's not even looking at us now while issuing his order. "My back is playing up and I can't keep carrying you up the stairs."

"I don't want to go out tonight!" I ground out damn well knowing I sound like a disgruntled teenager.

"If you don't go, Rae doesn't go."

"That seems hardly fair, considering we're not teenagers anymore. And he's in a grump!" Raegan says, not sounding too impressed with the way this conversation has turned.

"I know, but I never got to experience life with you two as teenagers, so… this is it!" Dad replies, extremely proud of himself.

"I'm out of here in search for peace and quite and some sleep." I get up from the sofa and start my walk towards the door.

"Oh Bran..?" I stop in my tracks, knowing the killing blow is about to come, I lift my head to the ceiling asking higher powers to give me strength to survive this. "did I mention that Indy is coming as well?" Yep. That'll do it. I turn back to face them. Raegans winning smirk is plastered all over her face. Dad is grinning, witnessing something new for the first time. "I should've started with that, ha?" She pretends not to be smug, but not doing a very good job of that.

I turn back to the door and shout over my shoulder "Come on then. Let's go out!" I hear a squeal from behind me and a rush of feet padding across the room with a shout.

"Catch!" When she launches herself at my back, making me give her a piggyback ride.

"Father! Your daughter is an absolute hellion!!" I shout.

"If I remember correctly son, you always wanted a sister!" There is zero sympathy in the old mans voice for my troubles.

"Come on! Giddy up Bran, I need to get ready!" Despite me shaking my head at her, I am smiling.

A couple of hours later we pull up to one of the most luxurious nightclubs in London - The Black Rose. Christian is still on duty and drove us here. I get out of the car and open the back door to help Indy out. I'm not sure where along the way I started to notice the tiny red head, but I'm not mad about it. What I am mad at - is Raegan seeing my attention on Indy. Indy is wearing a short, green mini dress, which is making men turn their heads, while we make our way to the entrance. I am really not in the mood to kill anyone tonight, but I might just have to.

Christian is leading Rae up the stairs to the entrance behind us. He is keeping her close.

"You sure you don't want to join us?" Raegan asks him.

"I'm on duty, I'll be working with Black Roses security team to keep an eye on things. Brandan you cleared it with Tobias?"

"I did, he'll meet us at the door."

"It'll be all right. Plus, Leo will be with you." I hear him explain to Rae, which puts her at ease.

I've known Christian for many years, but I've never seen him having as strong of a friendship with anyone like he has with Raegan.

"Hi mate, how you're doing?" Tobias- a childhood friend greets us as we arrive at the main entrance. We embrace and I have a sneaky suspicion Raegan will like him- she's a hugger as well.

"I'm good. Apologies for the last minute notice, but-"

"Aaa.. Don't worry. What are friends in high places for. Follow me." We enter the club, every decor, furniture and accessory is in the customary black and gold colour combination. Everything screams luxury and elegance. The waiting list to get in the club is months long. We round into a small alcove that drown out some of the music.

"This is my sister Raegan, the reason we are here tonight." Tobias eyes light up at the sight of Rae. Unknowingly she is wearing a little black dress with gold shoes.

"Pleasure to meet you Raegan." He kisses her hand. Christian is watching him like a hawk.

"You too." She replies shyly. "This is Christian, he will be working with your guys tonight."

"Of course, anything to keep you safe." He has not broken eye contact with Rae and neither has she. I wonder what Theo would say about this.

"And this lovely lady on Brans arm is Indy." He finally brings his attention back to me and my date. Yes. My date.

Kissing her hand "Nice to meet you Indy. Your two friends are already here and are in the booth with their drinks. Christian, this is Mark, head of security at Black

Rose, he will be your friend for the night." A man dressed in all black appears from the back and takes Christian with him.

"Right, let me take you to your table." He takes Raegans hand and tucks it in the crock of his arm "Follow me."

The club is exclusive, apart from months long waiting lists, it has several more criteria to be allowed in. Bank balance is one of them. The room is rectangular with a sleek modern bar in the middle and a dance floor behind it. A gold disco ball glitters above it. Private booths with plush seating are on the sides of the room, tucked up on a platform to separate them from the main areas. The rest of the space is filled with elegant bar tables and chairs. There are areas that have comfortable sofas for lounging. The lighting is dim and atmospheric, offering an intimate and exclusive atmosphere.

"This reminds me of a club up north." Raegan says to Tobias as we're making our way to the booth, that I can see Leo sitting at with a blond girl.

"Is it Azalea by any chance?" Tobias replies proudly.

"It is, how did you know?" Raegans voice has pitched a bit higher.

Tobias leans in closer to her ear "Because I own it." She turns to face him, with slight shock, but mostly surprise on her face.

"Rae, did you invite Theo?" That is like a bucket of cold water over Tobias. Tobias and Theo have never gotten along, neither have been willing to share the details when asked. That will cool him down for a while.

"I called, but couldn't get through, so I sent a message." Rae replies.

When we reach the booth and do another round of introductions. The blond girl with Leo is Elyse, his girlfriend, who seems to know Raegan already.

"How do you two know each other?" I ask the girls while taking a sip of my whisky.

"Leo and Rae walked into the bookstore I work at and spent a ridiculous amount of time and money there."

"I did" and "She did" Raegan and Leo says at the same time.

Chapter 30 - Brandan

I hate to admit it, but I am having a lot more fun than I care to admit. We've had several rounds of drinks, the girls have been mostly on the dance floor. Both Leo and I have been dragged on there few times as well. He is currently being forced to join in some group choreography which I luckily dodged.

"Hows the night going Bran?" Tobias slides in the booth opposite me.

"Surprisingly good, considering I didn't want to come."

"But your sister dragged you out?" He gives me a curious look.

"She did."

"I would have never of guessed that anyone could persuade Brandan Brentwood to do anything against his will."

I laugh and have to concede "She has her ways."

"So... is she actually your sister or..?"

"What do you mean 'is she actually my sister'?"

"Are you related or is she just sister in name?"

"We're related."

"I know it's not the eighteen hundreds, but you're cool if I ask her out?" I am not surprised by his question. I actually expected it, but that doesn't seem to ease me to just say 'yes, I'm cool with it'.

"Raegan can make her own decisions on who she dates." I take a sip of my drink. "But one hair on her head gets hurt, you won't be dealing with just me."

"I know." He looks back towards the dance floor at Raegan. "But I think she's worth risking the Brentwood wrath."

"And Theos." Definitely Theos.

He looks back at me with irritation written on his face. "I thought he had a girl?"

"He has."

"So what's his deal with Raegan?"

Isn't that the million dollar question? I keep my gaze on Tobias as I take another sip of my drink.

"Understood. Nice to see you again Bran, don't be a stranger. Hopefully we'll be seeing each other more often." He gives me a wolfish grin, I give him a tight smile, knowing his work is cut out for him.

Everyone is back in the booth apart from Raegan who is talking to Tobias at the bar, when my phone buzzes.

Theo Oakes

"What's up Theo?"

"Where the fuck are you, I can barely hear you."

"At the club."

"What club? And why?"

"The Black Rose and because it's a good night out." I am in a very, very good mood indeed.

"And you didn't think to invite me?" Is that a tinge of jealousy in his voice?

"Rae did, you didn't answer your phone or reply to her message."

"Raegan? She's there with you?"

"YES! It was her idea." Is it just my alcohol soak brain or can't other people keep up?

"What do you mean it was her idea? Why would you let her go out?"

"Wait. Hold on a sec." I pull my phone from my ear, take a photo of Raegan talking to Tobias at the bar and send it to Theo. "Check your messages."

There is a silence on the other end and then a low grumble. "Is that Tobias?" I don't respond. "I'll be there in fifteen!" He hangs up and I pocket my phone.

"Who was it?" Indy asks from my side.

"Theo." I take a large gulp of my drink. "He'll be joining the party."

"Is that a good idea?" Leo asks from across the table.

"Why wouldn't it be a good idea?" Elyse looks up at Leo with big doe eyes.

"You'll see when he turns up!" Leo replies and Elyse looks around the table to both Indy and I nod our heads in agreement.

Exactly fourteen minutes later Theo slides in the booth next to me "Where is she?"

"Calm down, have a drink and then go find her on the dance floor!" He gives me a look that says 'I won't be caught dead on the dance floor'. I look my friend in the eyes as I say "She is having a good time tonight, whatever you're doing - don't make it about you. She is smiling and laughing Theo. Don't ruin it for her."

He looks away, waving at a waiter to get him a drink. He doesn't speak until his drink is in front of him.

"That's the problem. I don't know what I'm doing. Not when it comes to Raegan." His admission sobers me up quicker than an ice cold shower and a shot of americano. I knew he had feelings for her for a while now, I assumed he knew that. Turns out I was wrong.

"I would suggest you figure that out first. I love you like a brother, but-"

"She comes first, I know."

Several songs later the girls and Leo make their way back to the booth.

"Look who decided to join us!" Leo exclaims as he slaps Theo on the shoulder "Elyse, this is Theo. Theo - Elyse."

"Hello mister grumps!" Raegan throws her arms around Theo, giving him a hug while balancing on her heels. I don't know how she hasn't tumbled to the floor yet. "Finally got my messages to join us?"

"I did." A very short answer from mister grumps.

"Come on, let's go dance!" She tugs on his arm, pulling him up and towards the glittery gold disco ball. Theo doesn't budge.

"I'm more in a drinking and sitting, than a dancing mood." Rae tilts her head to the right and I know exactly what will happen. The poor fucker doesn't stand a chance.

"Ok!" She exclaims, letting go of his arm straightening. "I'll go find Toby then!" All she manages is to turn before Theo throws back the rest of his drink, stands and starts guiding her towards the dance floor.

I laugh out loud, making sure he hears me. He throws me a deathly glare, which makes it even more funnier.

"He has it bad, doesn't he?" Elyse says while clinking her cocktail glass against Indys.

"The sad bastard doesn't even know it yet." Leo adds.

"Are you having a good time?" I turn to Indy. Her cheeks are flushed from the alcohol and dancing. But I'd like to think some of that flush is because of me. I've made sure to be close to her, nothing more than the occasional touch against her arm.

"I am. Are you?" She asks me over the rim of her glass.

I study her closely. It's not just her outer beauty that has me stunned, there is something more to this girl that I am drawn to. She is wise beyond her young years, loyal and absolutely tempting.

"It gets infinitely better when you're near." Yep! This flush is all mine "Do you go out often?"

She shakes her head and looks down at her drink "No, I don't usually have much free time."

"Patricia gives you days off, doesn't she?" If she isn't, she will be now, I'll make sure of it.

"She does. It's… other commitments." She is keeping her eyes downwards. The feeling rising up inside of me makes me unsettled.

"Indy. What other commitments?"

She finally looks up at me with a fake, shaky smile on her lips, and it cracks my heart open to see her like that. "I'm still tied up with my previous work place, but it's nearly at the end." She finishes the rest of her drink just as Theo and Raegan returns to the booth, stopping me to ask more.

"Raegan is going home." He says, holding her upright by her waist. She looks up at him with scrunched up eyebrows.

"Raegan is not going home!" Theo looks exasperated, arguing with a drunk Raegan is worse than arguing with a sober one. The chances of winning arguments now are only improved by a slight margin.

"You just downed two shots from another table and nearly tripped over your glittery heels. It's home time for Raegan."

She scoffs and looks at the rest of us. "Party pooper!" And elbows him in the ribs, Theo winces.

"Ok, then we'll go as well, I'll take Elyse home." Leo is up and guiding Elyse out of the booth.

"I'll order an Uber." Indy says.

"I'll drop you off on my way home. My driver is at the front. Rae- Christian will drive you home."

"I'll go with her." Theo adds, but I'm not sure Raegan hears anything as she is giving everyone a goodbye hug. Twice!

Chapter 31 - Brandan

"Honestly, you don't have to drop me off, I'm not on your way. You can just pull over and I'll-" Indy is getting increasingly more nervous as we're driving towards the south of the city where she lives. The spark that she had all evening is dwindling and I feel responsible for it.

"I am not letting you out on some random street at night Indy. I am taking you home." She turns to look out of the window, she is clutching her bag so tight, I feel like she will break it in half. "Indy?"

"Mmm?" She looks at me, there is coldness in her soft eyes. My gut is telling me, she doesn't want to go home, but I don't feel it's my place to say.

"Did your handbag offend you in any way?" I nod towards her clenched hands. She relaxes them and turns back to look out of the window.

We pull up outside a mid terrace house in south London. It's gone 2am, but the lights are still on inside.

"Thank you for the ride home and for the night." My driver is opening her door and I step out of my door. "What are you doing?" She asks suspiciously.

"Walking you to the door." I smile at her and a gut wrenching feeling tells me no one has ever taken care of her. No one has ever showed her kindness. I place my hand on the small of her back and we walk towards the front door.

"You really don't have to do this." Her voice is quite and shaky, which puts me on edge. We are only few steps from her front door when I hear shouts from inside. It's hard to decipher what is being said, but the tone of the voice is not welcoming. I glance at Indy, but her eyes are closed, breaths shallow and a lonely tear is trailing down her cheek.

"Indy? Are you safe here?"

She opens her eyes and gives me that shaky fake smile again "It's my home." Her voice catches on the word 'home'

"That's not the same thing. I'll ask you again and don't lie to me." She swallows and rapidly blinks her eyes "Are you safe here?"

She doesn't break eye contact with me while she shakes her head and whispers "No."

That's all I needed to hear before I lift her in my arms and carry her back to my car. My driver opens her door and I put her in the seat, put my jacket around her shaking frame and secure the seatbelt. I round the car quickly to get in beside her.

Tom, my driver, is already behind the wheel "Penthouse."

"Yes sir."

I reach over and take her hand in mine.

"I'm sorry." It's barely a whisper, I turn to face her fully. Indy is facing down at her clutched hands. Tears escaping her closed eyes. "I'm sorry."

I cup her face with both of my hands and turn her to look at me.

"Look at me darling." Vulnerability in her deep, brown eyes will be my undoing. I place a light kiss on her left cheek and kiss the tears away. When I move to kiss her other cheek, her eyes are closed. Her breath catches. I kiss the tears from her other cheek.

The Unspoken Darkness

I remove my hands from her face and sit back in my seat. Indys eyes spring open with confusion and irritation.

In a husky, low voice she says "I thought you're going to kiss me." I look at her with a promise in my eyes.

"There is only one thing of yours you will ever taste on my lips, and your tears ain't it." I twine our fingers together and kiss her knuckles. "You're under my protection now."

We've been quite the whole ride to my apartment, as we enter it I can see Indys eyes round at the space. She walks towards the wall displaying photos of mum, dad, Theo and most recently- Raegan and I. I fill up a couple of glasses of water and hand one to her.

"Come. The guest bedroom is equipped with everything you might need. There are also some of Raegans clothes in the drawers from when she stays here, I'm sure she won't mind you borrowing."

I show her to her room and let her enter the space while I stay outside the door. She needs to know and feel safe.

"Thank you Brandan." Her voice is quite.

"Good night Indy, I'll see you in the morning." I close the door and head to my own room to take an artic cold shower.

Despite the late night, I am up early, setting up my laptop on the kitchen counter to continue running any leads on the threat we are under. Unsure of how long Indy will sleep for, I order a spread of breakfast from the local bakery.

Not long after I lay out all the food on the kitchen island, Indy walks in the open plan kitchen- dinner- living room. She is wearing Raegans pyjamas and dressing gown.

"Morning" I say, my voice suddenly going husky "Come have some breakfast." She does. She sits down on one of the barstools at the island "Would you like some coffee?" I may not know how to cook, but I do know how to make a spectacular cup of coffee.

"Could I have some tea, if you have any?" One thing I excel in the kitchen and she doesn't want it. I supposed I will have to become proficient in tea making.

"Sure. How did you sleep?" I ask while I set about making Indy her cup of tea.

"Surprisingly well. I tend to have a very restless sleep in new surroundings, but I was completely knocked out as soon as my head hit the pillow." Thankfully she starts putting some of the food on her plate "What time did you get up to cook all this?"

I chuckle "Thank you for thinking so highly of my cooking skills, but this is from a local bakery."

She just nods in response and starts munching on her toast, I place the cup of tea in front of her and I watch her taste it.

Her face contorts slightly, which I am confident means it isn't very good.

"How's the tea?" I continue watching Indy, she takes another sip and tries to school her features to not portray her dislike for my beverage.

"It's good." Little liar.

"Really?"

"Mhm." She takes another sip and struggles to swallow. Other, more inappropriate images of her swallowing enter my thoughts.

"I'll give you a thousand pounds to drink the whole cup in one go." I'm testing her, to see how far she's willing to go to spare my feelings. Her brown eyes round up, like a cartoon character, which makes her look incredibly cute. "You don't like it, do you?"

"No, it's absolutely fin-"

"Indy!"

"It's bad. Like… really bad." She looks down at the cup, like it has insulted her whole being "Have you ever made a cup of tea before?" She blurts out. "I didn't know you could butcher a cup of tea so badly." She looks at the liquid in her cup and swirls it "Do you mind if I-" she gestures to the sink.

"Of course." I plaster my best charming smile, but I am fuming. How *did* I *butcher* a cup of tea so badly?

Indy tips the horrid tea in the sink and goes about making a fresh one. I'm watching her closely to ensure I learn everything there is to learn about how to make the perfect cup of tea for my little red haired liar.

We've been sitting in companionable silence eating breakfast when suddenly Indy asks.

"What's the time?"

"Nearly nine o'clock."

"Oh my God! I'm so late!" She jumps off the stool, nearly tripping over her own feet.

"Indy, sit down." I say calmly, she turns to look at me and I sip my coffee. Perfectly made coffee. "I told Patricia that you won't be working today and you also have the weekend off as well."

"What?" She stays frozen in place.

"Can you please come sit down?" She does, still looking in shock. "You will need time to unpack your things when they arrive later today and get used to your new surroundings, so I told Patricia you will be off."

"I... I... don't understand."

"Indy. I will not let you live in that hell hole of a house. It might be your home, but it's clear that it's not safe for you there. So.. you will be living here. There is plenty of space, you can pick whichever guest room you'd like, you can decorate it whichever way you want it. I will make sure I give you plenty enough notice before I stay here. And there is a guest room being prepared for you at the manor when you're working late and would rather not travel back to the city." Her mouth is open, I can see in her eyes how the words I've said are falling into place and what that means.

She looks around the room "I can't afford to pay rent for a place like this."

A small smile tugs at my lips "You don't have to pay any rent." She is looking at me, then around the room and back at me again.

"Brandan, I can't accept this. This-" she flaps her arms around "this is too much. You don't even know me. Why would you do this? Why would you help? I'm nothing-" the last sentence makes me snap, not at Indy, but whoever has told her or made her feel like nothing.

I take her face in both of my hands and my God that feels right. "Look at me. You are a gem. Everyone who has made you feel anything less than that, don't deserve to breathe the same air as you. You are special Indy and no, I don't know you, but I want to. I really do." Our faces are close enough that my nose brushes her "I don't need you to pay rent here or at the manor, but I'd like to have dinner, twice a week with you."

She blinks at me, still processing what I've said. It takes several long moments before she speaks "Will you be cooking?"

"No darling." Her cheeks turn the sweetest shade of pink.

"Thank God. Judging by your tea making skills, we would end up with food poisoning." Now Indy is smiling at me and I vow to myself to make as many bad cups of tea as needed, while they make her smile like that.

I kiss her forehead and step away from her, gathering my laptop and briefcase.

"Is there anything in particular you want from your house?"

She follows my movements and thinks for a moment "Just what's in my room."

"I'll make sure nothing gets left behind." I'm heading for the door when she calls me.

"Bran?" That's the first time she's called me that. Damn. "Thank you."

I smile back at her "Dinner tonight, let me know what you'd like and I'll pick it up on my way home."

Chapter 32 - Brandan

"I look ridiculous!" I growl in my final attempt to change my sisters mind.

"You look exactly what I expect a 9 year old Brandan would have looked like. Aaaand... not my fault you can't take the right measurements and gave me the wrong size *and* you're built like the Hulk!" She snipes back at me as we're making our way to our dads bedroom.

She has come a long way from when she first came to the manor. She has opened up and her personality is starting to come through. Raegan is extremely good at hiding her feelings and pretending to be fine, she never asks for help, so I make sure I'm always about when I know she's having a bad day.

It's Fathers day and we're at dads bedroom door, we have a trolley full of food with us.

"Wait!" She whisper shouts. I feel my insides light up in joy at the fact that she has changed her mind. "Do you think he has someone in there with him?" She screws up her face.

"What? No! Why would he have someone in his room?"

She looks at me with wide eyes like I'm an idiot. "What if he has a *friend* in there?"

"Eww.. no!! He hasn't got anyone! I thought you were gonna change your mind about this stupid idea!"

"Now you *are* being ridiculous. This will be the best fathers day George has ever had, so stop it and knock on his door."

"Why am I knocking on his door if he has someone in there?"

She only hesitates a second before firing back "Because you're older." Well... she's got me there. "And you said he hasn't got anyone!"

I knock three times and hear a grumbled '*come in*'. Rae opens the door, I follow in with the trolley and head to the right side of the bed.

Raegan is opening the curtains to let the morning light in. It is still fairly early and I'm not overly convinced dad is happy to be woken up by us. Dad sits up in the bed, still half asleep, not understanding what is going on.

We must be a sight to behold. His two adult children are dressed in matching short dungarees, Raes pink, mine blue, very stereotypical with white t-shirts. Raegan has her hair up in two pigtails and I have a bucket hat on, because my sister made me wear it.

"Happy Father's Day!" We both shout. Dad sits up a bit more in the bed. "We made you breakfast!" I announce as I lift the cover off the trolley. "We have pancakes, waffles, bacon, sausages, freshly baked muffins-"

Dad looks at me, raises his eyebrows and asks "You cooked?"

"I supervised." I answer, feeling slightly offended. No need to point out my only flaw. Even though Indy is slowly rectifying that.

"You ate half the things I made." My sister chirps up and snitches on me straight away, so I give her a shove and she lands on the bed. She sticks her tongue out at me. Yep, we're definitely kids again.

"And why are you dressed like… that?" Dad gestures to our outfits still not understanding what's going on. I look to Raegan for her to explain, as this is all her idea. I cross my arms and try not to look too smug, when this all goes up in flames.

"A while ago you said you wished you could've seen us run through the house together when we were little. So today- we're pretending to be just that." I'm looking at my dad who seems to be lost for words and I have to give my sister credit now, as I can see mist in his eyes.

She crawls up the bed and sits on his other side, while I get the tray of food and put it over his legs, then I crawl onto the bed as well. I pour us some coffee and orange juice and all three of us tuck into the food.

"Is Theo not joining us?" Dad asks.

"He's running late." Rae replies.

"More like running away while he has a chance." I mutter too loud and the hellion hears me.

Rae leans forwards and looks at me. "What was that Brandan? I didn't quite hear your grumbling while you're stuffing two waffles in your mouth!"

Dad chuckles.

A few minutes later there is a knock on the door and Theo walks in. Looks like he has made the same measuring mistake I did, as his green dungarees are a size… or three too small. From the corner of my eye I can see both, dad and Rae, trying hard not to laugh at him. Or me.

"Happy Fathers day!" There is little to no enthusiasm in his voice, while he gives his best death glare to Raegan "You!" He points at Rae "You and I are going to have a problem!" She laughs out loud, unable to hold back anymore.

"As I said to Bran, not my fault you gave me the wrong size!" He strides towards us and flops on the bed next to Rae.

"I didn't give you the wrong size, you ordered the wrong fucking size." He huffs next to her and picks up a muffin. Whatever issues they had before seems to have been worked out.

"I did not. And stop being grumpy."

We continue eating our breakfast a bit longer until Raegan pulls out three cards and some very badly wrapped presents.

"What's this?" Dad says while chewing on a waffle.

"These are cards that we made, but you have to bear in mind that our kid selves made these." Raegan says "And there are some presents that we probably would have gotten you at that age."

He finished chewing, wipes his mouth and reaches for the cards first. All three of them are bad and I can see him trying to hold back the laughter.

"We all tried to make them good, but turns out none of us were graced by the gift of art." I add

"I love them, they are great. I'll get Nora to frame them so I can display them in the office." Raegans and Theos expressions mirrors mine - horror - and we all shout simultaneously "NO!" Dad laughs. "Absolutely not." I add. Most things in life I can talk or hack my way out, but that would not be one of them.

He unwraps the first present, which is the tackiest 'Number 1 Dad' mug we could find. He turns to look at me "Why did you never get me a mug like this before?"

"Are you serious? All the gifts I've gotten you over the years and this is the one you wanted. A four pound ninety-nine tacky mug?"

He just chuckles and gets to unwrapping the second present which is a pair of socks that says 'Worlds Best Dad' on the sides and on the feet it says 'If you can read this.. bring me a beer'.

"I'll make sure I wear these today." Over the years I've gotten dad many different presents for fathers day, birthday and Christmas's. All of them expensive, exclusive or one of a kind, but I've never seen him happier than he is now, opening our fifteen pound presents. And it hits me, it's not the amount of money spent on them, it's the sentimental value. For dad to experience this with us- there is no greater gift.

Last present he unwraps is a framed print of all four of us. The photo was taken not so long ago in a restaurant we went for a meal. Dad is in the middle, Rae and Theo are on his right and I'm on his left, exactly how we are now. He is lost in his own thoughts while looking at the photo "This will definitely be going in the office. So, what's the plan for today?" He says and snaps us all out of our own thoughts.

Ever since mum got diagnosed with cancer dad has been in an attack mode. Whether it would be to fight the cancer, for a contract, or our competition or fighting to keep all of us safe. Now, for the first time in years I can see him relax and enjoy the moment, instead of waiting for the other shoe to drop. I hate to admit it, but what Raegan has planned for today is exactly what he needs. What all of us needs.

I take a final swig of my coffee as I say "We're gonna go to Brighton, spend the day at the beach, play same games and eat unhealthy food!" At that last part dads eyes light up, Patricia has him on a very short leash when it comes to his meals. Today is his cheat day.

An hour later we are walking to the Range Rover parked at the bottom of the stairs, as we reach the car Raegan goes to the drivers side door and gets in. Theo and I stop dead in our tracks, dad continues and gets in the front passenger seat.

She rolls down the window "Come on get in."

"You are not driving!" Theo says, a bit too harshly, but Raegan just narrows her eyes on him.

"Get in the car Theodore or I will make you wear a matching bucket hat to Brandan's." Turns out that was a threat enough to make my best friend nearly skip and hop in the car to escape the bucket hat.

"What are you going to threaten me with lil bear? I'm already wearing a bucket hat and you - are not driving."

She lets out a long breath. "You are not trained to drive if we are being-"

"Brandan Louis Brentwood, get in the car or-"

"Did you just middle name me?" I'm shocked, the only person ever to use my full name was mum.

"I did."

"Get in the car Bran!" Dad shouts wanting to get this show on the road and tuck into the unhealthy food we offered him.

"Or what?" I taunt Rae while trying to hide the fact that middle naming me, has straightened my spine.

"I'll have a little chat with Indy." My face and insides fall, because even if I think I can wriggle out of Raegans pressure, I won't from Indys. Fuck.

I stomp. And I do mean - I stomp to the back of the car and get in. I lean forwards and say to dad

"I'm going to say this again, just so it's out there, your daughter is a hellion."

He chuckles in response, zero sympathy for his eldest.

"Here." Raegan hands Theo a mint green cap, one to match his dungarees.

"No! You said I won't need to wear a hat."

"I didn't. I said you won't need to wear a bucket hat, I said nothing about a cap."

I let out a defeated breath. "Honestly mate, just roll over and take it. She'll chew you up and spit you out before you've even blinked." I say to Theo while putting my seatbelt on. "She probably knows your middle name and favourite way to die as well."

"What have I ever done to you to deserve this?!" He says, mostly to himself while taking the cap and adjusting to fit his head.

"You've made me cry once or twice, so this seems a fair pay back." Raegan says matter of factly as she puts the car in drive and sets of.

Dad and I give Theo glares of our own, which makes him sink in his seat "I said I'm sorry."

Chapter 33 - Brandan

The beach is busy with most of southern England having had the same idea - let's take dad to the beach. But Raegan is having us haul beach blankets, coolers with foods and drinks, an umbrella and games to a spot she's got earmarked for us.

She orders us around at military precision, I can see why she made a good teacher. Does she miss it? Miss her old life?

"Right! Who's ready for a drink?" She asks while sitting down on the beach blanket we've put down with several cushions for comfort.

"Yes please sweetheart." Dad says and she hands him a bear.

"Same!" Theo and I say at the same time.

Raegan had packed several different games to play, but we settled on Monopoly. I haven't played it since childhood, bringing back a wave of bittersweet memories with mum. We've been playing, eating our picnic and drinking and only now I notice - I've been scammed for the past two hours.

I am looking down at the property cards in front of me, then at Raegan, who is winning, with Monopoly cash piling up on her side.

"Raegan?" I ask, still looking down at my property cards.

"Yes Brandan?"

"Mayfair is one of my properties."

"Yes it is." She says confidently and I look at my deceiving sister, who is trying to be a picture of innocence.

"So why do I keep paying *you* rent for it? And double at that, because you have Park Lane?"

"No you haven't." She says nonchalantly. Liar. She is a bad influence on Indy.

"Yes I have!" I shout in a complete shock and, maybe, with a touch of humiliation. "You've cheated this whole time!" Dad and Theo are laughing, so I snap at both of them "What are you two laughing about, you've been doing the same thing!" Theo sobers as he looks at the board.

"Fucking hell Raegan! You can't do that!" Thank you. At least someone is on my side. While dad replies.

"I didn't. I knew what she was doing all along and you two suckers fell for it!" He laughs even harder.

"That's it. Give me back my money!" I say and reach across the board for her money.

"NO! Keep your paws off my money!" And she slaps my hand away "It's not cheating if you're attention to details is sub-par dear brother!" WHAT?

Theo tries to reach for the money, but she slaps his hand away as well, grabs the paper money in her greedy little fist and gets behind dads back.

"Give it back Raegan!" I stand, ready to pounce on her. I cannot believe she did that. Cheated her own brother out of Monopoly money. But the worst thing is? I didn't even notice it.

"No!"

Theo gets to his feet as well.

"Dad, tell her to give it back." I truly am a nine year old Bran again. "It's not fair."

"I am not getting in the middle of it, you need to resolve it between yourselves." He takes a long swig of his beer while re-counting his money.

"Bran, do you remember your 11th Birthday party?" Theo asks, eyes not leaving Raegan

"Yeah?"

"Do you remember that little weasel Johnny?"

"Oh… yes I do!" I smirk at my sister and there is a slight fear in her eyes as her smile drops.

"Boys no." Dad says sternly, as he remembers what we did to little Johnny. He kept sneaking inside and opening my presents, so Theo and I took him by arms and legs and threw him in the pool.

"She'll be fine. Or we can avoid it, if she hands the money back!" Theo taunts and steps closer to her. While her eyes are on him, I slowly step towards her on the other side. But she spots me and runs.

She ducks, runs and spins out of both of our clutches, but finally Theo gets her. He is holding Raegan under her arms, while she is trying to wriggle out of his hold. Even though she has been training with Christian and Leo for nearly two months, she is no match for Theo. I jog up to her and grab her my her ankles.

She is laughing and begging to be let go, as she has finally figured out what is going to happen to her as we're nearing the sea.

"OK! OK! Yes, I cheated! Don't throw me in the sea! Pleeease!"

"Too late Alora, should've fessed up sooner!" Theo says near her ear.

"Nooo!!" She is wriggling hard to get out of our hold, but most of her energy is going on her laughter. We are stepping in the sea when she shouts again "No!! Dad help!" I don't think she realises what she said, but I do. And I am hundred percent sure dad heard it too. This is truly the best fathers day he's had.

But I cannot linger on that too long, as we are over knee deep in the sea when I look at Theo.

"Ready?" He nods and we start counting in unison "One!" Swing "Two" Swing "Three" we swing her towards the deeper end of the sea and let her go.

"Aaaaaaaa!" Leaves her mouth, she lets go of the Monopoly money as she splashes in the water.

Theo and I are laughing hard when Raegan resurfaces with splutter. That makes us laugh even more.

"You two think you're funny?" She takes a couple of steps towards us and makes a big splash of water towards Theo, that soaks most of his mint green dungarees.

Then, she looks at me, I put my hands up in surrender "Don't you even think abou-" too late. She splashes me.

"Twinning!" She says while grinning at us and walks out of the water, where dad is standing, with towels in his arms.

I make a mental note to let Raegan plan all our family events and days out. Because this has been one of the best days of my life.

Chapter 34 - Raegan

Having an actual job to go to instead of spending my days at the manor has given me a purpose. I have a routine.

Every morning I get up at 5am and have a training session with Christian and Leo, which usually lasts about an hour. I then get ready and have breakfast with George, Bran and Theo when they're at the manor. Some days Christian and Leo take me to the office, some days I go with one of the guys.

I have been working in the media team since I joined Brentwood Global. My day to day jobs mostly involves proof reading media releases, contracts and even helping the senior leadership team with writing speeches. Despite the steady workload and days passing quickly - for the first time in my life - I feel content in my job. I don't feel like I'm missing out or having the nagging feeling in my tummy that this isn't my place.

This week I have been asked to go through our website and ensure there aren't any glaring spelling errors and update a few news releases. To save time, Bran has given me access to the backend of the website to correct things as I go along.

Brandan gave me a very quick, dummy guide to our website, which mostly included a list of things I shouldn't be touching or amending.

The Unspoken Darkness

Even though every sentence that goes on-line is read through by several people, there are surprising amounts of spelling and grammar mistakes. Even the ones I've been working on, I spot an error or two.

Hmmm.. this looks weird.

Our 'work with us' page seems to not want to load properly. I hit the refresh button a few more times to make sure it's not just a weird glitch. I click out of the edit mode and head to the live page. Same result. Weird gaps between our current vacancy adverts. Someone must've gotten a bit carrier away with spacing. I log back into edit mode and delete any extra spaces between the adverts, so the format mirrors our other articles.

Bran has upgraded my laptop with all sorts of security programs that not only keep my work and me safe from unwanted intruders, but it also allows me to check in on people from Julias life without a digital footprint.

Every time I am about to click the browser I stop myself. What if I have no self control and reach out to them? Which would undo everything I've done to keep them safe. What if I see them struggling? I know that will break my heart. What if someone sees it and connects the dots? But not knowing how they are doing is slowly killing me.

I click it.

I go to Lily's profile first and scroll through her latest posts. There aren't many. Post from last week is a celebratory dinner with Maya for Lily's promotion at work.

I follow the link through to Mayas profile. Despite her being the bigger personality between the three of us, her only post is the one with Lily from last week.

The looks they give the camera will fool everyone, but me. Their large smiles are bright, but their eyes are clouded in grief. So similar to the one I feel every day. It's the caption that stabs at my heart.

Even the biggest celebrations aren't the same without you. 🩶

I know.
I know.
I know.

I want to reach into my screen and grab them both, pulling them into a desperate hug. If they would learn the truth, would they ever forgive me?

I am pulled from my spiralling thoughts when another familiar profile pops up in the 'people you might know' section. The rolling waves of grief and sadness stops, being replaced by disbelief and hurt. So much hurt.

My breaths shallow. Heart is beating fast and loud. Tall walls of the office are caving. Windows looking out to the city are nothing but distant stars in faraway galaxies. Blood is ringing in my ears.

I need a release or I'll not survive another minute of this crashing doom. Even in this state my brain focuses on remedy - a sharp letter opener. Without a thought I grab it, pull up my skirt and sink it into my skin.

My lungs expand. Oxygen.

But wait... I think I broke a promise.

I look down to where the sharp point is dug into my upper thigh, between the scars that have made this their home. I haven't dragged the blade across my skin, it just punctured it.

Everything around me is a blurry haze as I rush through the office. People greet me or try to talk to me, but I have no capacity for that now. There is only one person I need right now.

His assistant doesn't even attempt to stop me. I march into Theos office, my gaze trained on him. Other people in the room cease to exist.

"Out. Now!" He issues in a dark voice, while rising from his seat and striding towards me. If there are objections or grumbles from people being dismissed, I don't hear them.

Theo stands just a few inches from me, his green eyes intent on me.

"I broke my promise." He looks down to where I am still clutching the letter opener in my shaking hand. When did I start to shake? Theo takes it out of my hand, looking at the tip, that is still covered in my blood. I didn't wipe it down before my march to his office. Is there a trail of blood drops behind me?

His voice is calm. Soothing me when he speaks. "What happened Alora?"

I open my mouth to speak, but no words come out. My lips tremble. I blink more than any human should be able to, wishing the mist away. I will not cry because of him. I try to speak again, but silence greets me once more. My lips unable to form the words blazing through my soul.

He cups my face in both of his hands and that loosens my vocal chords.

"He remarried." I don't attempt to blink the tears away "The fucker remarried that home wrecker, no more than two months after my death. Did I really mean that little to him?" I try to shake my head, but he doesn't let me.

Instead he leans in and kisses my forehead, pulls me close to him and holds me tight. I wrap my arms around his middle. My tears must've soaked through his waistcoat and shirt, but he doesn't say anything.

We stay like this for a while, until Theo lets me go from his embrace.

"Come here." He takes me by my hand and leads me towards his office wall. Wait… not a wall, a door. He opens the door and a bedroom greets me. I haven't got more than a couple of seconds before Theo pulls me into a bathroom, grabs me by my waist and sits me on a vanity. While he rummages in the vanity draws I scan the room I'm in. There is a shower in the right corner and toilet in the opposite one. And a vanity, which I'm currently sitting on, along the opposite wall. The decoration and fixings are sleek and modern, like the rest of the office.

Theo stands back up to his full height and steps in front of me with a pack of make up removal wipes in his hand. I reach my hand out to grab them and he pulls them out of my reach and gives me a scathing look.

"Just stay still." He says. I huff out a breath and try to get the wipes again "Will you just stay fucking still for a moment and let me do this Rae?" I'm taken aback by his tone. The harshness in it is not aimed at me and I know it. That is not what catches me off guard, it's the unapologetic sincerity and plea in his voice. One I have never heard from him. I fold my hands in my lap and relax my shoulders.

Theo gets to work on carefully removing my make up "Close your eyes." And he gently runs the wipes over my eye lids removing my mascara.

"When did you learn how to remove make up?"

"The night you kept telling me I was doing it wrong."

My eyes fly open in shock "What? What night?" He chuckles and it's my favourite sounds in the world.

"The night you went clubbing at Black Rose. Do you remember?" I scrunch up my face. My memories from that night in question aren't very vivid or clear. I don't fully remember getting home and in my bed. I shake my head and he smiles at me. A betraying heat is climbing up my cheeks.

"What happened? Why didn't you say I embarrassed myself?" I'm trying to rewind the memory tape of that night as I speak the words, but no clear memory emerges.

He continues cleaning up my face when he finally replies "Christian drove us home and surprisingly you made your own way up the steps. The quieter you tried to be when we got inside, the louder you got. You stopped in the middle of the hall, halfway to the stairs up to your room, looked down at your feet and said *"Shhh.. you're making too much noise!"."* I cover my face with my hands.

"I didn't?!" I peek through my fingers at a grinning Theo.

"You did. I tried to take your shoes off, but you were too drunk, so I picked you up and carried you to your room. But you wouldn't let me put you to bed until all your make up was off and your teeth were brushed."

I can feel my cheeks heat "I don't remember doing any of it."

"Well, that's because you didn't, I did. I took your make up off and then brushed your teeth. And put you in bed."

"Oh my God! I'm so sorry you had to deal with that. You should've just thrown me down on the bed to sleep it off."

"I would never do that to you Alora." I know he means every word he says and I don't know where I stand with Theo. Our relationship doesn't feel like the traditional friendship. Neither does the brother-sister one. There is a bond between us, one I cannot understand. Or maybe I don't want to understand. This, what we have now is good. Safe.

He is my safe space.

I break our eye contact and look around the bathroom and peek through to the bedroom "What is this place anyway?"

Theo lifts me off the vanity and we walk into the room "Rest stop for when I'm working late or running from one engagement to the next." He means his missions. Same as Bran. Reminder of the danger they put themselves in make me shiver.

"Come on, I want to show you something." He leads me out of the room and through his office "Cancel my meetings for the rest of the day." He says to Jacob without another look back at his office.

Chapter 35 - Raegan

We follow the route we took the night of our bike ride. I haven't been up on the rooftop since, didn't even cross my mind that I could come up here.

We step on the rooftop, even though we are in a middle of the summer, the weather is much more milder today. No sunshine, light wind, but I stop mid-step.

"What is this?"

Theo walks past me to where a little two seater outdoor sofa sits, picks up a throw blanket and wraps it around my shoulders. I look up at him. The lump from earlier is returning to my throat, but for a very different reason now.

"Theo, what is this?" I ask quietly.

"This, Alora, is your rest stop." I take an unsteady step forwards. The sofa sits facing south of the city for most sunshine. There is a coffee table and two armchairs surrounding it. A couple of throw blankets, one of them being draped around me and cushions. To make it more cocooned potted plants of all different sizes have been dotted around and solar lights strung between the taller ones.

I finally turn back to face Theo, a few steps away "Did you do all this for me?" He nods in answer. "Why?"

"Because you need it. No one else has access to the roof, just you and I. So no one will disturb you while you're up here."

"Will you sit with me?" He nods again and we take a seat on the sofa. A safe, rest place just for me. A place

no one knows about. I tighten the blanket around me when a gust of wind blows across the rooftop.

Theo is the first to break the silence "How did you find out he's re-married?"

"Bran installed this program, that allows me to check on my friends without any digital fingerprints. Every time I went to use it, I stopped myself. But today I finally got myself to click the button and check in on Maya and Lily. As I was scrolling through their social media Vincents profile popped up and there it was."

"Do you wish you never left?"

"What? No. Lily and Maya are the only ones who would ever make me regret giving up life as Julia Green. Seeing him married already to someone new, made me feel worthless. The life we spent together meant so little to him, that it can be forgotten about and move on in less than a couple of months. It made me think- did I imagine it all? The good and fun times we had together, was it just me that felt it? It makes me feel.. I don't know how to describe it… silly? Doubt myself of what I thought I knew." I take a deep breath and continue looking out towards the city. "He came and stomped all over my already broken heart again, making me spiral into my darkness. And the worst part about it? He doesn't even know what he's done."

Theo pulls me into a side hug and I lean my head against his shoulder.

"Raegan?"

"Mhm."

"Everything that happens between us is real. I don't ever want you to doubt that. I also don't ever want to hear you say you're worthless ever again. In case you haven't noticed, you are the centre of every Brentwood mans world. There is no worth big enough, to be assigned to you, do you hear me?"

"Mhm." My eyes are feeling heavy and my lids are drooping. I kick my shoes off and pull the legs on the sofa. I am content.

Chapter 36 - Raegan

Next three weeks pass quickly leading up to the annual Brentwood Summer Charity Gala, that is held on the third Saturday every July.

George is on another level of excitement, as this will be the first time I will be introduced to his world as a Brentwood. Despite me working at Brentwood Global for a while now, not many people know who I am.

Every dinner time Bran is laughing as George is bombarding me with intel on every person who will be attending. Who they are, what they do and whether we like them or not. I wouldn't be surprised if he gave me a test the day before.

We're still a day away from the gala and I'm having an afternoon tea with George in the sunroom.

"Hi!" I say as I enter the room walking over to George and giving him a kiss on the cheek. He has spent a lot of time with me, not just so I learn about the business, but so we can get to know each other and I've enjoyed every minute of it.

There are moments when he gets sad, because he wasn't there for my first day of school or teach me how to ride a bike or take photos before prom. And then there are times he apologises for not being there when I was growing up, but I don't blame him. I don't really blame my mum either. Not anymore.

Assigning blame to one or the other will not give us the missed time back, so I rather spend time with him and

Bran now to make new memories. I sit at a small round table that has a fresh flower arrangement in the middle.

"Is everything OK? You look worried." I ask.

As George is about to answer, Indy walks in with our afternoon tea. Indy and I have grown really close and I feel like she is my first real new friend. I know I have Leo and Christian in that group as well, but my connection with Indy is different.

Both of us have our own darkness to battle with. Neither of us talk about it, but we are there for each other to help the other get through it. We have also established a weekly girls night, either at the manor or at Brans penthouse, that Indy is living at now.

Bran is another topic we don't talk about, whether there is something more or not, both of them seem happy. And that is enough for me. But maybe my main reason to stay out of their situationship is that I am not willing to answer any questions about Theo and I. *Are* there any questions to be answered?

"I hear you will be joining us at the Gala Indy." George breaks me out of my thoughts as Indy is laying our afternoon tea on the table.

"Yes sir. Raegan was kind enough to invite me as her plus one." She says shyly.

"It'll be lovely to see you there tomorrow night." She nods and leaves the room. George reaches behind him and pulls out a box, not much bigger than shoe box and places it in front of me.

"What's this?"

He swallows several times and clears his throat "My wife is my soulmate. I didn't always know it or appreciate her, but when I finally realised it- I came running back to her.

I never told her about my affair with your mother. But I knew she knew that I had been unfaithful, yet she never mentioned it. I would have done anything she asked of me and I would never question it, just to earn her trust back. I loved her with all my heart, the day she passed a part of me died with her." My eyes sting from unshed tears for my fathers heartbreak. "It has been over four years since she died and I still have not forgiven her for not telling me about you. Maybe it was her way of paying me back for being unfaithful or maybe she just didn't know how to tell me. That box- she left that for you, I had to give it to you on a sunny day in our sunroom while having an afternoon tea." He gets up from his chair and turns towards the door.

"You're leaving?" I rush out as I don't want him to be alone and… and I don't want to be alone either.

"The final request was that I was to leave the room. It's just the two of you." He walks out of the door and I am left with a shoebox of unknown content.

Deep breath in. Deep breath out.

After few more moments I lift the lid and I'm greeted with an envelope addressed to me.

Dear Julia,

I've had over two decades to come up with these words, yet here I am still searching for the right ones. I always imagined to have this conversation face to face with you, but fate had different plans.

My illness has taken all of us by surprise, no one more than my George. When you are reading this letter I would hope you know the truth and your father hasn't ducked out of telling it to you himself.

I always wished for a daughter, but it was never meant to be. My only regret is that I never got to meet you in person.

When Brandan was little, he would always ask for a baby sister, it wasn't until his early teens when he stopped, so I know he will be the best big brother you could ever ask for. To most people he comes across as easy going and nerdy at times, but when he loves and cares for someone, there is no one better to have in your corner.

At the time of me writing this letter, I have not told my boys about you. I know it'll be a shock to both of them and I hope George will be able to forgive me for keeping you from him. And I hope Brandan will learn to forgive his father.

I have followed you from the moment I found your mother, the woman, I knew my husband was having an affair with. I held you the day you were born, you were so tiny with the biggest brown eyes I've seen, I had no doubt in my mind that you were Georges.

I visited the hospital where you were born, I walked in the room your mother and you were staying pretending I was looking for a friend. I left a white Hamleys bear with a pink ribbon- do you still have it? I got the same bear, with a blue ribbon when Bran was born. From the moment your big brown eyes looked at me I knew that you were part of our family.

I always checked in on you on all your birthdays and Christmas's, I hope your mother didn't throw the cards away.

I tried my best to make it to your school plays and graduations, you never saw me, but I was never far away.

If we would be having this conversation face to face, I'm sure you would ask me - why did you never tell George? And honestly? I don't have an answer for it, maybe I wanted to keep you all to myself or maybe keeping you a secret was my own payback for his infidelity. Looking back now- I wish I would have said something sooner, but hindsights a wonderful thing. I hope you'll forgive me.

I am incredibly proud of you, not just of what you've overcome and achieved, but of the person you've become. You have made me a very proud mum.

I'm sending you lots of love and the warmest hugs.

Here are two things I'd like to ask of you-

1. *Please look after my boys.*

2. *When you have a daughter of your own (I know you will, a mother always knows)- can you please have regular afternoon tea with her in our sun room? I wish I could have done that with you.*

Lots of love
Auntie Charlotte

Auntie Charlotte. Oh my God. I have received a birthday card for every single birthday from Auntie Charlotte. There hasn't been a Christmas that has gone by without a card from her.

The Unspoken Darkness

She was Georges wife. My tears are flowing freely over my cheeks as I clench the letter to my chest and close my eyes.

Emotions are overwhelming me. I am hit with a tidal wave of grief for a woman that I've never met, but has been with me my whole life. Knowing she has followed my life and was looking out for me, but is not here anymore- has widened the heart shaped hole in my chest. I look back down at the box that is still sitting on top of the table and I see pictures of myself looking back at me.

Me with a crooked smile on my first day of school and another where I've got a gappy smile. There are photos of every first and last day of school, from school plays and sports days. My prom and birthday parties and some photos of me with Vince. My university graduation photo. Charlotte has collected momentos from my whole life and kept them safe.

I sat at the table for over an hour, the tea was cold by the time I left and returned to my room. The morning after I came here, when Bran and Theo were leaving to get my divorce papers signed there was one thing I asked Bran to take from my old life.

My white old bear with a pink ribbon. Mum never really said where it came from, just that some woman gave it to her while looking for her friend, who had already been discharged from the hospital. That bear, Hammy, was never far away from me. I had to have it with me to snuggle up to every night. Even when growing older, it was always my emotional support bear who gave the biggest, warmest hugs. I squeeze the bear to my chest.

As much as I love my little bear hugs, I really need a big bear hug now so I pull out my phone and call my brother.

He answers on the second ring.

"Hi Rae, what's up? Everything all right?" Why does he think there is something wrong every time I call him?

"Yeah, all good. Just wanted to see where you are."

"We're just coming up the drive."

"I'll see you at the door." I hang up before he can say anything else or question what I'm up to. I drop the phone on my bed and run to the front door. By the time I make it there both, Bran and Theo, are walking in the manor.

"Hey, is everything all right?" Brandan calls to me when he sees me running down the stairs, his eyebrows are scrunched up and I regret not splashing my face with some cold water to get rid of the puffiness from crying.

I've never once seen them being at work and not wearing a suit and today is no exception, despite there being a heat wave.

It doesn't take him long to reach me with his long stride, he stops in front of me in the middle of the foyer with Theo not too far behind him.

"Can I have a hug?" My words catch him off guard for a moment, but he recovers quickly and open his arms for me to step into his big bear hug.

"You're sure everything's ok?" He asks his voice is muffled by my hair.

"Mhm, just wanted a bear hug." And I tighten my hold on him "Your mum left me a letter in which she sent me love and warmest hugs. Your hugs are the closest I can get to hers and this is what I imagined her hugs would be like- warm and safe." My eyes are closed and I'm smiling as my dark soul gets filled with light. Above me I can hear Brans breath catch, but his hold on me is tight. Both of us needed this.

Chapter 37 - Raegan

"You are so good at this!" I am absolutely stunned by how talented Indy is with a make up brush. She insisted on doing my make up as a payment for her outfit. Last week when George said he'd like for me to attend the charity gala, he was waiting until the last minute he felt safe for me to attend.

As exciting as the thought of going is, I absolutely did not want to go on my own. And yes I know the boys will be there, but I know they will get dragged away from one conversation to another and another and I will be left on my own with a bucket load of people I do not know.

So, in our last girls night, I made sure we both had a couple of glasses of wine before I asked her to be my plus one and come with me. She was reluctant, to say the least and I can't blame her. But after I bribed her with the third glass of wine, all expenses paid shopping trip to the city and that I will forever owe her one - she agreed. I do have a sneaky feeling that her saying yes, had to do with Brandan being there as well.

"I've always loved art and doing make up is a different sort of art. As you can imagine I didn't have much of anything growing up, so when I got my hands on any make up, I made sure to keep it safe." Over the past several weeks Indy has opened up about her past a little more. From the little glimpses she has allowed me to see, she grew up in an abusive family with very little support from anyone.

"Do you like working here? And you don't have to say yes, just because it's me."

"I love the security, and I don't mean it just financially." I nod at her, both of us threatening of being pulled in our own thoughts.

"That's enough of the doom and gloom conversation for tonight. We are going to a Charity Gala where we will eat very delicious food. Drink ridiculously expensive champagne. And we will most definitely be checking out the hot, single bachelors!" We clink our drinks glasses together "Let's get dressed."

We are getting ready in my little apartment in the manor, we have make up strewn about on the coffee table, all the options of our dresses, shoes and handbags laid out across all the sofas. I walk into my en suite and look up at the dress I'm about to put on. It's a dusty pink off the shoulder number, with pleated corset type front that snags my waist. The dress is skin tight from my hips to mid thigh, where the slit on my left thigh gives more freedom for movement. My long hair is put up in an elegant messy up do and I'm pairing my dress with gold strappy heels. Once I'm done, I swap places with Indy.

A knock sounds at the door so I just shout out 'come in' as I know it'll be Brandan. Last few dinners were spent deciding who will I be arriving at the Gala with. They tried to drag me into making the decision for them, but I refused. As a joke I said "why don't you just do rock-paper-scissors to decide?" And they did. And these are the men who run, literally, one of the largest companies in the world.

Bran walks in my room, both hands in his trouser pockets of his three piece navy tuxedo "Wow, you look gorgeous lil bear!"

I do a little twirl with a curtsy and my head spins a little, maybe having a drink or two wasn't such a good idea after all. He walks over to me and steadies me and places a kiss on top of my head.

"How many drinks have you had?" He asks while narrowing his eyes at me

"Just a couple, it was the twirl that got me!" Mostly.

"Mhm!" He doesn't buy what I'm selling, but before he can interrogate me more Indy walks out of the bathroom. She is wearing navy blue strappy silky number, that hugs her figure and flares out at the knees. The colour complements her complexion beautifully and her auburn hair is cascading down her back. She looks absolutely-

"Stunning!" Brandan says exactly what I was thinking, Indys cheeks flush the cutest shade of pink. With one look at my brother I know that Indys life has been changed forever.

The limo slowly creeps up to the entrance of Grand Connaught Rooms. The entrance has been decorated with floral arrangements and a red carpet has been rolled out. We are greeted by porters who open the door for Bran to get out.

I can see a few photographers being on the sides of the entrance trying to get snaps of the rich. He buttons up his jacket and reaches his hand in the limo for me and Indy to get out. I'm nervous. Self doubt creeping in with vicious thoughts, but I am also intoxicated by the thought of tonight.

Slowly and gently both of us exit the limo, with me on Brands left arm and Indy on his right, we walk into the gala.

Sound of music and peoples voices filter through and get louder with every step we take further inside the building. In the foyer we are greeted with a glass of champagne and because I helped with a few little bits to organise this - I know exactly how much each sip costs.

Marble steps on both sides leads to the first floor, where there are groups of guests milling about. We stop and say hello to pretty much everyone, being a Brentwood - you can't ignore the guests you've invited.

We make our way up the staircase towards the grand hall where the evening meal will be held, during which charity auction will be held to raise money for several local charities. And after all that, the lights get dimmed even more for a live band and dancing.

The grand hall is absolutely breathtaking. High vaulted ceilings, with art deco finishing and crystal chandeliers hanging from the ceilings. The room is made lighter with a decorative gold detailing. We weave our way through to our table, which is near the middle of the room.

Each table has 10 guests and I am about to meet ours. On my left I have an older couple, in their sixties and their granddaughter- Mr and Mrs Ratcliffe. They've been Brentwood partners for decades and we have a very strong legal working relationship with them. Opposite me is Theo and Heather. I haven't seen her since that fateful dinner. He is wearing a black tuxedo, has a day old stubble, which makes him look even more handsome than he already is. Damn it. Heather is wearing a red silky gown, similar to the one Indy is wearing, but the dress on Heather looks cheap.

To the right on the table are two gentleman, both wearing dark coloured tuxes, hair slicked back, with more hair product than needed. Their names are on the tip of my tongue, but I cannot recall.

"Good evening everyone. I'd like to introduce you to my sister, Raegan." Bran announces our arrival and everyones eyes snap up to me.

"Evening everyone." He pulls out a chair for me to sit down and gently pushes it back against the table once I'm sat down.

"And this is Indy, my date." Bran does the same for Indy, her cheeks rosy, mix of champagne and Brandans declaration.

"Hello." She says to the table and sits down between Bran and I.

The table falls into small talk after we've seated. I chat with Mr Ratcliffe about his granddaughters' upcoming summer camps. I look across the table and I am greeted with a dark expression on Theos face. His green eyes seem moodier, like they are holding a secret.

"Oh sweetheart, you look wonderful tonight." George is a couple of feet behind me, I rise from my seat and I'm greeted with a warm hug and a kiss on the cheek. I smile at him and straighten his bow tie.

"Thank you." He pulls my chair out and I sit back down, I guess Bran learnt his manners from his dad.

"Indy, so glad you could make it." He gives her a kiss on the cheek. "Can you do me a favour and keep an eye on these two?" he gestures to Bran and I. "They tend to get into trouble when left alone." Bran is already on his feet and giving his dad a hug as well.

"It was one time dad. And it was mostly Raes fault." He throws me an accusatory smirk I have become well acquainted with.

"I think we both remember events of that night very differently Bran." I say.

George doesn't bother shaking hands with the rest of the table while he walks towards Theo and pulls him into a hug "Looking very dapper son." When I first heard George call Theo 'son' I was slightly taken aback, as I didn't expect it. But for all intents and purposes, Theo is Georges son.

Heather is about to rise from her chair to get her acknowledgment from the main Brentwood, "Excuse me, I must return to my table." George turns away and makes his way to his table. I have to smother my giggle with a sip of a thousand pound a bottle champagne. A giggle has never tasted so good.

As our starters are being served Indy leans over to me and whispers "Is that the woman you caught Theo having sex with?"

"Mhm." I reply with a nod and an easy smile on my face. "I somehow thought he would have better taste in women." She says, slightly louder and I nearly choke on thin air "I suppose no amount of money can buy taste."

I've never heard Indy be so open and candid and I absolutely love it.

The conversation continues to flow steadily around the table.

"So, what trouble did you both get into?" Mrs Ratcliffe asks, looking between Brandan and me. "I must say, you don't just look like siblings, you look more like twins."

"Thank you and despite what Brandan says, it wasn't my fault at all for being kicked out of a club for throwing punches at random people, before I would even finish my first drink."

"It wasn't your first drink, it was at least your fourth" I'm about to open my mouth to argue, before he cuts me off with a look only an older brother could give "don't even argue, you were slurring your words and thought they were 'cute guys' to dance with, when dancing was the last thing on their mind."

I roll my eyes and they land back on the familiar green eyes, the face they belong to has a mask of boredom, but underneath it- pure rage. Theos jaw is tight and even from across the table I can see him clenching it.

"I thought they were cute! And it was you who bought me drinks, if I recall correctly?" I counter.

"I didn't know nuns drank." Heathers' dislike towards me was apparent from the moment I met her. I'm sure she has tried to find information about me online, but as I have no social media presence and Raegan Brentwood hasn't existed for more than than a few months - her assumption of me being a nun, isn't too far out of the realms of possibilities.

But mostly she is saying that to humiliate me, little does she know, I'm not overly interested in her opinion of me. So in return - I just smile at her.

Halfway through our main course she speaks again "Indy- is it? Didn't I see you when I popped round to Brentwood manor for dinner with Theo the other week?" Her tone is filled with venom and envy in equal measures.

Indy clears her throat "Yes, you did."

"But you were wearing a maids outfit." There is a callous look in Heathers eyes and I'm annoyed with myself, that it took me 10 seconds too long to figure out where she is going with this line of questioning. Her making jabs at me is one thing, but going after someone I care about, is not something I am willing to tolerate. Ever since I was little I've despised bullies, which is why I marched in Theos office to begin with. I put my utensils down beside my plate and level a stare at Heather. She is too much of a coward to look at me, so she continues to keep her eyes on Indy.

Brandan sits back in his chair lazily and drapes his left arm around the back of Indys chair, making it clear who's protection Indy is under.

Knowing how similar we are, I am very confident that Brandans look mirrors mine. From the reaction from the table- everyone knows a line has been crossed.

"Yes, I work at the Brentwood manor as a maid. But I didn't have to screw a Brentwood to get this invite." I've never been more prouder of anyone in my life that I am right now of Indy and how she stood up for herself. Theo chokes on his whiskey, but a smile is tugging at his lips, while Heather turns bright red.

"How.. who.." She is flustered beyond words, I am laughing loudly on the inside, but keeping my face schooled in the cold, fierce expression on the outside. From the corner of my eye I can see Bran smirking and Indy returns to eating her meal. Dismissing Heather like she doesn't even exist.

"How do you know that?" Heather is seething "Who do you even think you are!" Her voice is rising and my darkness is at the threshold of taking over.

"Heather, lower your voice and calm down." Theos monotone voice does little to calm her, I would even go as far as to say- it added more fuel to the fire.

"How can you tell me to calm down! Why aren't you doing anything?"

"What? Duel for your honour?" Damn. "Sit down and eat your food before you embarrass yourself even more."

She snaps her eyes away from Theo, points her finger and nearly shouts at me "You couldn't keep your fucking mouth shout, could you? What are you jealous of our sex life, so you brought the help as your wing-woman?"

Quietness settles and darkness rolls over me, I close my eyes, inhale and I open them. I am very familiar with anger and pain, which are two feelings I've lived with large portion of my life.

Fury however, is new to me.

"Shit, if looks could kill, you'd be a gonner Heather." One of the guys on the right adds, thinking of being funny, so I turn my gaze to him, my voice is lethally steady and I even give myself chills when I speak.

"Yet, you are talking." He blanches and turns his eyes downwards. I look back at Heather.

The Unspoken Darkness

"Heather, let me make a few things clear. You did not pop round for dinner at Brentwood manor - I invited you. You are only sitting here tonight, because I approved it. You do not raise your voice at me or any guest of mine. You do not sit at my table and throw insults at me, regardless of who you fuck." She is paler than pale and I'm half hoping she will get up and leave so we can all return to the evening as planned. "Have I made myself clear?"

She swallows, but doesn't speak, I don't break my eye contact until she utters the confirmation "Yes."

Waiters appear out of thin air to clear our dishes away, which is a welcome distraction to break the tension at the table. A voice booms over the hall to announce that the charity auction will start shortly. Conversation resumes at the table, but I don't hear it. I don't hear anything, I am being pulled down into the darkness again, letting *it* come forward has opened a gate I've kept tightly controlled for weeks. I am overcome with a mixture of feelings, my heart rate is accelerating. *It's* squeezing my lungs. I need to get out. I need to get out now.

Chapter 38 - Raegan

I mumble a distant 'excuse me' as I rise from the table in search of a restroom. I am having a panic attack and having it in the middle of an art deco grand hall is not a thing I have on my bucket list.

The ladies bathroom is busy with gossiping women, but all I need is an empty stall.

Bingo! I close the door and the lid on the toilet and sit. My eyes are wide, unblinking, my heart is off to the races and there is not enough oxygen in the world to help me get through this. The realisation of what I just did smacks me right in the face with embarrassment and shame. I am mortified of what I said back at the table. I press my shaking hands to my chest in a pathetic attempt to stop myself from spiralling, but at this point - it's a lost cause. I didn't just make a complete and utter fool of myself, I dragged Brandan and George and Indy right down with me.

Ouch. A sharp pain pierces me in the chest and I double over. A tingly achy feeling creeps down my left arm and the world is slowly caving in on me. Were the bathroom walls so close to me a second ago? There is a commotion outside my stall door and after a gruff 'Get out!' the voices die down.

Click.

Oh great, just my luck someone has decided to have sex in the bathroom where I am trying not to pass out in. At that thought my chest tightens even more and a new wave of pain rolls down my arm. I gasp aloud from the pain

"Raegan! Open the door." I think I've heard that voice before, but I can't place it.

The pressure inside of me is too much, I need to let it out. I reach my left hand under the slit of my dress to my left thigh. Feeling the cuts it's like placing my hand on the tap, I just need to turn it to make me feel better… so I dig my newly manicured nails into my thigh… and I don't let up.

"Raegan open the fucking door or I will kick it down!"

Words.

Threats.

"Raegan!"

The wood cracks as the door flies open. They are all miles away, all I feel is the honeyed life nectar coating my nails. It will soon feel better. Just a little bit longer.

My hand is yanked away from the sweet release and my eyes clear to meet an enraged set of emerald greens.

Theo.

"What the hell are you doing! We have an agreement - when you feel like this" he is crouching down in front of me, shaking my hand with blood covered nails between us "you come to me. You don't hide in the bathroom and hurt yourself. Do you hear me Alora? Don't look at the blood." he grabs my jaw and turns my head so I look back into his eyes "Look at me. You are having a panic attack and I need you to listen to me. Can you do that?" My head is fuzzy, words and actions are not linking up. The world around me has returned to caving in on me. I lurch forwards as another sharp pain wrecks havoc in my chest and a whimper escapes my lips.

Concern fills Theos whole being "Shit! Alora, baby, do you have chest pains?" I nod.

"Pain shooting down your arm?" I nod.

He releases my jaw and begins to hold both of my hands in his, right above my lap. He is drawing soothing circle with his thumbs on the tops of my hands.

"Focus on the soothing motion. Breathe in….. and out…. Breathe in….. and out…. Breathe in….. and out." Theo continues instructing me to breath until I can take a deep breath again and my heart is not racing hundred miles an hour. "That's my girl, you're doing good baby. Keep breathing." With every breath he tells me to take, I take a step further away from the bottom of the inky well. My head is clearing and memories rush back.

"I'm sorry." I murmur "I'm sorry for what I said to Heather, I… she…I…" I try to get the words out my breathing becoming ragged again pulling me back down.

"Don't you dare apologise for what you said."

"But I humiliated Bran, George and myself."

"What? Is that what you think you did?" He lowers my hands in my lap and cups my face and for the first time tonight, I see an open smile dancing across his lips. His very luscious lips. "Silly girl. You walked in that room under Georges and Brandans protection, but now… people will think twice before fucking with you. Not to mention who they would have to deal with if they piss you off." He kisses my knuckles.

"I don't think I can do this Theo." I swallow "I don't think I can."

"Yes you can." He places a soft kiss on my forehead "Yes you can baby."

"Will you stay with me?"

"Of course I will." Theo kisses my forehead again "I will never leave you." He is confessing everything in one sentence, but the haze covering my thoughts doesn't allow me to fully understand it. My tongue stays glued in it's place, unsure what to say. "Stay here." Theo gets up, grabs a handful of paper towels and run them under the tap. "Lift your dress."

I hike up the dress to expose three red half moon cuts. Blood is no longer oozing from the wounds. "Don't you ever do this again." He cleans off the blood and pads it dry with extra paper towels. "Have I made myself clear Alora?" His voice is stern, leaving no room for argument.

"Yes." He kisses my battle wounds, throws the used towels in the bin, gets to his feet and extends his arm towards me.

"Come, let's get back, I don't want to miss the yacht." The auction, which I have completely forgotten about.

"Why do you want a yacht? I thought you hated holidays?" I look at him in a surprise

The only reply I get from Theo is a roguish grin as he leads me back to our table.

As he pushes my chair back into the table, he lowers his head and whispers in my ear "I plan on taking *my* girl on a sailing holiday around Mediterranean." My heart stops, but for a very different reason.

Chapter 39 - Raegan

The next couple of hours pass quickly while the auction takes place. George is taking me around tables and introducing me to people. Most of the names I recognise from his tutoring leading up to the gala, some I don't recognise or have completely forgotten.

My panic attack from earlier has disappeared and once again, it was Theo who brought me back from my darkness. A mix of his gentleness and command tends to snap me out of the descent into the well of darkness.

"How are you enjoying your first gala?" My wandering thoughts are interrupted and brought back to present by Dylan, my current dance partner. He is the same height as me while wearing heels, green blue eyes and a million dollar smile. He works in the law division of Brentwood Global. If I would be interested in seeing people or even the casual dinner date, Dylan would be the ideal candidate.

"Who said this is my first gala?" But I mean a little flirting didn't hurt anyone, right? Champagne, as it turns out, is a wonderful courage booster.

"I assumed it was, as it's the first time I've seen you at a Brentwood event." I smile at him "Would it be immensely inappropriate to ask for your number in hopes for a dinner?"

"Yes!" Both our heads snap to the side as Theo is standing, looming over Dylan with a thundering expression on his face "I'll take it from here Dylan."

Theo has wrapped one of his arms around my middle and taken the other to lead us in a dance.

As we're getting into the rhythm of the dance I ask "Was that really necessary?" Dylan looked terrified when Theo lead me away.

"Yes. I didn't like the way he was looking at you."

"And how was he looking at me?" That questions earns me a scowl. "Like he wanted to ask me out on a date?" His hold on me tightens and he pulls me even closer to his chest. He looks down at me.

"Don't push it Alora."

"Why? I'm single for the first time in a long time, it's not just men who like to have some fun you know. And stop being such a bodyguard, I thought I had a night away from them." I take a sharp intake of breath before continuing to push Theos buttons "And last time I checked, you, Mr Oakes, have a girlfriend."

"You are driving me to the edge of sanity Alora."

"You and me both Theo, you and me both." I blow out a long breath "Where's your date gone anyway?"

"You scared her off."

"Eeekk... sorry about that. But... I tell you what-" I lean back a little to gain some space between us, we stop the dance and I raise my left hand in an oath "I promise I will be much, much nicer to your next girlfriend. How about that?"

"You promise?"

"I do."

"You can't break this promise to me."

"I won't."

"Deal." I return my hand to the back of his neck and we resume our dance. "Would you have really gone on a date with him?"

I shrug before answering "I don't know. It sounds exciting in theory when I've had few drinks, but I don't think I would have gone through with it in the daylight."

"Why not?" His voice has turned thicker.

"You know why." After few moments I add. "My heart got broken a long time ago, it took me years to put it back together and trust it to someone else. Only for him to go and tear it apart again. If I ever manage to piece some of the broken shards of my heart back together again, it will be mine and mine alone. I'm barely surviving this time, I won't survive another."

"What happened the first time?" I can feel him looking at me.

I look deeply into Theos eyes and give him a weak smile "Not tonight." I rest my head on his shoulder as we sway to the music. Brandan is on the dance floor with Indy, he hasn't stopped looking at her all night.

"What's making you smile like that?" I didn't even realise I was.

Keeping eyes on my brother "Seeing my brother fall in love." And that is the last sentence I utter before my world is tipped upside down. Again.

Bang! Bang! Bang! Bang! Bang! Bang!

Instinctively both of my arms wrap around Theos neck as he spins me around, away from the gunshots, shielding me with is body. "Hold on!" He wraps his arms around me, squashes me to his body, lifts me off the ground and carries me away.

Gunshots.
Shouts.
Screams.
Mayhem.

He puts me down behind one of the columns, brings both of his hands on either side of my face and makes me look at him instead of the carnage behind his back.
"Raegan! Rae, baby, listen to me. Stay here and don't come out. Whatever happens- do not come out. I will come and find you after-"
"What?! You're leaving me?"
"I have to. You know I have to." I start to protest but before I can even so much as open my mouth "I'll come back to you, I promise." He places a kiss on my lips and walks away.
"Be safe!" I don't know if I say that out loud or just in my head.

My back is against the cold column, I clamp my hand over my mouth to muffle my panicked sob. As the screams continue to build, my legs give out and I slide down to the floor. I close my eyes and pray to the God I don't believe in for it to stop. After several moments I turn to peek behind the column.

People are running, hiding, fighting, but there are two figures I would make out anywhere - Brandan and Theo. Their movements are fluid, synchronised. They're walking through the chaos with lethal precision and purpose. They kill whoever gets in their way.

They aren't just my brother and my friend or two of the directors at Brentwood Global.

They are two assassins, trained to kill without mercy. To protect their own.

Two gunshots ring out..

Bang! Bang!

My heart stops.

Chapter 40 - Brandan

"BRAN!!!" I would know that scream anywhere. "BRANDAN!!!" I jam a knife in one of the attackers eye, while shooting another three times for good measure. "BRANDAN!!!" Where are these fuckers coming from?

"GO!" Theo shouts from my side, with a nod I turn and run towards my sister, taking out a few more of the attackers in the process. When I reach her I come to a halt. It's not Rae who has me frozen in place, it's the body she is covering.

My dad.

He's laying on the floor, blood pooling under him. Raegan is pressing down on the right side of his chest trying to slow the bleeding.

"Dad! Dad stay with me. Help is coming." That's the second time I've heard Raegan calling him that "Dad please!" My sisters plea finally snaps me out of my frozen state.

I turn and see someone who I recognise, I don't know his name or where he works "Find me a car! NOW!" He runs off and I kneel down beside dad, he is conscious, but for how long?

A pair of feet come to my side and I look up to see Indy and her tear soaked gorgeous face. "Indy, find me any towels, napkins, any cloth to help with stopping the bleeding."

I place my hands over Raegans and press down. I don't care if I brake his collar bone, a rib or two to slow the bleeding.

Seconds later Indy returns with a pile of napkins in her arms, she passes a couple to Raegan who presses them into the wound. Dad reaches for my hand and I clasp it in mine, while applying pressure with the other over Raes hands.

"Get that gun." he grits out and my head swivels around until it lands on a glock behind Raes back. "it has your sisters prints on it." I look at my sister in question, but her sole focus is on keeping the pressure on.

"I got the car. Lets go. I'll lift the legs, Bran - the head, Rae- keep that pressure on, Indy - get the doors." Theo issues the orders like it's another day in the office. The training we've been through since childhood, has kicked in. Get the job done first, then deal with the emotions.

I quickly rise lunging towards the gun and tuck it in my waistband.

We move as fast as we can to get out of the building. Indy opens a door to the back of a Range Rover, I get in and scoot further in, while I keep dad as stable as I can. I'm holding dad in a tight upright grip, his head is resting against my chest, just under my chin. Raegan is crouching down on her knees in the footwell, not letting up on the pressure. Indy climbs in the front passenger seat and Theo jumps in behind the wheel.

Dad is still with us, his breathing is becoming laboured, but he is alert.

"Hey, I think your wife is mad at you." Raegan breaks the silence in the car that was threatening to shatter the windows. Both dad and I look at her with extreme confusion on our faces, she lets out a weird laugh, that borders on hysterical. "Charlotte left me a letter, that's what was in that box, among other things. She said that she hoped I knew the truth at the time of reading the letter and that you haven't ducked out of the task. It made me laugh, because you totally ducked out of it." Weak smile tugs at his lips. Rae reaches her right hand back and Indy places another bunch of napkins and she swaps the blood soaked ones out. "She was in the hospital the day I was born, she held me." She is smiling through the tears and she turns those golden brown eyes to me "She gave me exactly the same bear she got when you were born, just with a pink bow. That's the bear I asked you to take from my apartment, I never went anywhere without it. I named him Hammy."

An invisible hand is wrapping it's fingers around my heart and squeezing.
"I also want to start a new tradition." she continues. I'm in awe how calm she is. She isn't phased by the blood and if dad was right and not seeing things with his blood loss- did Rae use that gun I picked up? She is keeping this whole situation under control and not letting Theo and I spin out of control.

Theo might not carry the Brentwood last name, but he's as much of Georges son as I am. Theos dad was Georges right hand man and they've been friends since childhood. When we were 5, Theos parents finally decided to go on their long overdue honeymoon. Mum persuaded Elina, Theos mum, to leave him with us so they can enjoy the holiday, just the two of them.

Unfortunately on their 4th day of their honeymoon, they were in a car accident and both got killed. He was always part of our family, but from that day he become an honorary member of the Brentwood family. So even though he is driving the car and seems much more in control than I am, I know he is not. "I want us to have an afternoon tea once a month in the sun room."

"I think that's a wonderful idea sweetheart." As he gets his final word out, he coughs and splutters. Blood leaking out of the corners of his mouth.

"THEO!" Is all Raegan says in a tone of voice I've never heard her use, but it does the job and we are speeding through London at a breakneck speed towards the hospital.

We screech to a halt in front of the hospital, Indy is already out of the car and running inside to get the nurses and doctors. Seconds later a group of nurses rush out of the door with a stretcher and pull the back door open. Their movements are much more organised than ours was, within a minute dad is on the stretcher being rushed through endless sets of doors, with Ragean and me right beside them, still holding dads hands. Theo besides Rae.

"You can't come any further." One of the nurses stops and turns towards us, halting us in our step.

"But his our dad, we nee-" Raegan is interrupted by the nurse with softening look on her face

"Your dad is being taken into the operating theatre, you can't go in there." With that she turns and walks through the final double doors and follows the path of the stretcher.

The Unspoken Darkness

All three of us stand there, lost. Raegan leans her head against my shoulder and I pull her into a side hug. All the adrenaline from earlier is slowly seeping out of me, the weight of what is happening is settling on my shoulders. And I feel so extremely tired.

I have lost one parent, I can't lose the other. Flashbacks of mums final days crowd my head and the vise wrapped around my heart cranks tighter. Theo wraps his arm around my shoulder, reliving his own living nightmares.

"Guys, I found an empty seating area around the corner, near the nurses station where you can get updates on how Mr Brentwood is doing." Oh fuck, in all this, I forgot about Indy. How could I forget about her? I turn to look at the petite woman in front of me and for the second time tonight, a woman in my life is keeping me from collapsing.

She leads us to a seating area that is mostly empty, apart from couple of people. It is late on a Saturday night, unless it's an emergency- there aren't people here.

"Raegan, come, we need to wash your hands." At Indys words Rae looks down at her hands and it's at this moment when the realisation hits her. I can see it in her eyes that her already fragile world is starting to crumble down. She shakes her head while looking at her blood covered hands, it's the first time she is seeing blood on them.

Her fathers blood.

She blinks.

Again.

And again. Her throat working hard to swallow. Her breathing is picking up, which is a tell tell sign of her having a panic attack, so I cover her hands with mine and step in front of her, to halt the downward spiral. Her eyes rise to meet mine. I never thought I'd see this kind of pain in her eyes again, but fate is a bitch. She was keeping me going for the past half an hour, now it's my turn to take the baton.

"Rae. Go with Indy, get it washed off, I'll be right here."

I look where Theo is standing "We'll be here."

"Promise?"

"I promise."

Chapter 41 - Brandan

"Thank you for keeping her safe." I say to my brother sitting opposite me on the worlds most uncomfortable chairs. "I saw you two were dancing before the shooting started." Theo nods, he looks as tired as I feel.

Both girls are walking back to where we're sitting, both have washed all their make up off and Raegans hands are no longer cover in blood. As they reach where we are seated, Theo gets up and drapes his tux jacket around Raegan. She doesn't even notice that.

Raegan always uses 'please' and 'thank you' and is polite, the only time she doesn't do any of those things is when she is emotionally drained. Like now.

She sits next to me and Indy sits in front of Raegan. I lean forwards, resting my forearms on my thighs, my head hanging low. Powerlessness is a bitch. I act and react, resolve issues and get things done. I felt the same way when mum was ill and I hoped I'd never feel like this again. All I can do is sit and wait. I can't help dad. Or Raegan. Or Theo. Or myself.

"FUCK!!" The scream rips out of me before I get a chance to get a hold of my emotion. I run my hands over my face and lean my head against the wall behind me and close my eyes. I can't lose my head now. I'll count to ten and then I need to find a nurse to give me an update on what's happening in the operating room. I get to 4 when Rae leans her head against my shoulder and cover my hand with hers.

"Kids!" I blink my eyes open. Was I asleep? I shake my head to clear the mental fog. Carl is power walking towards us and for a split second I think it's dad. They look ridiculously similar. "Where is he?" With a few more long strides he reaches us, pulling me and Raegan in the biggest, bone crushing hug.

"He's in surgery." My voice has gone groggy from the power nap.

"He'll be all right Bran. He's a stubborn bastard, he won't give up, not now." I sniffle into his neck, which brings me back to when I was 5 and learning to ride a bike.

My hand eye coordination now is second to none, but when I was little - I could't balance for shit. Somehow uncle Carl pulled the short straw to teach me how to ride a bike, which was mission impossible for someone with zero balancing skills. After I'd fallen off the bike for the umpteenth time- I threw a top notch tantrum and declared that I will never get back on the damn thing. Seconds later I burst into tears as the level of frustration I was feeling as a five years old was way too much. So my uncle just held me and let me cry. Once I was done he looked me in the eyes and asked "You ready to try again?" I did try again and again, after a few more tries I learnt to ride my bike.

He releases us and before anyone gets a chance to see my misty eyes, I turn towards the nurses station "I'll go find a nurse for an update." I grit out between my clenched teeth, Carl claps my shoulder as I turn to walk away.

The station is empty, so I lean against the counter and wait. I watch Carl comforting Theo and even giving Indy a hug, he's still holding Raegan in a side hug. I don't hear the question, but I make out my uncles' reply "Yes, they're safe. Back home with extra security." I was so overwhelmed with fear of losing my own father, that I forgot to ask about my auntie and cousins.

"Can I help you?" My internal self scolding is interrupted by a middle aged nurse who is now standing on the other side of counter. Why did I want to speak to her? I give my head another shake.

"Yes, erm.. my father is in surgery, George Brentwood, do you have an update on his condition?"

She looks over me with very little sympathy on her face.

"What's your relationship with Mr Brentwood?" Is she shittin' me right now? I try to be a patient man, but the last few hours have drained me. Whatever patience I have left, I am keeping it for my family, not this woman.

"I Am His Son." I annunciate each word as I spit them out. She is not bothered one bit, but she does sit down and taps away at her computer.

Seconds later she picked up the phone "Can I have an update on Mr Brentwood?" The person on the other end speaks, but I can't make it out. She looks up at me from her desk ."Mhm, his son." There are a few more 'mhms' and scribbling notes down on her notepad. Finally, what feels like hours, she hangs up. "Surgeons are still working on Mr Brentwood. He has lost quite a lot of blood, which is making their job more complicated as he needs transfusions. But rest assured, they are doing their absolute best."

I know the meaning of the unsaid words. In autopilot I ask "Is there a time frame how long surgeries like these take?"

"It'll be at least a few more hours." I turn my head to look back at my family and a suffocating lump climbs up my throat. I think I murmur 'thanks' as I make my way back to them. How the fuck do I tell them all what I was just told? The uncertainty is what I fear most.

My face must be doing a grand job of mirroring my thoughts, as everyones faces drop even more. So I tell them what the nurse just told me. We're in a vacuum as we all process what I've just learnt. We all find our uncomfortable seats and sink into our own quite hells.

"Here." My eyes fly open as Indy hands me a cup of coffee.

"Thank you Indy." She goes to hand cups of coffees to Theo and Carl. She keeps one for herself and places a spare one on an empty seat. Raegan is asleep and slightly drooling on my shoulder. If this would be in any other setting - I would make sure to take a picture and torment her with it's existence for years.

As I'm about to finish my cup I hear voices coming from the corridor we saw dad being taken down, moments later a doctor in scrubs is walking towards us.

"Rae…. Rae…. Raegan wake up, doctor's here." Her eyes pop open and she stands in one go, I'm surprised she didn't get light headed from the fast shift.

"Brentwood family?" Doctor asks and we all answer with 'yes' "George is out of surgery and is being moved to ICU. He lost a lot of blood so we had to do blood transfusions. The bullets didn't touch any vital organs, but did cause a lot of damage. He is stable, the next 24 hours are the most crucial ones so we will monitor him closely. I would suggest you all head home and rest, it's been a long and traumatic night for you all. I'll ensure a nurse calls you as soon as there are any changes."

"Can we see him?" Raegan is the first to speak.

The doctor thinks for a second before answering "I can only allow one of you to see him and it'll be from behind a glass."

"Carl, would you like to go see him?" Rae turns around to face our uncle, who is visibly surprised by her question and offer.

"Would you like to Rae?" He tentatively asks, as if not to scare her.

"I do, but if that was me in that room, it's my brother who I'd like to see."

Carl looks at Rae for a long moment before speaking. "Thank you. You kids head home and have some rest, I'll stay. I'll call you if anything changes."

Chapter 42 - Brandan

It's morning when we arrive back at home. The staff are awake and going about their daily tasks, but the atmosphere is bleak. None of us are good company as we make our silent ways to our rooms, in a hope to wash the night away. Tux off. Shower on.

Scrub.

Scrub.

Scrub.

I know I should try to get some sleep, but I can't, there are too many things I need to take care of. With dad being in hospital our competitors will want to use that to their advantage. There aren't many, less than a handful of people that know who we really are- those are the ones I need to keep my family safe from. When a tragedy like this strikes - people use it as an opportunity to strike. We've already been taking hits, now we are exposed.

Issuing statements, making calls, replying to emails, seems like an endless slur of 'I'm so sorry' and 'How are you holding up?' And 'Is George going to be OK?' Like any of those fuckers give a damn about him.

I've also set up a program to run the security footage from the gala to analyse every second and check every single person through facial recognition. It's been running for a few hours when I make my way back to the screen.

I sit on a sofa and place the laptop on the coffee table as I rest my elbows on my thighs and watch the scene in front of me.

Rae and Theo are dancing. She is looking at someone and smiling, but what catches my attention is Theos intense gaze on Raegan and the smile tugging at his lips. I unmute the video just as the gunshots go on.

There is zero hesitation in Theo as he wraps his arms around her, turning her away from the direction of gunshots. Protecting her. Raegan has wrapped her arms around his neck and nestled close to him "Hold on!" Theo shouts as he lifts and carries her away. They leave the sight of the camera on my screen and I switch to the next one. He's taken her to the furthest corner he could and put her behind a column, out of everyones sight. She is trembling and in shock. He cups her face, forcing her to look at him and not the destruction around them. "Raegan! Rae, baby, listen to me. Stay here and don't come out. Whatever happens - do not come out. I will come and find you after-" he doesn't get a chance to finish his sentence as Ragean interrupts him.

"What?! You're leaving me?" She's scared, I can see it in her eyes and hear it in her trembling voice.

"I have to. You know I have to. I'll come back to you, I promise." He kisses her and walks away towards the gunshots.

I look back at the screen where I've hit pause and look at my sister. She's in shock.

I hit play and concentrate on Rae, she is looking around the column to see what is going on, fear written all over her face.

She turns her head sharply to her left.

2 gunshots ring out.

"NOOOO!!! DAD!!"

She is running.
I switch the cameras again to follow her, I know where she will end up, but the scene that is playing out in front of me is not what I expected.

Dad has been shot, but is fighting a large man while another, presumably the shooter, stands to the side, gun still aimed.
Raegan is running towards them, in her gown and high heels. She doesn't slow as she approaches the two men. In one swift movement she grabs the centrepiece vase of flowers and smashes it over the guy with the gun. He falls to the floor. Unconscious.
There is no hesitation as she jumps on the back of the man who is now, beating dad. Our heavily bleeding dad.
I believe this is what they call 'she's gone feral'. Raegan is clawing at the man, scratching his face. He loses balance and they fall, with Raegan hitting the floor first, but she doesn't let him go. He lifts himself up and lets his body slam into the floor, hoping she'll let go. Fuck! He does that a couple of time, before she digs her thumbs in his eyes.
They both scream.
His - pure pain.
Hers - pure rage.
Finally he rolls off her, she scrambles away on the floor, picks up the gun that was dropped from the vase guy.

Aims.

Closes her eyes.

Pulls the trigger.

Breath is lodged in my throat. Despite this happening hours ago, a chill runs down my spine.

She drops the gun and rushes over to dad.

"Hey, hey. It's going to be ok. Stay with me. Stay with me dad." He doesn't reply, just looks at her and clutches her hands, that are pushing down on his wounds.

"BRAN!" The same gut wrenching scream from hours ago, echo through the speakers.

I pause the video again, I know what happens next. I am too wired up, too many emotions swirling inside of me.

Anger, because someone had the audacity to think of hurting us.

Reminder of the pain and suffering of losing a parent.

Failure of not protecting my family. How will I make this right?

People are looking to me now to lead them, to keep calm and not be fazed by all the shit we've just been through. Yet I can't even lead my own mind to start sorting all this out.

I hang my head low.

Knock - knock

I don't want to deal with anyone right now.

Knock - knock.

"Bran, it's only me. Are you awake?" my sisters voice filters through the closed door, sharp pain splits my chest. I could have lost her. I failed her and the promise I made. I've learnt long ago that life is fragile, the only difference now - I am on the receiving end of it.

I can hear the door open and soft footfalls coming to where I'm sat on the sofa.

"What's happened? Bran, you're scaring me." She's knelt to my side and pulls on my right arm. "Is it dad?" I can't look at her. Heaviness sits sturdy on my chest and I don't know how to cope with it. "What's going on?" Her voice is trembling and I know I should answer, but words are failing me.

I lift my head and meet the same golden brown eyes that match mine filled with concern.

"No, no change in dads condition." My voice is croaky and it's in this moment I realise I've been crying.

"Oh, come here bear." In one swift motion she's next to me on the sofa and pulling me in for the biggest, tightest hug. Her much smaller arms are wrapped in a death grip around my shoulders, pressing my head into her shoulder.

"I got you. I got you." She repeats in a soft whisper against my head and I cling to her as my life raft in a storm. And for the first time in nearly 5 years I let myself cry. I let all the emotions I've kept inside me out. Last time I allowed myself to cry was when my mum died.

We stay like that for a long moment, Raegan doesn't say or ask me anything. I know she doesn't judge me either. She understands.

"I'm scared." Words leaving my mouth surprise me "I… I don't want… I can't-" I'm trying to find the words to apologise for what I just said, I'm supposed to be the big brother and take care of everything. Not sob like a three year old toddler and burden her with my worry.

"Me too, but you're not alone. I am here. I won't go anywhere."

"Promise?"

"I promise." Her little pinky grabs mine and we're locked in a promise.

"Rae?"

"Yeah?"

"You can't close your eyes when you shoot a gun." She chuckles a little.

"I've never had the official training."

"We'll change that."

"Ok. Have some rest now, I'll be right here when you wake up." I do just that. Tiredness pulls me under and within seconds I am slumbering in a dreamless sleep.

Chapter 43 - Brandan

After waking up from a 4 hour nap and reassuring Raegan that I am fine, I finally need to track down Indy. First I check the room she has been staying in here at the manor, but I find it empty. My next stop is the kitchen, if she isn't there - Patricia will know where I can find her.

"Morning Patricia." I say with as much gusto as I can muster. Before coming here I called uncle Carl to check on dad. No change to his condition, still in ICU. Raegan and I agreed to go to the hospital in an hour to relieve Carl and let him get back to his family.

"Afternoon Brandan." She replies solemnly "Is there any news on Mr Brentwood?"

"He's being monitored, but he's stable. Do you know where I can find Indy?" I don't know why I don't tell her the truth. Maybe it's more for my benefit than hers.

"You're always looking for that girl." She gives me a questioning smile, which on any other day I would return with a smile of my own or a witty comment, but not today "She's in the greenhouse."

Greenhouse? Didn't know anyone ever went in there apart from me. Correction. All the staff knows that I don't like people venturing into my greenhouse.

The greenhouse was the only space where mum and I would spend hours potting, grafting and experimenting with different plants, how to achieve best blooms, or be more fragrant, or just lasting longer in the vase. Ever since mum died, I have kept everything in the greenhouse as it was the last time we were there together. Having someone enter my sanctuary and move things about. Touch pots or plants. The chance of someone wiping away the last remnants of my mum makes my heart beat faster and my strides longer.

It's located at the back of the house in the middle of the old gardens. It's not small by any standards, but with the plants surrounding it, they make it seem smaller.

I'm about to pull the door open when I see Indy sitting in the middle of the greenhouse on a pile of the compost bags. She looks lost in thought. And I want to know what she is thinking about. What is making her bright face dim? I want to know and I want to rip it apart.

She doesn't hear me enter and I sit down next to her. She doesn't flinch or move, still far away in her thoughts. After a moment she speaks "Yesterday was the first time I felt scared since I moved out of my old home."

"I wouldn't have let anything happen to you."

She looks at me and I can see the fear in her eyes. My heart drops. I want to pull her close to me, but I hesitate. Does she no longer feel safe with me?

"I wasn't scared for my self Brandan. I was scared for you." Fuck and fuck my hesitation. I pull her into my lap and she clings to me like a baby monkey. I can feel her trembling, but she doesn't cry. Indy hasn't told me what her past was like and I have kept my word to her to not investigate it. I don't want to just earn her trust to know her past. I want to earn the right for her to want me in her future. Because as much as I try - I don't see mine without my red haired girl in it.

"Will it make you feel better if I told you that I'm good in dangerous situations?" I speak against her hair. Feeling myself relax in her warm cocoon.

She shakes her head "That only makes it worse." I chuckle softly, while still holding Indy close to my chest. "I wasn't just scared for you being injured, I… I didn't want you to lose your dad." Double fuck.

No one has ever pulled these deep, guttural emotions out of me. With just one sentence she has cracked my soul open, planted herself in the middle of it and closed it back up. She is absolutely undoubtedly intertwined with my whole being. I pull her face from my chest to look into my future she holds in her eyes.

"There are two sides to me darling. One, the gentleman who you know, the other - is a powerful man who takes what he wants. And what both of us want- is you. But I want you to want me to take you." I kiss her with a chaste kiss for the first time. Her lips are as soft as I imagined. I whisper against her lips "Tell me what you want darling. The choice is yours. It will always be yours."

"I want both of you." Triple fucking fuck. This woman. I pour all my raw emotions she has awaken and I kiss her.

The desperation of our kiss is all consuming. It's longing and deep. I'm savouring every swipe of my tongue, touching of our lips. The little vixen even bites down on my lower lip. This is perfection.

I pull away and lean my forehead against Indys "You are mine and I am yours. Is that clear Indy?"

"Yes." She answers without hesitation.

"You will stay here, at the manor."

She scrunches up her nose before speaking "What if I want to stay at the penthouse?"

"Safety is one, non negotiable topic. You will do as I say, there will be no arguing. If you want to be mad at me for it, that's fine. I'll take it. But your safety is paramount to me. Do you understand?"

"I do." I kiss her forehead.

My phone buzzes in my trouser pocket and I know it'll be Raegan saying I'm late for our visit to hospital. I rise with Indy still wrapped around me "I have to go, we're going to the hospital."

"How is Mr Brentwood?" Worry has crept into her soft, lust filled features.

"He is still in ICU in critical condition." I plant another forehead kiss on her and I start to walk towards the door. Gateway back to reality.

Reality feels too heavy at the moment. I wish I could stay with Indy in this green bubble for a while longer.

"Brandan?"

"Yes darling."

"Promise me we're real." I stop in my tracks and look at my girl, legs wrapped around my waist, one arm wrapped around my neck, while the other is running its fingers across my eyebrow. In an attempt to convince herself that this is indeed real.

"There has and never will be a fake thing about us. You and me Indy, we're it. My life is yours and yours is mine." I place a kiss behind her ear and she melts into me.

Chapter 44 - Raegan

I have faced many different challenges in my life. A couple of them have been life altering, but neither compares to the past 24 hours. The absolute fear of losing George, dad. I called him dad.

I called him dad for the first time when he was shot. Why did I not do it before? What was I waiting for?

My darkness is pulling me hard towards the abyss, but I won't let it win, not this time. I anchor my feet. When I saw Bran in his room, my brother, bigger then life personality, drowning in devastation and self blame. It broke my already shattered heart.

We are back at the hospital, heading to the ICU unit. Uncle Carl hasn't left the hospital since he arrived not long after the shooting. He looks as bad as we all feel. His hazel eyes are sunken and dark surrounding his eyes. The tuxedo he's been wearing since last night is all crumpled up.

He pulls us both into a hug and holds us there.

"Any news?" I ask

"He's stable, but no change. The doctor said if he stays like this, they should be able to move him out of ICU this time tomorrow." Carl replier

"That's good news. You go home, we'll stay here." Bran adds.

The evening and night passes at a snails pace. Bran continues to work, his program is running checks on the surveillance footage of last night. I am not trained in the same way Bran and Theo are, but I still want to contribute, so I am helping look through the footage as well. Nothing in particular catches my attention. The Gala wasn't a secret, many people knew it was happening and where it was being held. Yes, the security was tight, but there were also a lot of vendors and staff, coming and going with supplies and staff changes. If someone was organised and well versed in how the night would flow, they could slip in without attracting unwanted attention.

Which is what happened. The attackers were wearing masks, so identifying them from the feed won't be possible, but the bodies of the killed have been moved to a facility to be identified. But that has been made more complex due to police involvement. The mega spectacle the attack created, has got not only police and other authorities involved, but the media are going wild. The only saving grace is - there were no phones or cameras allowed inside. Mostly to protect my identity, giving media no footage of what happened inside of the Grand Connaught.

It's been a week since the attack and I am on my way to the hospital to see dad before work. He was moved into a private room from ICU 3 days after the shooting. I've given Bran and Theo strict instructions to not tell him about work or the investigation or anything, that will get his blood pressure up. He needs to stay in as calm of a state as he can to speed up his recovery.

I am by his hospital room door when I hear voices inside.

"Are the police close to finding out who's behind it?" Dad asks and I scowl. Christian and Leo behind me stiffen, they know how I feel about them talking to him about this.

"No, they are going down the route of bad blood between us and some old competition that are no longer in business. They are however not willing to share much about the identities of the assailants." Bran replies, giving him more information than he should.

"If their IT security is too much for you Bran, maybe we should take a midnight trip to the MET?" Theo sounds way to excited about the prospect of breaking into the Metropolitan Police Headquarters.

"Their security isn't too much for me, I just don't trust what it says. If you're offering a brotherly night out, what about a trip to the morgue?" He counters with an offer of his own, like an actual bidding war.

"You should do it sooner rather than later, whoever is behind this, will want the bodies gone, so they can't be tracked back to them." Dad is actively encouraging this. Unbelievable.

Enough is enough, I open the door and walk in. Three heads turn in my direction.

"I am disappointed in you." Theo and Bran attempt to turn their expressions to pure innocence."Don't you even try to do the puppy dog eyes at me, that won't help you." So they look at dad "Dad won't help you either."

Dad smiles, some of his usual colour and olive complexion returning to his face. "I should've gotten shot sooner if I'd known that was all it took to get you call me dad."

"That is not funny." I say sternly, the three of them are on top form today.

"Like in the upper arm, nowhere vital." He continues

"Have they changed your medication today, because you are talking a load of rubbish." I walk over to him and on the way I slap Bran around the head.

"Hey!" He exclaims "That was uncalled for!" Since dad has been moved out of the ICU, an invisible weight has been lifted off Bran.

Even though life has been relentless, I've continued to work, regardless of Theo's insistence I take some time off. He knows better than most that having a routine is good for me. So I settle in my office and start going through media releases planned for tomorrow.

One of them is about us expanding our support for local communities through the charity work Brentwood Global does. It also mentions that there are three roles being filled to support this extra work at Brentwood Global and it encourages people who are passionate about their community to apply.

I am well aware of the businesses we conduct. I've accepted that the work the Citadel does is the darker side of my heritage, and there is a strict vetting process in place on which jobs get accepted and completed.

Which makes the charity work BG does more special to me. The available positions intrigue me and I head over to our website to check them out.

Once again I am greeted with the view of not so long ago, the formatting is all weird, different spacings between the currently live job adverts. It looks incredibly messy and suspicious.

After I fixed the page last time, I went to check it a day later and it had reverted to how it was before, but I put it down to me not saving the changes I made. I repeated the process and ensured all my changes have been saved and uploaded onto our live website.

Now I know someone is doing this on purpose.

I follow the link through to edit the page and this time - I am paying a lot more attention to everything I can see on my screen.

I've spent the better part of two hours reading through every word on the page, every page there is a link to and each job advert. Nothing looks odd, but the nagging feeling in my stomach tells me I am close to something. I need a shot of caffeine to reenergise my brain, I reach over to grab my mug and accidentally click and move the mouse.

My mouth falls open.

A hidden text has been written in the 'gaps', the font is smaller and white, to match the background of the page. But there is definitely something there. I highlight everything in the empty space and paste it into separate document, changing the colour of the text to black.

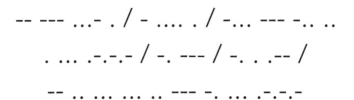

What in the world! Is that a morse code? A quick search on google lands me on a morse code translation website and cold sweat covers my body.

Move the bodies. No new missions.

I clasp my hands over my mouth in shock. This is how they have been sending information to whoever is after us. They are using our own website against us.

There are more irregular gaps, which I am confident will have other messages embedded.

... .- ..-. . --..-- / -. --- / .-.. . .-
-.. / - --- / ..- ... .-.-.-

Safe, no lead to us.

-. . -..- - / ... - . .--. ... ..—..

Next steps?

This time I leave the hidden messages as they are and click out of the website. I reach for my phone and call my brother.

"Hey, what's up?" He answers on the third ring.

"I think dad was right."

Chapter 45 - Raegan

"About the bodies…?" He asks cautiously.

"Yes. If you think the info MET has in the files is incorrect, we should check the bodies ourselves."

"How come you changed your mind?" Bran is asking suspiciously.

"I didn't, I never disagreed with what he said, I just didn't like you stressing him out." I try to cover my changing mind.

"What's really going on?" Maybe I was a bit too snappy with my reply, I need to change the direction this is going.

"You know it takes me longer to process *these* sorts of things. I want to find whoever is doing this as much as you."

There is a long moment on the phone where neither of us speak, I know he is not fully buying into what I'm telling him "Ok. But promise me you will tell me if something is bothering you?"

"I will." The lie tastes rotten in my mouth. In the short amount of time I've known Brandan, I've never lied to him. I never had the need to.

For the next two days I continue checking every line of our website, but the only place where the coded messages are posted are the vacancy page. I have left them there as they are not wanting to draw any attention to the fact I've found them.

Knock - knock.

"Come in Leo." Leo pokes his blonde head through the door and steps into my office.

"Ready for lunch?" It's only him today, Christian has been called away on a different assignment, which I have learnt is a code word for doing work under the Citadel.

"Come in and close the door." He does as I've asked, but gives me a suspicious look "Pull up a chair next to me."

"Rae, what's going on?" He's sat on a chair next to me now at my desk.

"I need your help and I need you to leave the bodyguard Leo on the other side of that door. Can you do that?" I am nervous about sharing the information with Leo, but I know I can't do this on my own. "Please Leo, I wouldn't ask if it wasn't important."

I can see the conflicting on his face. He pulls his hand down his face and releases a big breath "All right. But… if there is even the slightest risk of danger, I'm telling Bran."

"Deal."

I re-tell the sequence of events and show him the messages. He is quite for a long time, processing the information I've just shared.

He startles me when he finally speaks "You need to tell Bran. Like… right now!"

"No. I can't tell him this yet, I need more evidence. Or a name or-"

"Rae, this is some serious shit. He can deal-" I shoot up from my chair and step away. I am a ball of anxiety ready to explode.

The Unspoken Darkness

"I can't tell him, Leo. He has already so much on his plate right now. If I tell him about this - he will be all over it. He doesn't need another thing to do or to worry about."

"Listen" he tries to placate me "I know you're trying to help, but this is so much bigger than you think, he needs to know Raegan. Needs to know, not wants to, needs to." My throat is closing up and my eyes are burning.

"He broke." I swallow "I saw my brother break and all I could do was wrap my arms around him and hold him tight." I clamp my lips together to prevent my tears from spilling "But I can do this. And I need your help Leo. You are the only one who can help me."

"You mean the only one who won't tell the big three?"

"Yes."

"Are you sure you know where you're going?" I whisper to Leo as we are weaving through one of the offices to get to the server room. For the past week we have been gathering evidence on who might be the one adding the messages on the website. The list of names is surprisingly long, but we're planning on making it much shorter after our trip to the server room.

"Yes." He answers confidently "Well.. mostly." Another minute or so later "Bingo! Told you I knew where it was." I just roll my eyes at him.

"Good. Now get us in there before anyone sees us."

"Everyone has already left, relax."

"Whoever is doing this, will know about the backup files, so excuse me for being vigilant."

"Wow! Someones a bit sassy today!"

I glare at him "Will you just get on with it!" I will admit that I am more on the edge as the last couple of weeks have progressed. But I am also excited to be able to share our discoveries with everyone.

Finally Leo cracks open the server room and we slip inside.

"Do you know what *you're* doing?" Leo asks smugly, with a wide grin on his face

"Absolutely." Not. "I just need to find where the back up files are stored, then find the websites back up and copy all available files across. Easy." Not.

We spend over an hour finding our way around and getting the files we need. Our website is backed up daily, but it only stores the last 30 days, that should capture the ones I deleted without realising it.

We go back to my office and I lock my laptop in the safe.

"Are you all right if we stay at Brans penthouse tonight?" I ask Leo as we exit the building "I want to have an early start tomorrow."

"Yeah, no objections from me. We could have that Thai take away from around the corner."

"Oh yesss.. That sounds like a really good plan."

Chapter 46 - Brandan

"Where's your sister Brandan?" I look up from my phone to see dad sitting down at the dinner table.

"I think it's Theo you should be asking that." I smirk at my friend who is sitting across from me with very little expression on his face. The only person that face lights up for is my sister.

My phone buzzes "Speaking of the devil.. Hello lil bear. What's up?"

"Hey, is it all right if we stay at your penthouse tonight?" Theos ears perk up at the 'we' in Raes statement.

"Who's 'we'?" He growls from across the table and Raegan hears it, so I switch my phone to speaker mode and place it in the middle of the table.

"Leo and me. We're only just left the office and I need to be back in early, so I would rather have an extra hour of sleep than drive all the way back home."

"Yeah, not a problem, Indy is at the manor." I reply

Dad chirps up "Sweetheart, don't you think you're working too much?" His face is covered in concern. It's been nearly 4 weeks since he was shot and recovering well. But all three of us are babysitting him at any given time to stop him from going back to work too soon.

Raegan is quite on the other end of the line "Sweetheart?" Dad repeats, perking up more in his seat. I can hear Raes deep inhale "I... I think I found something." A weighted blanket falls over us "There are some things happening on the website." Website?

"Rae, what do you mean?" Theos voice is calm, but carries a wave of urgency.

"I don't want to talk over phone, I need some extra time in the morning to check a few more things and the- Leo WATCH OUT!!"

Loud metal crunches and screams of Raegan and Leo booms through the phone.

Three of us are now standing with my phone still in the middle of the table. Hearing the aftermath of an accident.

"Rae? Rae baby- you still there?" It's Theo who finds his voice first. "Raegan? Leo?" Urgency in his tone rising.

No reply, just moans.

"Raegan wake up!" Dads strong, authoritative voice seems to do the job.

A weak voice speaks "Leo…Leo wake up." There is rustling of seatbelts.

"I'm awake…. I'm awake.." Leos breathing sounds laboured "I'm here." Raes breathing can be heard through the phone "Rae, my leg's stuck. Get out and call for help. You need to get out."

"I'm trying, the fucking door won't fucking open-" she is near enough screaming and then she falls silent. Her voice steady, but quite. "Leo… they know… they're coming for us. We need to move. NOW!"

"Rae, get out of the fucking car and run!"

"I'm not leavening you. Come on, help me pull your leg out." Sounds of frustration and rising panic filters through the phone.

There are no words.

Just pure terror that has settled over our dining room.

Helplessness fills my veins again.

The Unspoken Darkness

Bang!
Bang!
Bang!

Gunshots.

From how close they are to the microphone, they must be Leos. "Get out of the car Raegan." Leo grits out. "They're after you, you need to run."

"The passcode is the bear. Brandan do you hear me? It's the bear."

More distant gunshots ring through. They don't have much time. What passcode is she talking about?

Raegan screams. What sounds like a door is wretched open. Her screaming sounds more distant.

"Get your fucking hands off her!" Leo shouts.

"Aaa… aren't you just the… best bodyguard. Allowing me to capture Mrs Brentwood so easily!" A voice I do not recognise has come up to the car. The voice is crisp and vile. I can hear Raegans struggle in the background. "I suppose, to Miss Brentwood, you were the worst bodyguard."

Two shots ring out.

Another scream rips from Raegan. But this is guttural. Primal. I can feel her pain through the phone. And I am shaking with anger by not being there. Not being able to protect her. To stop what has happened to Leo.

One of our units closest to them were dispatched as soon as the car crashed, but they are still 10 minutes out.

Footsteps fade away from the car.

"Miss Brentwood, I will kindly ask you to calm down. We will become very close friends while you tell me everything you know about Darheaven Citadel. We can do this the civil way or… the painful way. The choice is yours."

"You've just made the biggest mistake of your life." I'm not sure how her voice is steady when she speaks these words.

"No one will come to save you, because no one will be able to find you."

A dark laugh burst from Raegan.

"There are monsters and then there are those, who even the monsters are afraid of Mr..?"

"You can call me Mr Bright."

"Mr Bright, you've just awakened three of them and you will not come out of this alive, I promise you that."

Bang!

Quietness.

"Why the fuck did you shoot her?" Cold sweat covers me and I'm not breathing. No one in this godforsaken room is breathing. "Answer me!" Mr Bright bellows.

"I..I thought she was reaching for a gun." The man who shot my sister answers.

"You thought she was reaching for a gun? Her hands are tied behind her back and she has NO GUN on her you imbecile! Stop her bleeding, we need her alive." People rustle and move to follow Mr Brights commands. "Give me your gun!" Mr Bright demands.

Bang!

"I can't deal with this incompetence. Take his body with us, I don't want any leads left behind. Is she stable?"
No one replies.
"Is she stable?" Mr Bright bellows.
A woman finally replies "She's losing a lot of blood and her pulse is weakening. We need to get her to The Room."

"Let's move!"

The microphone picks up Mr Bright and his teams retrieval.

We stand around the table for few more seconds, the last three minutes pulling the rug from under all our feet.
I look at Theo who is fury incarnate.
Dads eyes are focused.

He looks both of us in our eyes "Whatever it takes, we bring her home. We bring Raegan home alive. I am not losing my child."

Chapter 47 - Theo

When we arrive at the scene I am still in the haze of what has just happened. My Alora has been taken.

I walk to where I can see a patch of blood in the road.

It's Raegans blood. I know it.

I crouch down and run my index finger through the red liquid. I've spent months of keeping the blood from being spilled from her body.

"Leo is being rushed to the hospital. His status unknown." I didn't even hear Bran walk up to me. He crouches beside me "I made a promise to Raegan that I will keep her safe." He looks at me and I nearly fall to the ground as I often forget how similar their eyes are, it feels like it's Raegan who is looking at me. "I need you to help me bring her home."

I break my gaze from him and look back down at the blood that should have never left her body.

"She is my home."

Flashback to the morning after Brentwood Gala

I walk Raegan to her rooms, I don't want to leave her side. Not only to keep her safe, but because I am selfish and don't want to be alone tonight. We're in her little living room, she still has my jacket draped over her shoulders.

I stand in front of her as I drop to my knees, I rip the split on her dress up to her tiny waist. I have a clear view of her five horizontal markings and the three half moon shapes she made with her fingers in the bathroom earlier.

I run my right hand up the back of her leg, stopping below her bottom and gripping her thigh tight. Telling her without words that she is not to hurt her. Her eyes never leave mine, but I break our eye contact as I lean forwards and lay light kisses on each of her scars. I can hear Raegans quick intake of breath, which gives me extra satisfaction. After I pepper her with 8 kisses I get up and turn to leave, but she grabs my hand, eyes still on me.

"Did you win the yacht?"

Her question catches me off guard, I clear my throat and give my head a nod.

"I did." I look into her golden brown eyes, that are still red from the crying "I just need to win my girl now." I might as well say it, there is no point in holding back. But does she know I mean her? Our relationship has been anything but smooth, but deep down I know she is my person. She looks at me, then blinks and drops in a crouch in front of me.

She undoes my shoe laces and loosens them, then motions for me to step out of them. I do. She straightens and I drop to one knee in front of her, she places her foot on my knee and I undo the strappy shoe. There is still blood on her feet. Once I'm done with the first, she swaps her feet and I undo the other.

She takes my hand and leads me into her bedroom, the sun has risen and the curtains are half drawn, letting in enough light in the room without needing to turn on a light. We stop in front of her dresser and she turns to me.

Raegan takes my right hand and takes out the BG gold cufflink. She follows the same motion on my other sleeve and places both cufflinks on her dresser. She next reached for my collar and lifts it up removing the loosened bow tie still dangling around my neck. Rae doesn't make eye contact, but I know she is well aware of me following her every movement. Drinking her in.

One by one she undoes my shirt buttons, instead of just pulling the shirt out of my trousers- she takes off my belt. Undoes my trousers and eases the shirt out. Finishing the last few buttons before she takes the shirt off, folds it and sets it on her chair. I must've had my eyes closed for longer than I thought as my trousers are off, folded and placed next to my shirt and so are my socks.

I am standing in my boxers in front of *my* girl. She turns her back to me and looks over the shoulder. I take my jacket off her shoulders and place it next to my other clothes. With gentle fingers I set to undo her dress, once it's loose enough I pull it over her head. She isn't wearing a bra and steps out of her underwear in one swift motion.

She walks in the bathroom, turns on the light and starts the shower. She moves back to the mirror and starts taking pins out of her hair. I take my boxers off and help her with the last remaining pins.

The Unspoken Darkness

Raegan takes my hand and we step into the waterfall shower. We stand under the falling water for a long moment before she wraps her arms around my waist and lays her head against my chest. I don't think twice about wrapping her in a hug of my own. This feels right. I've only ever had snippets of her, but Rae, my Alora, feels right in my arms. We stay in our embrace for several long minutes before she makes me sit on the stone bench and starts washing my hair. Then my face and rest of my body.

As I'm taller than Raegan I easily wash her hair without her needing to sit down. Her body feels fragile in my hands, but I know better than most, that she is a survivor. She hasn't told me what caused her to cut the first time, but she will.

After we both have rinsed off, she plants soft kisses on my body. It takes me a while to realise she is kissing my scars. Scars from training and missions. There are a couple of bruises forming along my ribs from yesterdays attack, and she kisses those as well.

She shuts off the water and steps out of the shower, wrapping a towel around her and passing one to me. We dry off quickly, but I see her putting on a pair of underwear and pulls over her towel wrapped hair one of my t-shirts. Without another blink of an eye, she passes a pair of jogging bottoms to me, these are mine as well. A caveman satisfaction rolls over me, not just from the sight of her wearing my shirt, but her having them. She must've come into my room to get these.

The Unspoken Darkness

While I put the bottoms on, she has moved in front of the mirror and is brushing out her long hair. I step to stand behind her, take the brush from her and finish brushing her damp hair. She reaches in one of her drawers and pulls out a spare toothbrush for me. It's clear she doesn't want me to leave and I would be a fool for wanting to.

We step back into her bedroom, I close the curtains to fully sink the room in darkness. She rustles the bedding while climbing in the bed. Raegan keeps the duvet back letting me get in her bed, I lay down on my back and pull her legs across me. Wrapping my arms around her with her head on my chest. Just like the first night I held her.

"Why do you have my clothes Alora?" I whisper.

"They help me sleep."

"And how long have you been stealing my clothes from me?"

"For months."

Fuck. I kiss the top of her head and she lets out a sigh that makes warmth spread through me. One of her hands is holding my left arm and the other rest on my neck. I lean into her warm touch.

Chapter 48 - Theo

It's been four weeks since the shooting and I've spent every single night wrapped in Raegans limbs. We follow the same routine as the very first time- shower, change, bed. Both our bedrooms now has the other persons clothes and bathroom items. At first we didn't talk at all, but with each passing day we opened up more and more. We haven't done more than that, we haven't even shared a kiss. I know she has been hurt before, so I am giving her all the time in the world to trust me enough to let me in.

She sits up on the bed, folds her legs in front of her and looks at me with those gorgeous golden brown eyes.

"We need to talk Theo." My heart doesn't just skip a beat, it stops all together.

"No." I don't want to talk, talking never ends well.

"We do. You know we do." She takes my hand in hers, she is still so slim. She's been under constant stress for months and hasn't been eating. "In the past, I have given my heart to those who didn't deserve it. At the time, I thought they did, so I gave it my all. My heart is no longer one piece, it's hundreds and thousands of shattered little pieces. I am piecing it back together, but this time it's harder. However much of my broken heart I can salvage and make it into a living, beating thing- I don't ever want to give it away again. So I cannot promise that I will ever love you, but… you are the only one who makes me feel less broken. And safe. When you look at me you don't see the scars and the trauma, pity and all the horrible things, you just see me. You see who I am. I know you want and deserve more than I can give you-"

I'm up like a shot, slamming my lips against hers before she goes and says something stupid like 'I need to find someone else'. I hold her face in my hands and kiss her deeply, with all the want and yearning I have for her. I make her feel my love for her.

If she thinks she doesn't love me, she is delusional. Only a person in love will put the others needs above their own. I will, however, not tell her that. She needs to work it out for herself. And that makes me smile against her lips, her hands are in my hair, pulling and tugging me. I pull her into my lap, making her straddle me. Raegan pulls her lips away from mine.

"Theo-"

"Shhhh baby! You talked, I listened. You said it yourself - I see you." I kiss her again and a soft moan escapes her lips, I capture it with mine and I groan unashamedly. "But I am a gentleman for you and as much as this hurts me-" the little devil grinds against my hard cock knowing exactly what she is doing with the cheekiest grin on her puffy lips "You're making it hard for me to be a gentleman right now baby." I nip at her jaw which makes her giggle.

"I'm sorry. Go on." But her eyes says anything, but sorry.

"I want to do this right, I want to take you on a date."

"At least three?" She asks quirking her brow and I pull her closer, my arms around her torso.

"However many dates you want to." This time it's Raegan who is putting her lips on mine, soft and gently and kissing me senseless.

The Unspoken Darkness

First thing on my list the following morning is to see George and ask his permission to date Raegan. He has been my parent for most of my life. I have never called him dad, but he knows he is one to me. That is exactly why I need to talk to him.

Despite how close of a call it was with George, he is recovering well. To be honest, most of the progress is due to Rae being an absolute menace with doctors, nurses, even Bran and me to keeping him calm, stress free. And under no circumstances talk about work. She nearly pulled Brandans ear off while pulling him out of the room when she overheard him giving George the latest on the investigation progress. She might be half the size of him, but he wouldn't have won that fight even if his life depended on it. After that, neither of us dared smuggling information to George.

"Morning Theo. What brings you to my gilded prison." Even though George has been released from hospital, Raegan is running a tight ship on his routine. He is not allowed to leave his room, unless accompanied by someone. Mostly to prevent him from sneaking into his office and start working.
I make my way to the chair next to his bed and sit down "I wanted to talk to you."
"Aaaa… finally." I must've looked as confused as I thought, because George just shakes his head and laughs "I've been waiting for you to come and talk to me for over four years now." What is he talking about? "That's how long you've been in love with my daughter, that's why you're here, aren't you?"

I sit back in the chair and slouch down. Yes. Yes he is 100percent right, but…

"How… when…what.." I'm trying to get the words out, but they are just a jumble in my head. Have I been too obvious? Surely walking around with hearts for my eyes were only a thing in films.

He chuckled "I know my children. And by all intents and purposes- you are my son. So, tell me."

He knew. The old man fucking knew. Well.. there is no point in denying.

"Yes. I love Raegan and I'd like your permission to date her."

"On three conditions."

"I'm listening."

"One - even though Raegan is an adult and doesn't need my permission, I'd like you to ask me for her hand in marriage before you propose. Two - her safety is paramount. Three - you will always honour her wishes, whatever they might be."

"I will." And I finally let myself smile. A matching smile is on Georges face.

"I presume if I would ask you to fill me in on the progress of the investigation..?"

"I won't tell you a single thing."

"Smart man."

I'm walking out to the car and dial Brandan. He answers and I say what I need to say, without any greeting

"I don't need your permission, but I would like you to know that I'm going to ask Raegan out on a date. George knows as well."

He is quite for a second before replying. "Took you long enough!"

"Really? You too?"

He laughs "Oh, did dad say the same thing?" I sigh, loudly, which makes him laugh even more. "Stop throwing a toddler worthy tantrum and-" I hang up, I'm not in the mood to listen to him.

Me: Midnight drive tomorrow, be in the garage in your leathers at 23:55.

Alora: Is this our first date?

Me: Yes.

Alora: I can't wait.

Present

"Guys, we got something!" I'm pulled from my memories, when one of our operatives waves us over to a dark side street. Two other guys are surrounding something by the wall. As I step closer I realise, it's not a something, it's someone. Someone I recognise well.

I crouch down in front of him, while he is clutching his leg, that's been shot. At least Leo got one of the fuckers.

"Hello Dylan. How much pain are you willing to endure, until you sing like a pretty little bird and tell me everything I need to know?"

Epiloge - Raegan

I thought I had more time in my life.

I thought the choice to go will be mine.

I thought I had more time with him.

With them.

I was wrong on all accounts.

In the flash of a gun, it is not the bright light at the end of the tunnel that greets me.

It's the unspoken darkness that finally claims me.